To share,
Enjoy!

New York City Days, 1965

Henry Intili

PublishAmerica
Baltimore

ISBN: 1-60836-954-4
PUBLISHED BY PUBLISHAMERICA, LLLP
www.publishamerica.com
Baltimore

Printed in the United States of America

SEPTEMBER 1965

September 7, 1965

New York City
105 East 15th Street

Age: 20   Height: 5'3"   Weight: 129
Waist: 29"   Shirt Sleeve: 29" Inseam: 29"

See all those 29s? That's a good number for me. 29. 2+9=11. Eleven has always been my star-born lucky number. I was born on 11-11-44. That makes 4 and 8 lucky numbers as well. But not as lucky as 11. Take today's date for instance: 7-9-65. 7+9=71. 7+1=8. Should be a good day, not a great one. In fact, I did make some money today, although at an annoying price. A typical 8 day.

Classes at Washington Square, New York University don't start for another week, and I need money for rent and food and other basics. So I agreed to work with my father for a few days. I have not worked with him in his electrical business as much this year as in the past. Not my choice or my fault. This summer he did not contract the volume of business that has been his staple work diet.

Work with my father started when I was eleven years old (there's that number again). Every Saturday from May to October I carted wire, metal boxes, drills, and anything else a small and willing boy could manage. I began each day with the unloading: I stretched into the dark interior of my father's Chevy panel truck, pulled out the boxes and coils of armored cable that my father had carefully loaded the night before, and struggled with them like a willing donkey across rough-graded dirt to the construction site. After that came any task my father wanted. "Hank, hold this wire...bang on the floor with a hammer here when I call you from below...nail this box on to that stud and make sure the bottom is as high as your hammer." He paid me three dollars a day. Hardest three dollars I ever earned in my life. Coils of steel cable can be damned heavy when they weigh nearly as much as you do.

In those years my father worked from six in the morning until six at night.

He drove his 1950 dark green Chevy panel truck in the dusky morning while I slept in the back curled up like a cat on his old, dirty work coat. The combined smells of sweat and cigarette smoke were imbedded in that coat's quilted fabric. When I was eleven, I had so much respect for my father, so much pride in being allowed to work with him, that even breathing in the musty odors of that ratty coat was pleasurable. If there wasn't enough room on the truck floor, I stretched out across the coils of wire, trying to blend my body shape into the cable doughnuts, feet in one coil, rump in a second, shoulders against a box of plugs and switches.

Year by year I was allowed more difficult, more responsible tasks from installing the plugs and switches to running wire and finally designing circuits from blue prints. Two summers ago, between my freshman and sophomore years at Dickinson College, I practically ran the entire operation in the Morristown subdivision. We both made good money. I made a nice cash salary, and he made an equally nice profit from my labor as a quality employee. A good arrangement; the top of a long growth curve.

The summer would have been more enjoyable if we had been talking to each other. A whole summer driving from our small house in Short Hills that he built with his own hands to the housing development in Morristown in the morning and back again in the late afternoon with hardly a word between us. Well, he started the fight, let him find a way to end it.

As I said, the usual volume of work wasn't there this year. With his children living on their own, maybe he didn't need the income. In any case, that lack of work left me so desperate for money to replenish my bank account for this school year that I stayed extra hours stocking shelves at Jack's Deli here in Manhattan through the summer.

My mother called last night. "Dad could use your help tomorrow in Morristown. Do you have any plans?"

I told her we would use the usual arrangements: He would meet me at the Morristown railroad station which is on the way to the housing development. Half a dozen times this summer we've successfully made these arrangements of where and when to meet in the morning. The Lackawanna train pulls into the station just before eight in the morning, and I wend my way through the assembled executive types over to Morris Turnpike and we meet up. Easy, right?

The hard part for me this particular morning was pulling myself out of bed at 5:30. Last night was hot, I had to sleep with the window fan blowing on me to stay even halfway cool. Needless to say, I didn't sleep well. Tossed and turned under a damp sheet, body sweaty and itchy. Damn near impossible to force the eyes open and the body up and out when the alarm screamed at me.

I walked halfway across Manhattan on a deserted Fourteenth Street. Wind-blown newspaper fragments snapping their displeasure in the gusty sea breeze shared the eerie morning light with an occasional plume of tumbled steam from a Con Edison vent. Another hour and the street would be alive with delivery trucks, store workers, and taxis. Another hour and I would be in New Jersey riding the train.

The Sixth Avenue PATH tubes, clean and efficient compared to the regular New York City subways, took me to New Jersey in time to catch the empty reverse commuter train to Morristown. The electric trains of twelve passenger cars are stored overnight in the Hoboken yards and run to Morristown in time to bring the executives from Morristown, Madison, Summit, Short Hills, and the other bedroom communities back to Hoboken for the trip across the river to Manhattan. If I had taken the train the night before to Short Hills and stayed the night at my parents' house, today would have been easier. But I haven't felt like being part of that place lately.

The trip through New Jersey that I sometimes enjoy for the morning scenery was tiresome today. The slate roofed stations at South Orange, West Orange and Maplewood, the cane backed train seats, the blue capped conductor announcing the stations in full voice to an empty train car—all monotonous this morning and not the least interesting. My head throbbed with a cottony vagueness; each clack of the wheels set off a small explosion inside my head. I had a book with me: *Giants in the Earth* by O.E. Rolvag. I couldn't concentrate on the words of this wonderful novel. I wish I could write as sparsely and cleanly as he does.

An hour out of Hoboken the train decelerated into the Morristown station, and I saw my father's panel truck waiting by the side of Morris Turnpike. The conductor and I shared the squealing, steel herringbone platform between the cars. As the only passenger on his train car I felt a personal attachment to the conductor. He walked down one set of steps holding on to the vertical grip as I moved down the other with my toolbox in my free hand. We both swayed and bounced as the cinder filled grass passed by. I was deafened by the screeching of sparking steel brakes on shiny steel wheels. Our cinder grass became pitted cement, then canopied station.

I jumped off the train (as usual) before the cacophonous beast stopped and watched my father's truck pull away from the curb not a hundred yards away. He disappeared into the morning commuter traffic. I ran, yelling, waving my free arm, shouting, my metal toolbox scraping my thigh. Nothing. Dozens of business types with their briefcases and long quarter folded newspapers looked over at me. See the circus freak escaped from the local mental hospital. And what's worse, I didn't have enough money to take a train back to Hoboken and then the tube back to Manhattan. I was stuck. I would have to hitch a ride to the subdivision and track my father down. What a real pain in the ass is he! How could he leave me there when the train was pulling into the station!

Busy morning traffic filled the four-lane road. Curler-haired wives driving dark suited businessmen to the train. Damn him for leaving me there! I stuck my thumb out for a ride, then pulled it in and switched to wild arm waving.

Coming towards me I saw the unmistakable blue Panzer Tank of Helmut the Painter. My younger brother Anthony christened Helmut's panel truck the Panzer Tank. Anthony came to the conclusion that Helmut the Painter, this large, mild man with his deep German accent, blue eyes and blonde hair, was in fact an escaped Nazi. And his truck, filled with the tools of his painting profession, was a German tank is disguise waiting for the secret signal from the hidden Fuehrer.

> *"Helmut, Ich bin zuruck gekommen," says the Fuehrer as he informs our painter of his impending return.*
>
> *"Ya, mein Fuehrer." Sound of Helmut's gum soled painter shoes trying to click together. Only a dull thump is achieved. The Fuehrer stands unimpressed.*
>
> *"Sie mussen von New Jersey Blitzkrieg machen." The leader intends to return his far-flung Germans to the Fatherland. "Ein Volk!"*
>
> *"Ya, mein Fuehrer!" A smart salute to the tip of his spotted painter's cap. Helmut exists to obey.*
>
> *"Sie mussen die Oligarchs von New Jersey todt machen." The Fuehrer remains the champion of the common man, the scourge of the Capitalist Oligarchs who control his long lost German Volk. He turns his brown, leaden eyes away from Helmut and looks to the far Kittatinny Mountains. Then Helmut realizes as tears flash into his own eyes that The Leader understands him because The Leader was also a painter of houses.*

I flagged Helmut to stop for me and jumped into the passenger's seat after he stretched across the truck and opened the door. "Does your father not pick you up?"

"My train was late; he must have gone on without me." I said the lie, though I can't think why I should defend him. "Can you drive me to the job site?"

"Ya, of course. Dat is no trouble. Und how did you do with frauleins in die Big City? Get them all yet? Hah?"

"No, Helmut, not yet. I'm working on just one and she's more than I can handle."

We drove to a section of the subdivision that is nearly complete, a section where Helmut would be working today and where I was sure my father had planned for Anthony and I to complete at least two houses by installing plugs and switches; easy work, almost boring.

Helmut and I passed a yard being raked smooth by a team of small, swarthy men. The men were dressed in faded plaid shirts and brown pants; each man had a rolled headband. Summer labor from Mexico. Maybe a dozen men in a row across the future lawn, bent over rakes, their heads always down. Behind them watching lazily stood a larger, full-bellied man. His left hand hung at his side holding a cigar. With steadied, unconscious regularity, the hand swung upward to preciously place the cigar between his lips. His chest expanded in a deep inhalation. The downward swing of that pendulum arm was matched by an exhaled cloud pointed high to the maple and oak trees that had been left in the yard. For years I have watched this same man and what seemed to be this same crew (how can you distinguish one man from another when they are bent over, performing the same raking movements on small stones and debris?), always hard at work when we arrive, always at the same tasks no matter what the weather, and always there toiling when we leave in the evening. Peasant work.

My ancestors too were peasants. Laborers, brick layers, drayage men. My father had started work as a brick boy to his father. My grandfather had come to America as a drayage partner to his future father-in-law, Giaccomino Anello. This was a business arrangement no one ever thought to discuss with my grandmother. Her revenge on them both would fill up the pages of a whole novel.

For me labor constituted a means to finance part of my college education. My father still pays the tuition. I wish I didn't have to take his money.

Helmut found my father's truck within a block of the Mexicans. He wished me well and drove off down the block to another house in the same development. Dad was at the back of his panel truck removing boxes of plugs and switches. He said hello to me as if nothing had happened. No explanation for the train station. Not even a mention of his ill-timed departure that left me stranded. Typical of him: no real talk about important things. Well, since he won't talk about it, neither will I.

My younger brother Anthony stood to the side waiting for someone to tell him exactly what to do. Until that happens he wouldn't lift a finger. He's not nasty or insolent, just lazy. When you're paid by the hour, why do anything until asked? Dad gave me instructions for the house and drove off to work on another project. I was annoyed with him giving me instructions; I know as well as he what has to be done.

When his truck turned off on to another street and we were alone, I asked Anthony what happened at the train station. "Didn't you see the train?" I grumbled as we carried several boxes across the neatly raked and seeded lawn.

"Yes." He yawned and shook his head.

"Well, why didn't you wait?" We stepped through the open door into the uncarpeted house. Splotches of spilt drywall plaster covered the plywood floors. The house smelled fresh and cool.

"I told dad to wait. I even saw you get off the train. But he wouldn't, he just drove off." Anthony dropped his box on the floor. A great cloud of plaster dust accented the hollow explosion as the box hit the floor. Anthony believes in the indestructibility of electrical parts. He sat on the miraculously undestroyed box. Through the naked window a leaf-dappled sunlight sparkled in the rising plaster cloud.

"That doesn't make any sense," I said, more than a little angry. My voice rang in the empty room. I carefully lowered my cardboard box of switches and my steel toolbox.

"He said he wasn't going to wait all day for you."

"All day? The train was on time. He said he wouldn't wait?"

Anthony yawned. He was bored by this. It happened, it's over. Why bother? "His exact words were: 'I'll be goddamned if I'm going to what all day for him. If Hank's so damned independent let him find his own way.'"

Anthony shrugged his shoulders when I looked at him with complete disbelief. "Hank, I'm just telling you what he said. Listen, let's go out back and see if we can find some bottles to throw stones at before we start on this house."

Smashing glass bottles sounded like a great idea. We were in luck: The back yard wasn't graded and cleaned yet. The place was littered with boards, cut shingles and plenty of soda pop bottles, even some quarts. We gathered a dozen bottles and stood them in a line on the top of a dirt bank. Too bad for the bottles that our aim rated high this morning. Glass bursting in the morning sunshine. What a mess. "Let the Mexicans rake it under," Anthony said. I didn't share his contempt, but neither did I feel like cleaning up. We never do. Broken glass is as much a part of construction sites as the scraps of lumber, shingles, Helmut's empty paint cans, and even our own electrical detritus.

The dozen bottles failed to satisfy us, and we searched the area for more. In the garage we located an unexpected treasure: a stack of Eddie The Tin Knocker's uninstalled heat registers. We stoned them behind the house too, only we used big rocks so that the registers were mashed and not just dented. We hate the damn heating and cooling man aka the tin knocker. The bastard always messes up our wiring to put in his heating ducts. Last year at the end of the summer we filled his air ducts with small nails on half a dozen houses. Must have taken him days to locate the rattles when he turned the air on. Smashing Eddie's heat registers made me feel better. We returned the smashed registers and carefully stacked them in the garage. Didn't want him thinking the heat registers were stolen or lost.

The workday was a perfect definition of simplicity. Plug, switch, light socket, plug, switch, light socket, ad nauseum. Afterwards I went home for dinner rather than catch the train from Morristown back to New York City. The ride to Short Hills was quiet. Nobody spoke. Anthony was in the back propped against boxes and coils; I was in the passenger seat trying again to read the Rolvaag book; dad was driving, his ubiquitous cigarette stinking up the truck. No radio. The truck doesn't have one. Never did. Probably never will.

My mother smiled and kissed me sweetly, happy and surprised to have me home. After the usual dull dinner around the kitchen table, dad left the house for the rear garage to unload the truck from the day's work. Anthony drove the family Ford off to some last minute party (he leaves for college in a few days).

"Do you still hide the wine in the broom closet?" I asked.

Mother laughed and flashed her wide grin. "I don't hide the wine."

"Then why do you keep that bottle of clear liquid in with the mops and rags?" I opened the long, narrow broom closet door and reached into the back on the floor to find the gallon bottle of sauterne. Mother likes her wines on the sweet side,

"It's not hidden on there. The bottle is too large to fit in the ice box."

"Refrigerator, mother. Ice boxes went out years ago," I said correcting her. She smiled again, this time so broadly that you could see the space for her missing bicuspid. That space has always fascinated me. How did she loose the tooth? I've never asked her. Someday I'll have to. "This isn't the bottle I brought you last time is it?"

"No," she answered, "That one's gone. This is a new one." I gave her the eye. She punched my arm. "Don't look at your mother that way. I am not a drinker, God forbid. I like my glass of wine at night before I go to bed, that's all."

I poured us both a glass and spoke as we washed and dried the dishes. I told her what happened at the train station. The last dish dried and put up in the cabinet, we sat at the kitchen table. She had been listening quietly. Finally she sighed: "Your father has not been well this summer; he's not been himself lately." I don't need her to tell me that.

"Are you staying tonight? Your bed is made up."

"I can't stay tonight," I answered.

Her eyes dropped slightly. I was flooded with guilt. Total, instantaneous. "This is still your home."

"Dad doesn't need me tomorrow. We finished everything today." That was not the answer to the statement she was really making. But there is no way for me to answer her straight, to tell her what I really want to say:

> *Mother, listen, I can't stay here. It's overwhelming for me here. I'm sorry about Rusty. The pain I caused you that I can never erase. I can't even face or comprehend that pain. I don't know how to return to what was there between us in high school, between dad and I. The world exploded for me that year, and the pieces won't go back together. I can't return to the Church or your dreams for me. If I could do it and make you happy, I would. But nothing works that way anymore. Can't you see that?*

Silence. She sipped her wine. My mother uses silence the way Jim Bowie wields a knife. No one can conquer it. My father, who never yields an inch to any of his kids, is regularly defeated by my mother's silences that can stretch for days. Tonight she was giving me a minute waltz.

"Well," she said at last, "Whatever you think best."

"I have a lot to do in the City tomorrow." I heard myself speaking on the defensive. "And it's much easier to take the train in tonight than to fight the executives tomorrow morning. So I had better look for the 8:05 tonight." I looked at the clock above the sink. 7:30. (7+3=10; 1+0=1. 1 is not a good number.)

"Do we have to leave now?" she asked.

"No, I have a few more minutes. Will you drive me to the station?"

"Of course."

"I'll come for a weekend before school starts." Even as I said the words I had this awful feeling that I'm throwing my mother a bone.

"Come anytime." She looked at the clock. Sipped her wine. "There's some meat sauce for you in the freezer. Take that back with you."

"Thank you." We sipped our sweet wine as time stretched out in the elastic silence. Maybe she wanted some reassurance. That's what I told myself although why she would need assurance baffled me. Or maybe I needed to say something, anything, to bring her back to the smiles. "I always use your sauce. JoAnn and I will cook it up one night this week."

"Hmmm. How is JoAnn?" My mother likes JoAnn. After the mess with Rusty, my mother really likes JoAnn. Even though JoAnn's not Italian, she's still a "nice girl."

"Say good-bye to your father before you leave." Her voice was soft. Her eyes drilled into me. She made more than a demand. This was a half-silent absolute command.

"I'll be back in a minute," I said rising from the kitchen chair.

He was in the rear garage. I heard him loading metal boxes and tools. Every night for every year I have ever worked with him: After supper, unload from the day, load for tomorrow. The garage is his. He built it himself: poured the concrete, laid the blocks, trussed the roof. His tools, his truck, his garage. Clean, orderly. No calendars, no pin-ups, no radio, nothing personal. Just the tools of his electrical contract business.

He pretended not to hear me walk in and concentrated only on loading the truck for tomorrow's work. Adding a coil of this, a batch of that. I watched the solidity of his frame flowing in unwasted movements. A body born and honed for ceaseless work.

"Dad, I'm leaving."

He looked up. His face was deeply lined; his curly black hair now peppered silver. And always the cigarette hanging from the corner of his mouth. He nodded. "Let me pay you for today." He took out his wallet and handed me a few bills. I didn't count them. He would never make a mistake. He coughed twice, a hacking cough, and then dragged deep on his cigarette to clear his throat. "Do you need money for school yet?"

"No. Not for another week."

"Well, let me know. I'll write you a check. I have the money now." We stood for a moment, poised, waiting for something that didn't happen. Couldn't happen. Waiting for words that I cannot say:

> *Dad, don't you understand that I needed your support. That I looked up to you more than anyone in the world. That I really didn't know what to do. I was three or four people. You had to finally for once in our lives sit down with me and talk to me about what was right. Talk to me like you never did in high school. You never sat me down ever to talk with me. I needed that. And I needed it with Rusty. And when you didn't, I saw that there wasn't anything there between us. There was no father-son. There were just rules. Your rules that didn't have anything to do with the real me. The same rules you have for wires and drills and hammers. That's why I didn't talk to you all that summer. That's why I still can't. It has to come from you. You have to talk to ME.*

He nodded, raised his hand to me an inch or so, and returned to his work.

In the car on the way to the railroad station, I noticed as I sometimes do what a beautiful woman my mother is: Small, firm, nicely shaped. I never saw her as a woman until Thanksgiving of my sixteenth year. There she was in the kitchen by the stove smiling and laughing; and for the first time I noticed her beautiful body: Athletic and full breasted. The last realization embarrassed me totally.

I'm tired tonight. And it's hot again. I can't afford an air conditioner this year. At least I have a big fan in the window. JoAnn should be over for lunch tomorrow. I could use some catching up in the sex department.

September 8, 1965;
Late

I was deep into the fourteenth century with Sigrid Undset and her splendid book *Kristin Lavransdatter* when my sister Rose called tonight. "Helloooo," she chimed when I answered the phone.

"Hello, Rose. How are things down in South Jersey?"

"In South Jersey? What new ever happens here? That's a joke. There's nothing here but tomato farms and DuPont. When Carl and I want to do anything, we have to drive an hour to Philadelphia. And that isn't very often. Oh, well. So much for me. Hope I'm not interrupting a wild evening of sin and debauchery in the Big City."

"Ha! Now that's the line good for a laugh. If you think Jersey can be boring, try New York when you're alone in your apartment with only four walls to look at."

"JoAnn's not there tonight? That's a surprise. Is everything all right between you?" My older, married sister being an older sister. Sometimes I think I grew up with two mothers.

"Everything's fine with us. She gave me the night off."

"Gave *you* the night off? She's the one who probably needs the night off." Rose likes JoAnn. Everyone likes JoAnn. Rose asks us to visit her from now and then so that she can spend time with JoAnn. Talks more to JoAnn than to me.

"Sure," I answered. "Can't have a whole lifetime of Sodom, Gomorrah, and wonton behavior. Can't all be Chinese."

"Chinese? I don't understand. What do they have to do with your lifestyle?"

"That's a pun. Wonton. Chinese. Better Chink than extinct." No response on the other end of the line. So much for my literary merits.

"What I called about," said sister Rose back in control, "is an idea Carl and I had. The house at Sea Isle City is unrented after Thursday of this week. Summer season's over. Carl thought you and JoAnn might want to join us there Friday night. That is if you can stand being chaperoned for the weekend by us old fogies."

"Sounds great to me. The part about the house. You can keep the part about chaperoning. I don't see enough of JoAnn as it is. I'd love a weekend at the Jersey shore. And JoAnn doesn't have anything planned that I know of. Will your in-laws be there?"

"No, thank goodness. Carl said his family won't drive over until after the weekend. The house will be ours. Well, almost ours. And that's the part about the chaperoning. Mother wants to go, too. Can you pick her up in Short Hills and drive her down with you? That's assuming you're driving." Another typical older sister trait: last minute complications. Why can't people keep their lives simple? Or my life simple since now I have to coordinate everything with JoAnn and my mother (why isn't dad going?). More phone calls to make. More questions to answer or dodge.

Mother in the house at the shore means JoAnn and I will be in separate bedrooms. Rose lets us sleep together when we visit her place, but my mother's presence will change everything even though mother certainly knows my couch here has other uses besides being a place where we sit and hold hands.

"Hello." JoAnn has a mellow, legato voice. I phoned her private line rather than bother her parents at this hour by using the house line. Not that I would prefer to talk to them.

"Hi, sweets it's me," I said.

"Hi! This is a nice surprise!"

"Not too late for you?"

"No. I'm here reading a book. Nothing big going on. A work by Jessamyn West." If she wasn't doing anything "big" tonight, then why didn't she offer to spend the evening with me?

"I don't know that author." JoAnn is always finding books by obscure writers. "My sister Rose called. She and Carl want us to join them for the weekend down at Carl's family house at the Jersey shore. Want to go?" I felt like I was selling the idea.

"That sounds like fun. We haven't been any place new or interesting in ages. Life's getting into a rut. When do we leave?"

"Friday afternoon, I think. I guess we'll be back Sunday night.'

"No problem here. You want to take my car?"

"Unless you want to walk." Silence. Why does she always let conversations drop? She knows I'm not good at forcing talk. "There's a complication that Rose put in. We may have to pick up my mother in our way down."

"That's OK, Hank. Maybe I'll have her sweater finished by then."

"What sweater?" I asked. JoAnn is always knitting people sweaters. Usually big, bulky things for winter. I have two myself.

"The one I've been knitting for the past two months. I told you about it. Can't believe it's taken me this long." More silence.

"What are you doing now?" I asked

"Nothing. Why?"

"Want to go out for a beer?" Why do I always have the feeling that I'm pulling and tugging at her?

"Well, yes. No. No, it's getting late. And by the time you got up here it would be far too late. My parents are already in bed. I'd like to, but not tonight. It doesn't sound like a good idea for tonight. What are you doing tomorrow for lunch?"

Tomorrow. What good is tomorrow for today's living?

September 9, 1965, *Thursday Nite.*

Worked at Jack's Deli this morning. Stocking shelves, washing pots, organizing used soda bottles. Highly intelligent activity for a college student. Since Jack's store is only a half dozen blocks from JoAnn's place, I went over there for lunch. Her parents were off to work. Annie the maid had gone shopping. Definitely a good time to catch up on some neglected sex time.

We decided to take a bath together. A sexy, romantic idea at first. We soaped and rinsed each other. Her breasts felt wonderfully slippery, her pussy hidden and inviting. One thing led to another and I was on top of her in the bathtub. With her legs pressed against the tub sides and me squeezed in between them, spare room was at a premium. And maybe we had too much water in the tub because whenever I would stroke up too hard, she would slide down under the water. Instant readjustment while she sputtered and choked and I tried to avoid cracking my skull against the chrome water sprout. That left us with only little pushes, a tempo which wasn't going to lead anywhere.

We finally worked out a good rhythm that promised a pleasant finale when we heard the front door open and slam shut. "JoAnn!" shouted Annie in her deep black voice.

"I'll be there in a moment!" answered JoAnn trying to lift herself out of the tub. Not easy to do with me wedged between and in her. I'm only a stroke or two away and not in any rush to leave. "Hank! Please!" she whispered loud in my ear, "Let me up!" That entreaty deflated me in all departments. Hello, scrotum pains. And no time later to complete the day's exertions. JoAnn had to go out with her parents tonight, leaving me footloose again.

"Hank, Annie can't find you here. She'll tell my parents," whispered JoAnn in a panic as she toweled herself dry. I watched ruefully as her hairy triangle disappeared into white cotton panties. Goodbye my friend! "You have to sneak out." Flop, flop breasts into bra, hook up the back.

"How?" Meaning: Are you sure we can't take another minute for me?

"Hank, get dressed!" she whispered. Skirt and blouse in place. Abandon All Hope. "I'll go in the kitchen and distract her. You sneak out the front door. Quietly!"

"But…"

She silenced me with a kiss that tasted faintly of soap. "I love you. Call me later."

September 10, 1965

This will be a strange entry. Part of my New York City education. Down the hall from me lives an older man, maybe fifty years old, small in stature like me and in fine physical condition. He always dresses stylishly, his dark, tailored business suits complimenting his drawn, lined face and wavy, pepper hair. Whenever we pass in the hall or meet waiting for the clunky old elevator we say hello.

About a week ago we met in the elevator as he was coming home from his Wall Street job and I was returning from Jack's Deli probably smelling of garlic or onion. He invited me to come over for a drink later in the evening.

I had a pleasant two hours talking about the City and school. He told me his name was Andre and he was from a Hungarian aristocratic family. Flip and pert, he spent the evening smiling, laughing, and making small comments and compliments about my fine physical condition and "smart little body."

He shares the apartment with a sausage dog that he calls "corky." An intelligent and lively dog; "Cute" to use Andre's favorite word. Corky ran back and forth the length of the apartment on his tubby legs at the slightest command. Andre clapped his hands and Corky danced around. Never barking, always playful.

This evening Andre called and asked if I was free to join him for dinner. Why not? JoAnn's off someplace with her parents and Andre insisted dinner was his treat. We hailed a cab to a West Twelfth Street restaurant that was crowded with densely packed tables. You couldn't stretch your arms without intruding your neighbor's eating space. Forget privacy. Without wanting to I heard about this one's vacation and that one's newest silk shirts and sport jackets, about movies and plays. And I had to keep my mind on Andre's stories. At least the food was excellent.

Then we walked down a busy Sixth Avenue to a basement bar and night club on West 8th street. Again the place was packed with customers. Andre didn't want to sit at one of the tiny tables near the stage. I didn't object because I didn't see a single spare seat much less two. Not that I could see much of anything: the place was as dark as a theater before the curtain rises.

We stood in the back, far away from the stage, at a cramped and smoky bar. Through the blue haze we watched a marvelous floor show. A slinky, sexy lady singer in a very low cut red dress performed song after song to ear-deafening applause and cheers. I loved her bawdy jokes except for the ones that I couldn't understand about the "boys" in the band.

We stayed a couple of hours. I had a glass of wine or two. Andre drank half a dozen Tanqueray and tonic. On the way home as we walked quietly up lower Fifth Avenue towards Union Square, Andre suddenly exploded at me.

"This cutie act has gone on far enough, Hankie."

"What act?"

"You know what I mean." His voice shook.

"No, I don't. What did I do wrong?" I couldn't figure out why he seemed so angry. Did he expect me to pay part of the tab, even though he kept grabbing for the check? "Did you want me to pick up some of the bill?"

He shook his head: "Don't be stupid. Of course not. This has nothing to do with the bill. You can't be that naïve about this evening. No one can."

"Naïve about what?"

"I suppose you didn't notice that everyone at the restaurant was male?"

"There weren't any women there? I guess you're right. I didn't notice that. Maybe my mind wasn't on girls tonight. It hasn't been a good week for me in that department. I didn't even talk much about JoAnn."

"And putting your arm across to the next chair as if you were stretching out and relaxing. Most tacky way to behave in a restaurant. You're going to tell me you didn't see the faces everyone was making at you."

"No. Why should anyone be making faces?"

"And you didn't notice everyone at the bar was male."

"That's right, they were. Weren't women allowed? Isn't that kind of exclusion illegal? I must have been to busy watching the singer to pick up on the lack of women. She was gorgeous. And what a great singing voice. 'Fly me to the moon and let me sing among the stars.' Wonderful"

"You just can't be that naïve. Even Jersey can't produce them that stupid."

Well, I guess I am. Apparently Andre thought we were on a date together and I was leading him on. How strange. I certainly didn't mean to. And I certainly have no feelings in *that* direction. I have enough problems with women. I know I talked to him about JoAnn when we met the other night. Why would he ever think I was bent *that* way?

Speaking of problems, we did not return to the apartment building in time for the last elevator. This damn place has a damn elevator that quits at one o'clock and doesn't start up again until six in the morning. Well, the elevator itself doesn't quit. This is a manual elevator that requires an operator. He goes off duty at one. Andre told me that wasn't legal. There must be someone on duty at all hours or they must install an automatic elevator.

Personally I don't mind the walk upstairs. Keeps me in shape. Andre was huffing and puffing by the fifth floor. He smokes too much. I slowed down and waited for him at every landing. We had a friendly parting in the hallway. I hope he has better luck on his next date. He seems so interesting.

September 13, 1965

The South Jersey shore is so delightful in the fall. The water is clear and warm, the beaches of white sand tail out gradually forever. The seaside towns lay quiet and empty with the end of the tourist season. We lived with the sound of crashing surf and unstoppable wind. Only a boarding house of black habited nuns shared our section of the beach. Very idyllic.

The drive down The Garden State Parkway from Short Hills to Sea Isle City, far past Asbury Park, Atlantic City, and Point Pleasant was tedious and interminable. The next town is Cape May at the very bottom of New Jersey. Fortunately, the Friday afternoon the traffic was light and so was the trip.

My mother was pleased to see us when we picked her up in Short Hills. Doubly pleased to see JoAnn. She likes JoAnn. Everyone likes JoAnn. She threw up her hands and oohed and aahed at the sweater. "This is something I can really use this weekend. That breeze will be chilly in the evening." My mother was packed in a small suitcase. "I don't need that much and I didn't know if you had room for more."

"Mother we have a whole car."

"Well, I didn't know that. I just wanted to be sure."

We stood around the Formica and chrome table in the kitchen of my parents' house. I rolled my eyes to the round ceiling fluorescent light and spoke to it in disbelief: "What would we take in the car that could possibly fill it up? An elephant?"

She laughed and slapped my arm. "You know what I mean."

My mother was in a talkative mood as we drove to the shore. She insisted on sitting in the back seat so that JoAnn could sit up front. I drove. She asked the usual questions about JoAnn's parents and school, standard Polite Talk 101.

20

We arrived at the shore early enough for JoAnn and I to take a swim before dinner. Before my mother fixed dinner. In her suitcase she had managed to pack two quarts of meatballs and sauce. My stomach was thankful that my sister Rose was there to oversee the cooking. In case I didn't mention it, for all her meatballs and sauce, my mother is an awful cook. Maybe that's not a nice thing to say about your mother especially since she does try.

Her cooking could best be described as halt cuisine: "Halt! Or I'll shoot!" Leftovers always taste better than the original. Two day old leftovers, the best. By that time the various components of the dish have melded together sufficiently to mask their original preparation. I expect double reheated pork chops to be a twin to shoe leather; I don't expect the originals to have that taste and texture. Crusty cream corn, mushed lima beans, lumpy mashed potatoes: these are far more palatable the third time around.

Sleeping arrangements at the shore lived down to expectations. Rose and her husband Carl had one bedroom, my mother and JoAnn another. I had the choice of the attic or the lounge on the screen porch. I chose the porch for sleeping and the attic for clothes and changing. That way I could come and go as I pleased, early or late, and not have to tiptoe up the stairs past bedrooms.

Carl's house is the second in from the beach. Several years ago, before hurricane Donna, this small bungalow occupied the third position from the beach. That monster storm removed the first house and pushed the beach back until no trace of the original beachfront remained. Carl insists this same erosion occurs relentlessly in the old towns on the South Jersey coast.

JoAnn and I walked from our small house past one other until the road terminated in the sand dunes. A bisecting path formed by thousands of feet, bare and sandled, led across the grass tufted dunes. White sand and crunchy, round yellow pebbles covered the lawns, sidewalk, and street like drifted and blown snow in January. A constant, unrelieved wind sound was inescapable, as was the wind that caused it. The muffled thunder of slow, steady surf suddenly became distinct as we crossed over the dunes to the clean, white beach.

That first afternoon the water was wonderfully warm. JoAnn and I swam and body surfed in the shallow water and low waves until the sun slipped into a pink and ruddy sky behind the distant houses. The wind cooled quickly without the September sun. We kicked and splashed our way back to the beach and toweled off the salt water. The grit and dried salt waited for the showerhead at the side of the house. After mouthfuls of salty ocean brine, that initial taste of fresh water running into my mouth was so insipid! A pale, bland imitation of primal liquid.

The first ten seconds of fresh water were fine. That spray had kept the warmth of the outside pipes. But I had forgotten that the outside shower has no hot water and instantly blanched as the water temperature plummeted. JoAnn watched me dancing like a whirling dervish and decided that torture wasn't for her. She washed the sand off her feet, ran up the gray wooden steps to the porch, and went into the house for a hot shower before dinner. The screen door with its loose spring slammed behind her.

I stood for a moment covered with goose bumps and decided that being a he-man has certain drawbacks. I too retreated to the house and a hot shower. In the bathroom I had to face the one great drawback of life on the beach: no matter how much I shower, no matter how much talcum powder I use, at the shore I always feel clammy, always end up with sand and grit in my crotch.

After dinner JoAnn and I volunteered to wash and dry dishes. Then everyone settled down for a game of 500 Rummy. The dinning table had a cover of seashore plastic oilcloth. An old tiffany lamp added charm to the musty, salty house smell. My mother insisted we play for pennies. In her suitcase she had managed to stuff a jar full of Lincoln heads. She doled out fifty coins to each of us in exchange for two quarters. Then she promptly won the pennies back and we had to buy another 50 pennies. No one beats my mother at cards, especially when she chooses the game.

'How did you learn to play cards so well?" Asked JoAnn as she purchased another fifty cents worth of pennies.

"What else did we have to do when I was young? We couldn't afford to go to the movies, and my aunt wouldn't let me go out with the girls in the evening. And God forbid I should even think of going anyplace with a boy. Or even having a boy over at the house."

"My mother was raised by her aunt Anna," I explain to JoAnn.

'That's mostly true," said my mother. "Rummy! Count your points." I was down 50, JoAnn 75, Rose and Carl about even. My mother racked up another 200. Carl's turn to deal.

"I don't understand," said JoAnn. I was going to warn her that talking while playing cards with my mother only made things worse. The discussion would interfere with your concentration; my mother's mental card computer wouldn't miss a tick.

"Oh, it's such a long story. I don't want to bore you."

"Mother, you might as well tell it," said Rose. "JoAnn hasn't heard it, Carl only knows it in bits and pieces. Tell the story and put it all together. And we might as well stop the game now you're beating us anyway. At this rate we won't have enough money to pay the mortgage next month."

"But we haven't finished," my mother complained looking dolefully around the table. She was reluctant to stop and leave some pennies on the table.

"We can finish later," Rose said in an older sister tone. "Let's go sit on the porch and enjoy the breeze." Rose pressed her point by rising from the table. Carl followed suit immediately. My mother showed less enthusiasm. She knew that once the card game broke up, it wouldn't go on again that night. But with the scratching of chairs on linoleum she knew her chance had passed. She too left the dining room for the front porch with the distant sound of surf.

"Oh, I'm so glad you made me this sweater, JoAnn. First night I have it, and already I'm warm as toast in the pure wool. You're so talented." My mother settled into her chair. "All I need now is a glass of wine. Do you think my son would be nice to his mother and bring her a glass from the kitchen?"

"Yes, mother, I'll get your wine. Anyone else?" My mother started the story while I was in the kitchen. I could hear her clearly through the screen door.

"My mother's family name came from Naples. They settled in Newark, New Jersey, near Bloomfield Avenue. I don't know why they came to America or what brought them to Newark. I suspect life was much better here than there. Where they settled is a residential part of Newark that was completely Italian.

"My mother had two older sisters: Anna and Bessie. Their mother's name was Frances, which is my name too. My Grandmother Frances. Bessie was married to Frank Vucola, a sweet man who must be over eighty now and is still very much alive. Frank and Bessie had a flock of children, your Newark cousins: Yola, Marie, Vera, Elsie, and the rest of the seven girls. I was always in their house. I remember that big brick house as my real home. And Uncle Frank was the father I wish I had. 'Papa' I always called him. You both remember Bessie," my mother said to Rose and I. "We would visit them all the time."

Rose nodded "I remember a big house in Newark with Aunt Bessie always cooking. Sheets of pasta dough stretched out on a table ready for dabs of ricotta cheese to make ravioli."

"Yes, Aunt Bessie could cook. That whole family loves to cook and eat. Everyone except my mother's sister Anna. She was very religious, even as a little girl. She entered a convent when she was a teenager. A very strict convent. Aunt Anna always wanted to be a nun.

"My mother's name was Asunta Panico. That's a pretty name. Asunta. Everyone told me that she was a very attractive girl. But she had what they used to call "weak lungs'."

"Weak lungs?" I asked.

My mother shrugged her shoulders. "I don't know what that phrase means exactly. No one had the money to go to the doctor in those days. You did what you could. That's what everyone said your grandmother had: weak lungs. That's all I know. You didn't question what your family said. For instance, my mother was introduced to her future husband in the old fashioned way: The meeting was arranged. I think the year was 1919 and she was seventeen years old. The man they arranged for her to marry had already been married before. He was also from Naples. A tailor by trade, Salvatore Capaldi made suits and coats and shirts. Not a successful man. I don't know if he worked for himself or for someone else.

"Salvatore had three children by his first wife. After her death, (I don't know anything about her), he put the children in a catholic boarding school run by nuns. Not the same one as my Aunt Anna. These were teaching nuns. The ones that use the rulers on your knuckles. Salvatore was a small, gentle man and married my mother because he needed a wife. He wanted his children from his first marriage back with him again. Everyone knew that. He thought he was very lucky to marry a young, beautiful girl like my mother. He must have brought some money to the family for the match. But I certainly never heard the truth about that. What I do know for sure is that they never told him about my mother's weak lungs.

"I was born a year later in 1920. My mother never recovered from the birth. I doubt she ever got out of her bed again. She died from influenza in the winter of 1922. Her weak lungs. Salvatore's children by his first wife never had the chance to leave the nun's school. Now he has twice a widower with children from two marriages.

"What happened next is hard for me to explain: my mother's family blamed Salvatore for her death. How could he be responsible? If anything they were wrong not to tell him his future wife lacked the strength for childbirth."

"Mother," I asked, "could Salvatore have asked for his dower money back if he could show that Asunta was weak and ill when he married her? Maybe they had to blame him for her death. Otherwise they would have had to return his money. And maybe they didn't have it anymore."

"I can assure you that if anyone took his money, they didn't have it to return. So maybe you're right. This is something I've never thought much about. Sometimes I don't understand what families do.

"What could my father do? They told him to get lost and that was that. He couldn't go to the police who wouldn't do anything anyway. What did they care about the endless domestic squabbles of the poor immigrants? And my father had no means to care for an infant. He wasn't married, there was no woman to look after me except my mother's family. He had to accept their decision. Not that he had much choice. They hid me from him. Refused to let him see me. Refused to tell him where I was.

"I lived with my grandmother Frances until I was seven. We were poor. Very poor. My grandfather had died years before. I don't know how my grandmother made the few dollars she brought in. We lived in two rooms. I slept in the same bed with my grandmother. That's how I knew she died. I woke one morning to find her lying next to me stone cold dead. I rolled over as I always did to kiss her good morning, and I kissed a corpse. I n my mind's eye I can see the lips of that little girl touching the cold shoulder of her grandmother." My mother crossed herself before continuing. "I screamed and screamed. What an awful thing to happen to a small child.

"Aunt Anna had to come out of nunnery to care for me. Aunt Bessie's family could not afford another mouth to feed. Or that's what they said. Aunt Anna hated me for taking her from her monastic life. She only came out because the family told the prioress of our problems. The prioress ordered Anna to leave the cloistered life. The convent order agreed to keep her as a lay sister, but she had to leave the nunnery. The order of the prioress could not be argued. This was a cloistered order that practiced total obedience.

"Let me tell you: She took the nunnery with her to the outside world. We had candles and religious statues in the house. We went to mass every morning and confession every evening. Too much. Too much for a young girl. Aunt Anna worked in the Westinghouse factory between morning and evening church. She kept her vows of chastity and piety. And she expected me to do the same. Pray, pray, pray, that's all we ever did.

"Over and over my grandmother had told me that both my parents died during the influenza epidemic. Bessie and Anna said the same thing. They never told me anything about my stepsisters. So I always believed that the death of my parents from influenza had left me an orphan.

"Whenever my father Salvatore made inquires about me to Bessie and Frank, which he did all the time, they wouldn't tell him anything. He didn't know Anna had come out of the convent and had no way to find me directly. And of course no one ever told me that he had come around asking for his daughter.

"Salvatore married a third time. This wife wanted all his children to live with them. His oldest girl by his first wife didn't want to leave the nuns. She stayed in school there and became a teaching nun herself. The second and third girls went to him. One is your Aunt Mary in Springfield, the other is your Aunt Felicia in Suffern. My father and new stepmother tried to find me, but again my aunts refused to tell them anything. And I was the one that most needed a family of my own."

The breeze had not dropped as the evening cooled. A few lights in the house across the street, a street lamp at the end of the road, and the constant roar of the surf were our only company on the dark night. JoAnn went in to fetch some blankets and the ladies wrapped them around their legs. Carl and I wore long pants. My face was pasty and my hair stiff from the constant salty air.

"When I was fourteen I had long, dark hair and a pretty figure. I had energy and brightness. But life with my Aunt Anna was hell. I would talk to a boy and she would call me a whore and a slut. Awful things. And beat me! Then I had to pray and pray to keep Satan from me. What devil? I was just an ordinary girl. We fought and bickered constantly.

"The fights must have spilled over into the family as a whole because my Aunt Bessie fought with her sister Anna about me. I began to stay with my cousins more and more. That was nice. The girls were my age; we would play and laugh like kids everywhere. One evening when it was time for me to go back home to my Aunt Anna the girls didn't want me to leave. They threw me on the bed, took off my clothes and left me only my slip. I stayed. What else could I do until they returned my clothes?

"Then came the afternoon that changed my life. I was at my cousin's house playing some silly game upstairs. Aunt Bessie called me down to the kitchen to help her. She was making pasta that day; the wide, thin strips of dough hung down from strings all over the room. She told me to sit in a chair at the table and eased her huge body into the chair next to me. She brushed her coarse black hair from her face with the back of a floured hand.

"'Frances,' she said, 'there is something I have to tell you. God forgive me for saying it. Something you should have been told years ago. A lie that's been eating at me. And now I think you're old enough for the truth. Your Aunt Anna doesn't want you to know, but I do. I've lived with this lie long enough. You have a right to know.' She took a deep breath before she continued. 'Your father is not dead. He's alive and well.' She took another deep breath. I was frozen in my chair. 'He lives three blocks from here with his new wife and children. There, now I've said it.'

"I must of looked pale as a ghost because she continued talking. 'I know this is hard to believe. What I am telling you is the truth. He comes here often to ask of you. Yesterday he came by again. He stood in my doorway with his hat in his hand and begged me to tell him about his daughter Frances. Tell him anything. Was she alive? Was she well? Anything. His eyes filled with tears as he pleaded with me. I sent him away, and at the same time I knew that this is the end of the lie for me. I cannot torture him, cannot torture myself, anymore to keep his lie. I promised my mother, I swore on her future grave not to tell you anything, ever. God forgive me for breaking my oath.'

"I didn't say a word to Aunt Bessie. I didn't say goodbye to my cousins. I left their house and walked down the block to our apartment. I remember a beautiful, warm Sunday afternoon; I remember Aunt Anna in her rocking chair by the front window with her half-glasses down on the end of her nose crocheting or tatting. That's how she spent every Sunday. I walked in the door and started screaming. Maybe I screamed for an hour, or maybe it was only five minutes that seemed like an hour. I threw back at her every ugly thing she had ever said to me. I called her a hundred ugly names I wasn't aware I knew. Over and over I demanded to know how she could call herself a good Catholic when she had lied to me for all those years.

"'He killed your mother,' she answered impassively. 'He forced her to be a wife when she had no strength to bear children. He killed my beautiful sister Asunta. I hope he suffers forever.' No remorse, no sympathy, not the slightest waver of apology appeared in her voice.

"I demanded to know where my father lived. She refused to tell. I think that's when I started throwing things. Sometimes you say things or do things, even as a child, that you can't take back, you can't retreat from. I screamed that I wouldn't obey her or live with her unless she brought me to my father. Of course she wouldn't tell me. In her heart and in all her actions she was still a nun, and they learn to be as stubborn as mules. The next time I saw Bessie, she wouldn't talk about my father. I guess the sisters had met and Bessie had been forced into silence again.

"Well, one thing led to another, and within a few months it was clear I could no longer continue to live with my aunt. I wouldn't obey or talk to her. Rebellious and angry. Very angry. Finally they sent me away to live with a family in Caldwell. That's where I met your father. In high school. Actually I met your Uncle John first. He was in my class. But when I met his older brother, I knew he was the man for me."

"Humph. I have a feeling, mother, that you are leaving out all the juicy parts," I said, "and stopping just when the story becomes interesting."

"You don't need me to tell you about that stuff."

JoAnn asked, "Did you ever meet your father?"

"Yes. Fifteen years later. We were living in our house in Short Hills. The children were in school that day. The doorbell rang and I went to answer it thinking a neighbor was coming over for a cup of coffee. When I opened the door, there was this little man, neatly dressed, with thin, bright eyes. And his face was so familiar, like one I had seen my whole life. In a flash, before he could say a word, I knew who he was. I almost fainted. I didn't know what to do or say.

"'Frances?' he asked. I nodded my head. 'I am your father, Salvatore Capaldi.' I started to cry. He started to cry. We stood there in the open doorway crying. We didn't know what to do. He was a stranger who owned a face that was an older version of my own. Finally he came in, I made him coffee and we talked all afternoon. You children came home from school and I introduced you to your grandfather, but you didn't understand who this man was.

"That's when I learned about my sisters—stepsisters. I had a whole family I never knew about! He told me that Aunt Anna had come to him a month before and told me where to find me. Just like that. My Aunt and I hadn't said more than a few words in twenty years, and she finally breaks down and tells my father where he can locate me if he wants to. The pain of talking to Salvatore must have burned her heart like acid. But that action of hers led me to a new relationship with her, thank God."

Everyone sat in silence. The wind and surf were our companions in thought.

"Enough talk for one night," said my mother. "I'm tired. Who's going to bed?"

"JoAnn and I are going for a walk," I said.

Rose and Carl decided to call it a night.

We walked down to the beach and sat on the dunes above the high tide. A gibbous moon rose above the horizon, painting the frothy oceans waves with silver. The cold wind precluded any lovemaking although I very much wanted to.

The next morning I rose early from my porch couch/bed. Cold, damp morning with a haze above the ocean. I ran a mile down the beach in the soft sand. Exhausting. And then walked back along the high tide line collecting shells and oddments.

September 14, 1965.

Registration today at Washington Square College, NYU. Classes start tomorrow morning. Full schedule for me this term: English: World Literature; German; Greek thinkers; Organic Chemistry and Lab, and Physiology.

I also need to talk to the Employment Office at school and locate something better than working part-time at Jack's Deli during the school year. Can't complain about the sandwiches and free meals, but the work doesn't strike me as college level and it's too far uptown. Or maybe I'm tired of selling soda and beer and pastrami, washing pots and sweeping that one small asphalt tile floor.

Yesterday, at the used bookstore on Broadway, I located some of my school books. That helps the bankbook. This year I only asked my father for tuition money. Everything else I am determined to supply on my own.

Andre phoned this evening. "Hankie, how would you and your girlfriend like to join me for dinner tomorrow. Isn't her name JoAnn?"

"Yes, it is."

"And you're free for dinner?"

"Yes, I think we are."

"Then it's a date?"

"Yes," I answered. After I hung up, I realized how smoothly he had led me through a series of yes answers. When I subtract our misunderstanding last week, I have to admit that was an enjoyable evening with an intelligent, witty man.

JoAnn and I were already planning to get together anyway tomorrow. This invitation saves us the problem of figuring out what to do. Should be most interesting.

I called JoAnn. "I would love to meet someone who finds you as attractive as I do." Very funny.

September 15, 1965.

Long, busy day. Classes in the morning starting at eight. Work in the afternoon at Jack's Deli for some pocket money. Plus a huge roast beef on rye with potato salad.

Late in the afternoon I opened the apartment door as the phone rang. The college job placement office has a listing for a part-time evening position at Beth Israel Hospital. That would be convenient. The hospital is located a few blocks east of here. I could walk from school to work and back to my apartment. They want me to interview tomorrow. Sounds great to me; plus the job has to be more interesting than the deli.

JoAnn came over at five. We chatted about new teachers and school schedules. There are a few days every week when we can meet for lunch or a break.

About five-thirty we were interrupted by a knock at the door. I opened the metal beast to find my elderly neighbor from across the hall, Mrs. Keller. She admits to seventy-five and curses the infinities that age brings. At least once a week I visit her for tea. Her apartment is the same size as mine, but that's where the resemblance ends. She lives with magazines and books; they share every corner, every table; she's an intellectual pack rat.

"Mr. Intili, I was wondering...Oh, I see you have company. I'm sorry to bother you, please excuse me. I'll come back later." She's old enough to be my grandmother and she insists on calling me "mister." Not that she looks my grandmother. My father's mother was short, fat, menacing, and the undisputed ruler tyrant of her home. Mrs. Keller is thin, white-haired, and as nervous as a bird.

"No, no, please, Mrs. Keller, don't go. Come in and join us."

"No, I couldn't do that. You two don't want me to disturb you. I'll come back again when you are free."

"Mrs. Keller, why are we standing in my doorway arguing? JoAnn and I have plenty of time. Do you need something?"

"Hello, Mrs. Keller," chimed JoAnn sweetly.

"Oh, hello darling," answered Mrs. Keller. She likes JoAnn. Everyone likes JoAnn. Mrs. Keller didn't budge from the doorway as she continued her discussion. "When you have time I want to show you something."

"Mrs. Keller, we have plenty of time." I was repeating myself. "Did you want me to come over and see whatever it is?" I noticed that her door was open.

"Only when you are free."

"We're free now, if JoAnn can come too."

"Of course JoAnn can come. At my age what would I have to hide?" she said laughing. A big, wrinkled smile showed her teeth of which she is proud. She claims every one of them came with the original package deal.

I glanced at JoAnn. She raised her eyebrows to say: why not? So we crossed the dim hallway to Mrs. Keller's apartment. Of course, her abode offered no place to sit; her three chairs were occupied with magazines except for the one cushioned Morris chair with an upholstered footstool in front and a floor lamp next to it. Her reading chair.

"This is what I want to show you," she said taking a large, brightly colored magazine from the footstool and presenting it to me. *Soviet Life*. JoAnn pressed her breast against my arm; we looked at the magazine together. We read the title, and gazed at the cover picture of a healthy, smiling, female doctor bending over a youngster. Mrs. Keller smiled too. She stood there, arms wrapped around her thin figure, her right index finger tapping her left forearm, anticipating our surprised reaction.

"You didn't expect that did you? Well, I have certainly been learning quite a bit today, let me tell you. I have my little secrets. A month ago I heard about this magazine on a television program. So I called my daughter and told her to find me a copy. Well, she didn't like that, but what are daughters for? I didn't show you the first one she brought me, did I? No, I didn't think so. I think I laid it over there in that pile under the window. Well, we can find it later. That's not important.

"After I read that first copy, I knew this was something I had to have. Told my daughter to order me a subscription. She absolutely didn't like that. No, she didn't. Told me the FBI keeps track of people who read this kind of material. Well, I told her, if the FBI wants to come around and investigate this old lady or bug my phone, they must be pretty hard up for criminals. Investigate me for reading a magazine! Made me so angry, I think I'm going to order the *Socialist Daily Worker* and maybe that other one, I think it's called *The New Republic*. Then let them come snooping around. I'll tell them a thing or two. Open their ears up, I bet."

"I don't think the other magazine is called *The New Republic*, Mrs. Keller." I commented quietly.

"Well, whatever. This *Soviet Life*, now that tells a story you don't see in our papers or on television. The Russians aren't completely bad the way our government wants you to think. And what the magazine says about that awful war in Asia, that makes sense to me, it does. Never could understand what we're doing there. Could you? So if you want to borrow this, just let me know. That way you can read it and the FBI won't come after you. What a disgrace. Do you want some tea?"

"Not this evening. We have dinner plans."

"Oh, how lovely. Well, you just go out and enjoy yourselves. This old body of mine isn't good for anything but reading and looking at television. I don't know what I'll do when my eyes give out. There are only a few parts of my body that work anymore. Well, that's no concern of young people like you. You just enjoy. Wish I had done more of that when I was young."

From Mrs. Keller's small, cluttered apartment to Andre's large one with its paintings and antiques was a small step in physical distance and a great leap in culture and attitude.

"Come in, come in," said Andre, his arm outstretched, his fingers waving us by him, "Don't stand out in the hallway. Corky, let them walk down the hall!" He shouted to his sausage-dog that was running back and forth, jumping in the air, and letting out tiny yelps that seemed in perfect proportion to his size. "All the way down the hall, kids, straight through to the parlor."

"You must be JoAnn who Hankie tells me all about," said Andre when we reached the parlor/living room. He brought his feet together and bowed his head slightly as he shook JoAnn's hand. "You're such a lovely girl! He's so lucky!" JoAnn glowed in the simple compliment. She wore a black cashmere sweater with a gold chain and ivory pendant that rested between her headlights.

"Oh, may I?" said Andre as he reached to lift the pendant from its comfortable bed. I would have never dared to reach that close to a girl's boobs for fear of touching them. He did it easily, smoothly. "Very beautiful. This is valuable jewelry. A family piece? European?" He was looking right into JoAnn's eyes, level, the pendant rolling in his fingers. To my mind, the chain, the pendant, the fingers, the question, his eyes: these formed a bond that linked them completely. The atmosphere glowed with a sexual aura.

"It was my grandmother's. She emigrated from Bavaria."

"Of course, yes, the quality shows. And the warm glow in the ivory suits your sweater and your color perfectly." He returned the pendant to her sweater, caressing it between his thumb and index finger. The white orb relaxed in JoAnn's soft cradle.

"Well, boys and girls, this is my little domicile. How nice to have you here."
Andre was dressed casually in tan shoes, tan slacks, and a blue silk shirt opened
three buttons to reveal a gold chain twisting through his thick chest hair, gray and
black.

"Would you care for a glass of wine? A very nice Johannesburg Riesling I
found today at that tacky store around the corner." He spoke to JoAnn who
nodded her head yes, yes. I had a feeling he could have asked her anything at that
point and she would have said yes.

Would you take the dog for a walk?
Can I borrow Hankie for a month?
Would you suck my big toe?

Yes, yes, yes.

"I won't ask Hankie about the wine. He'll just have to accept what we girls
give him. His poor macho ego won't recover for a week. Anywho, JoAnn would
you take three crystal glasses from that cabinet against the far wall, while I open
this bottle?"

"Yes," answered JoAnn. What else could she say after this cake icing of sappy
flattery and attention?

She secured three engraved goblets while Andre opened the wine with an
ornate silver corkscrew. The bottle made a respectable "pop" when the cork was
extracted. "I know we should wait for the wine to breathe," Andre said with a
conspiratorial whisper to JoAnn, "but do you think we could dispense with
proper etiquite this one time?"

"Yes," she giggled. Giggled, for Christ sakes. I was forcing myself not to
vomit or shake my head at such silliness. Another yes.

"Shall we make a toast?" Andre asked. "To new friends." First he clinked
glasses with JoAnn then with me. I'm certain he winked at her.

The wine was superb. So much for "tacky" stores.

"About dinner. Since there are just the three of us getting to know each other,
I thought we might eat in. I could prepare a simple chicken paprikosh.
Everything we need is in my tiny frig. That way we can nosh some cheese and
crackers, chat, and enjoy our wine."

"Only if you let me help you cook," said JoAnn.

"No, no, no. That's not necessary. The meal will only take me a moment.
Everything is ready. And anywho, I don't want you to mess up that beautiful
sweater. You stay right here, I'll disappear for a moment into my kitchen and

prepare a few munchies. Corky," he said to the dog who was sitting in the corner, "you play with these delightful young people while I'm gone."

Somehow JoAnn and I ended up in the kitchen helping Andre cook. His apartment has a real kitchen, small but furnished. There's a table, two chairs and the usual kitchen appliances. I sat at the table with my glass of wine. JoAnn and Andre prepared the carrots, potatoes, chicken, peas, and I forget what else. Wine clouds my memory.

"Isn't Andre a French name?" asked JoAnn, scraping some carrots over the sink.

"More than just French, my dear. Mine is a common name in Hungary, too. Which is my original family home, though it would be impossible for me to go back there. I left just before the war broke out."

"The Hungarian uprising?" I asked.

"No, Hankie. Although the suggestion is most sweet of you, I was referring to The War, the Big War." Andre pared meat from a quartered chicken he had boiled earlier. "Don't look at me like that, it isn't polite to stare at someone when he is revealing his age. My parents sent me to college in Switzerland after Hitler marched into the Sudetenland. They knew another World War was coming, and they did not want me to fight in it. So you see, Hankie, You're not the only one who doesn't want to fight in a War that butchers young people."

"What happened to your parents?" asked JoAnn. She had completed cleaning and slicing the carrots and had commenced operations against the red skin potatoes.

"They died. I don't know where. So many people died. Everyone of talent and intelligence. Every family of my class. The German baboons destroyed Eastern Europe. The Russians inherited only the dumbest and the lowest. I escaped the war. In the early 40s, while the rest of the world burned, Switzerland was a vast holiday for a wealthy, cute, young man with a full Swiss bank account. You cannot imagine that world.

"We vacationed on Lake Geneva in the summer. I was not the only rich boy avoiding the chaos. One summer—I think it was 1944—we drove into a town in my maroon Mercedes with the top down. A great convertible with smooth leather seats. First stop, the local police station. I placed a stack of Swiss francs on the desk of the police chief. The police look so stuffy proper in their starched uniforms, with their fleshy complaisant faces. On his desk I dropped a pile of bank notes. That's the universal language of the police: Swiss cash. I told him I was paying for my tickets and fines in advance. He nodded politely.

34

"Then we partied through the summer in a rented villa overlooking the blue lake. A dozen boys. And occasionally a young girl, too. We weren't that choosy. Something you wouldn't understand, Hankie."

Andre smiled at me, winked at JoAnn and filled our glasses to the rim. "Hankie's so lucky to have a cute girl like you," Andre said to JoAnn as he clinked glasses with her again. Then he leaned over and whispered something into her ear. I couldn't make out the words. She laughed, blushed, and bobbed her head. Yes, yes.

"Well, by the end of the war my bank account was empty, my Hungary destroyed, and my family…no more. Eastern Europe raped and held in bondage by the Russians. Stupid Americans, so naïve to trust the Slavic barbarians. In Switzerland the big party broke up the way the best ones always do. One evening we had full wineglasses in our hands, gentle lovers in our beds; the next morning we parted with the mist.

"I had managed during the war to obtain a college education at the University of Basil. But at the end of the war, I had no money and no job. So I sold my Mercedes to my ex-banker. Do you know he had the cutest, most charming wife, and sometimes he would come over to visit us girls on the sly?" Andre was directing his talk to JoAnn again; she shook her head in commiseration. "Don't even trust your banker."

"Especially not your banker," JoAnn added definitively. I looked at her in amazement. Where did that come from? Her eyes remained only on Andre; she wasn't acknowledging my presence at all.

"In 1946 I decided to try my luck in America, in New York. There was no place in Europe fit to live in except Switzerland. And no broke Hungarian could find a job there. Anyway, the party was over, and I pride myself on knowing when to say goodbye.

"Now, JoAnn, add those wonderful vegetables that you cut so expertly to the pot. We cover it, wait 30 minutes while we talk about you and your plans, and then dinner will be ready. Hankie! You haven't set the table! You're impossible. Cute, but impossible. How does this girl put up with you?"

We didn't return to my apartment until nearly midnight.

"Oh, Hank," she said, taking off her blouse, "He has such charming manner and savior faire."

"I think the dog Corky is more interesting," I responded as I turned back the couch cover.

"Do I hear the patter of green demon feet?"
"No, but you're going to see the hairy monster."

September 17, 1965.

Last night JoAnn came over to my apartment for dinner. We cooked up a pot of spaghetti with my mother's frozen sauce that was her parting gift on my last visit home. Doing my laundry and sending me off with Ragu sauce and meatballs—my mother's elixir of need.

The closet-sized kitchen in my apartment approaches its theoretical limits when you fix dinner for two. Actually my dwarfish kitchenette is a converted closet. You open what appear to be ordinary closet double doors and find yourself in front of a tiny stove, sink and refrigerator. A hundred years ago my apartment building was an exclusive residence with two large apartments on each floor (much like JoAnn's building). These ample dwellings were chopped up into smaller units; now six apartments occupy each floor. In the last century my hole in the wall bedroom, bathroom and closet were part of a large elegant apartment that defined the front half of the apartment building. What remains of this urbanity is a truncated vivisection. The beauty, like blood, spilled on the dissecting table; and the shabbiness, the remains of a pale corpse.

After dinner JoAnn and I cleaned up the apartment. She put the leftovers into the refrigerator for my dinner tomorrow night. I collapsed the card table legs one after the other in succession, folded up the metal chairs, and stowed them in the next room behind the bathtub. Most evenings when I have dinner by myself, I sit at the desk near the window and look out over Union Square. The City sounds of cars, horns and shouts, the Con Edison bell tower ringing out the quarter hours, the flapping of pigeons in circular flight around the trees, below—this activity outside the window leaves me less lonely. But on nights when I have guests, I take out the card table and chairs and place them in the middle of the room.

We stood side by side in the closet-kitchen to wash and dry dishes. The warmth from her body swelled my interest in the right places. A growing interest that would have to wait until we finished our tasks. JoAnn likes to complete one project before she starts another. Asking her to do otherwise is a one way journey down a road named Frustration Alley.

Eventually I washed the last pot and handed it to her. While I drained and wiped the sink, she toweled off the porcelain pot and put it away in the tiny cabinet above the tiny stove. She wiped her hands dry on a towel that hung from the back of the closet kitchen door. Then she stepped back from the kitchen, scrutinized the scene for a moment and closed both doors. JoAnn's final actions when she completes a task have a way of saying: this is complete, there is no more, time to move on.

JoAnn crossed the room to my combination couch/bed. This one large piece of furniture is covered with a tan corduroy fabric sown to fit (well, almost fit) by my mother. A "house warming present." She also sewed matching (well, almost matching) covers for the foam bolsters. My mother wants to ensure that no one deliberately mistakes my couch for a bed. Or maybe she wants to remind me that this particular bed is sometimes intended for use as a couch. Very particular sometimes. Like now when I'm alone with a girl.

JoAnn sat far back against the wall bolsters with her legs pointed straight out across the couch. Then she crossed her legs. Absolute sign this wasn't a romantic interlude. Talk Time. My mother would be pleased the bed/couch retained the couch identity. When JoAnn sits on the couch and tucks her legs under her, then the evening has promise. Not tonight. My heart sank along with another part of my anatomy. No sense sitting next to her on the couch; so I parked myself in my desk chair on the other side of the room.

"Hank, I want to talk to you about a long conversation I had with my parents last night. Mostly with my father, the way these conversations always are. It's so repetitious. This quote talk unquote" (JoAnn draws quote marks in the air around her word) "was a discussion about boys, eligible boys and other boys."

"Meaning me," I said.

She answered with a long gaze and then continued, "It was a one-sided quote talk unquote that continued for several hours after dinner. Maybe it started with dessert. A real 'fine al cake'. My mother played second chorus to my father's lines. Maybe they even rehearsed them. It was awful. Finally I gave up and went to bed. I was so tired."

She shifted herself around and tucked her legs under. There was no secret signal in her movements; the evening was dead in that department. "So this morning I wake up and what do I find pushed underneath my door?"

"Ten tiny reindeer?" I asked to be funny.

"I wish. I find notes. Pages and pages of written notes. My father's writing. Dated the middle of the night! He must have stayed up continuing the conversation with my ghost. Why does he make everything so difficult?"

I didn't answer her. However, I did notice that her deep brown eyes lack their usual lustrous sheen this evening. She looked past me to the window and talked to whatever spirit abides in the trees around Union Square. "I guess I ought to read some of this to you. Maybe you can tell me what to do. Pass me my purse, please. I left it on your desk."

Her dark elegant purse stood upright on my garage sale desk where it held down a mess of school papers. I reached over and grabbed it. The leather was wonderfully supple; it seemed to melt into my fingers. As always I felt awkward handling a woman's purse. Why couldn't she fetch her own purse? I didn't ask her to take chunks out of our time together to read letters from her insomniac father. She removed a folded mass of crinkled onion skin paper from her purse. At least a dozen sheets. He must have written half the night! Who would lecture his daughter for hours on her choice of boyfriends and then continue the lecture long after she's gone to bed? She shuffled through the pages until she found a place she wanted to read, had obviously planned to read.

JoAnn's long brown hair was brushed straight down this evening. When she combs her hairs that way, the sharpness of her facial features are overemphasized, her nose appears larger and her chin more pointed. When she wears her hair up in a bun, she can be quite pretty.

Ready to read, JoAnn tossed her hair back from her face and over her shoulder. Her voice, although basically legato, had a sharper edge than when we were chatting of this and that over dinner. I guessed she was under some strain.

"*Boys in general have a lot to do on their own, they are interested in their future, not in girls. Girls have to really go at them if they see some spark. Some guys are like absent professors. They don't think of girls because they are so intent on their own futures. Other guys are looking to feather their nest. They see a nice girl, well off, sweet and simple, no airs, and they cater to her in every way. Some girls think it love when they are chased for their money and possible future position.*"

JoAnn looked up at me. "I really don't think that about you. I've told them a million times you don't care about 'feathering your nest'. They think I don't know how to tell about boys. But no matter what I tell them, it doesn't do much good, does it?"

She moved on to the next page. The onionskin had a crisp lettuce sound as she shuffled the pages around.

"*You are getting to an age where you will be going out with boys older than you: 26-27-28. If you don't click with them, you should arrange for them to meet your girl friends and vice-*

versa. Of course the boy's financial and social background must be such that you are not afraid to introduce him to your friends. "

How can I ever live up to their ideal of background? I know my ancestors were peasants. They didn't come to America because Italy was a paradise. Our home didn't have a library or Saturday afternoon opera on the radio. My parents didn't go to college, although they made sure their children went. My large library of books and my collection of classical records are from my own directions. Doesn't that count for something? And of course I'm not Jewish.

We lived on the south side of the railroad tracks in Short Hills. Not poor and certainly not wealthy. Talented, hard working blue collar. I went to Dickinson College on scholarship and worked through the school year for this professor or that, anything to make spending money. Summers I worked for my father, even if we weren't talking. I had to have that money. JoAnn's father paid her college bill in cash. Now that JoAnn and I have both transferred to NYU, I'm working even harder to support my apartment and buy the basics. Her father opens his bottomless wallet another inch. How can I ever measure up to those standards?

"*Social work in hospitals, blind, old age, etc. is fine and can be done when one is married to her own cultural, and social background; and when she has time to assist. We believe in integration, in equal rights, in the poverty program, and all that; but it doesn't mean one has to travel in these unfortunately low circles where men will make play for any gal who shows a bit of class. Naturally only the smart ones will make the play and give you plenty of logical reasons why it should be.* "

"That's enough. The letter goes on and on. The same stuff he was jawing to me about last night. That went on and on, too. I wish they would leave me alone. Hank, what do you think?"

I felt cold all over, even though the apartment was warm from the day's heat. I was immobilized like a bronze statue in Union Square covered with white pigeon droppings. "Well, besides the length and contents of the note and its deliberately negative tone, I am troubled by your acceptance of it."

"That's not so; I don't accept what he has to say."

"Yes, you do."

Her voice sharpened. She ran her hand through her hair as she snapped at me: "If I accepted the contents of these pages of notes, why would I read them to you? Why would I be here? That's not a fair thing to say to me. I take hours of his garbage on this subject last night. That's hardly my idea of accepting his opinions."

I said nothing. Just looked at her. After a minute or two of cold staring, she shrugged her shoulders and handed me the pages of writing. "Throw them out. Burn them, get rid of them. Anything. I don't want them. It's not worth fighting with you. I wanted your help. Is that asking too much?" I took the pages without answering her barbs and stuffed them into the trash bucket by the door. We've been dating for three years, and I'm still at best an imitation of an acceptable person.

It seems clear from her father's note that someone like her old high school boyfriend Murphy is his idea of an acceptable boyfriend: Jewish, pre-law at Yale, polite, rich family. I told her that after I dumped the notes in the trash basket. "Murphy is your father's ideal mate for you."

"Murphy! No way. He's so boring. How can you even think that I would prefer Murphy to you?"

"It's not what I think. My thoughts have nothing to do with the dynamics of the situation or with the logic of how your parents think."

"Of course it's what you think. Don't you understand that's the real difference between you and Murphy? Between you and most other boys. You think. I would never go out with Murphy again. I tried it once in high school. That was enough. I really don't know how you could believe for a second that I would go out with him, or even want to. You're the only one I want. Sometimes you don't understand anything." She chopped her hand in the air with her hand. There it was, one of her finality gestures.

On any other night I would have argued the point farther with her. That air chop combined with a friendlier look in her eye separated this evening from the pack. No way was I going to continue a pointless conversation. Perhaps the evening had changed in my favor. So I moved across the room to the couch. Good move. She pulled me down to her and almost popped the buttons on my shirt. She buried her face in my chest and I felt her crying.

I held her for a moment, but cuddling was not what she wanted. She loosened my belt and had her hand down my pants to grab and stroke me. We made love for an hour with incredible intensity. She wanted more and more and more.

We never took my mother's cover off. Even though it was still technically covering my couch, my mother would not approve of the stories her corduroy could tell.

September 20, 1965.

Yesterday was a beautiful day. JoAnn and I rode the Staten Island ferry back and forth across New York Harbor. Best five cent boat trip in the world.

Riding the IRT subway far downtown on a Sunday afternoon is worth a trip by itself. The old stations with their wonderful mosaics and tiles. Such artistry. Peasants, stone masons and plasterers from Italy in the latter part of the last century. Probably paid pennies to produce the wondrous art of subterranean lower Manhattan.

"Look at this art!" I shouted in JoAnn's ear. You always have to shout into someone's ear to be heard over the wind-roaring, wheel-screeching IRT. Needless to say, I don't mind having the excuse to be close to JoAnn. She always smells so fresh.

"Yes," she shouted back, her lips brushing my neck.

"Do you think the Wall Street types who jam into this train every Monday to Friday even see this work? Or care about the people who had the talent to produce it?"

"Did the artist have enough money to invest into it?" She answered me.

"They didn't immigrate from Italy because they were prosperous. Certainly my grandparents didn't. They left because they needed work. Where would they ever get the spare cash to invest?"

Sometimes I don't know if JoAnn is being perceptive or dense. Was she making a jibe at my lack of money and her own inherited investments? Or was she telling me that there are different kinds of wealth and differing appreciations?

The train screamed into the Wall Street station. The doors opened. I pointed to the fancy stucco. "Maybe the City could commission modern masonry in huge dollar signs."

"How about bulls and bears?" She spoke as the subway doors close.

"How about unbearable bull?" I shouted into her ear as the train roared out of the station. We laughed into the squealing noise and stale wind.

We walked up and out of the last and most ornate station at Battery Park and strolled down the deserted Riverside Park in the warm noontime air to the ferry ship. On the trip out to Staten Island we stood at the front of the ferry boat and listened as the bow slapped and slashed through the gray harbor water. The strained throbbing of the ferry's engines massaged our feet. Side by side we watched boats of all sizes and descriptions moving past, reminding us this is a major world port.

"Have you heard from Chris lately?" JoAnn asked.

"I've written a letter or two, but I haven't received an answer."

"Did you say anything to him that would anger him?" For some reason her question really annoyed me.

"Why the hell would I do that?" The sun was in my eyes as I tried to look at her. I squinted and could only make out the darkened image of her face under sparkling, free blowing hair.

"You don't have to jump down my throat over a simple question, Hank. I was only asking. You're being over-sensitive."

"No, I'm not. Sensitivity has nothing to do with it." I turned my back to the harbor and fixed my gaze at the Statue of Liberty. Wish I had my liberty, I'm thought; my freedom from this albatross.

Maybe I ought to explain about Chris. I first met him in my sophomore year at Dickinson. He was a senior, a Senior spelled with a capitol S. The major student figure in the Mermaids Players Theatre Group. He probably had his eye on me from my freshman year when I dated Rusty. Any dark, short freshman who could snare and date a red headed senior was worth Chris's attention. That Rusty had been a part of the theatre group and had dated some of his friends only increased his interest.

Chris roomed down the hall from me in the non-fraternity dorm. With little effort on his part he became my idol. My confidant. My mentor in the amorous arts. I was attracted to his confidence and poise. He was the only person that year I confided in about Rusty's abortion, an issue I never even discussed with JoAnn that year although we dated steadily all through my sophomore (her freshman) year. Another full year passed between JoAnn and I before I could talk to her about Rusty. And then only in pieces.

Chris dated a delightful girl named Joanie. She graduated the year before (with Rusty's class) and lived in town teaching at a local high school in order to be close to Chris. When I first met Joanie she knew about me from Rusty as well as Chris. Joanie was instant family to me. And since she, Chris and I are short folks, under five-five, we had that added bond as well.

Chris's Great Scene occurred sometime past the middle of the school year. I know that because JoAnn and I had been together for a number of months. First I heard from a friend that Chris had suddenly jumped into his car and mysteriously driven off from school; then I heard he had thrown a desk through a classroom window. Strange stories filled with the germ of truth about Chris's unpredictable nature. He was nowhere to be found for several days. Not in his room, not in class, not at the theatre. And Joanie wasn't answering her phone at her apartment in town.

"Did I ever tell you the story about Chris throwing the desk through the window?" I said to JoAnn to break the silence between us.

"I was there at Dickinson when he did it. Everyone heard the story."

"Oh, yeah. And do you know about the note that started it all?"

"The note Joanie left on his windshield saying she was pregnant?"

'Oh, you know about that, too."

"Yes, Hank, I knew about that. And as fond as you've always been of those two, I always thought that note was wrong of her. I can imagine what she felt, any girl knows that scene in her mind. But she shouldn't have told him that way." JoAnn looked down at the water rhythmically splashing and spraying against the front of the ferry right beneath us. My eyes are on the water too.

"Did I ever tell you what Chris said to me when he returned from his honeymoon?"

"No, that story I don't know."

Even as she answered, my guts froze. I had gone too far. This is an area I'm not comfortable discussing, I can't find the right words, and I continued to stare out at the water and the front spray. Maybe a fish would appear and I could change the talk. Even some interesting garbage would help.

JoAnn pressed against me; she must have sensed I was having some trouble. "Maybe you told me once, but I don't remember. What did he say?"

"He said: 'You solved your problem one way, Hank, and I solved mine another.'"

"He was talking about Rusty?"

I looked away from the water and away from JoAnn. The Statue of Liberty had my complete attention. I shouldn't have started this conversation. There had to be a way out. Rusty is an issue I never talk about. Only once or twice has the subject been mentioned in the three years JoAnn and I have been together. And those talks where brief and oblique.

"That wasn't a nice thing for Chris to say," JoAnn commented.

"It was a true statement."

"Well, since I'm on the pill it won't be our problem. I just wish the damn pill didn't make me gain this weight." That's my cue line to grab her tight and hug. It's not difficult to notice that she is somewhat chunkier these days. But there's no way I would ever admit to that, at least to her face. "You feel fine to me."

"That's not true."

Oops. I know that tone of voice. Time to steer clear of those shark infested waters. "Do you remember when Chris and Joanie moved off campus into a trailer? He didn't want to move into her apartment, even though she thought it was OK for them to do that. He said something about needing a place that was theirs from the start. Chris is such a syrupy romantic.

"Well, one evening after they had been there only a few weeks, Chris called me up. Said he had to talk. Very important, very hush-hush. As usual I was bored to death of schoolwork and welcomed the break. My car was parked a dozen blocks away on some hidden street in town. I couldn't park the car on campus because I was on scholarship and wasn't supposed to have a car at school. God, what a beast that '56 Pontiac was. Can't believe the Dean never caught me with it."

"Hank, Dean James knew all about your car."

"He did?"

"Of course he did. Everyone knew about your old car. No one minded because you were so eccentric. Sneaking a car off campus was deemed a natural part of you."

"Are you sure?"

"Certain. Dean James even talked to my father about your car. They had a big laugh about it."

"They did?"

"My father is a big alumnus donor. Dean James tells him everything. But never mind about the car. What happened that night with Chris? I haven't heard this story."

"I met Chris at the front door to the trailer. He yelled to Joanie that we were going out for a beer, and we drove off. We hadn't gone a block when he slapped his hand on the dash and said in his best John Proctor voice that he had to talk to me about a serious problem, a problem he can't discuss with anyone else. He made me swear I would never tell his situation to another soul. I agreed. What choice did I have? Since there wasn't a chair in the car, he might throw his shoe through my window."

JoAnn laughed at my scene. We locked arms and watched the seagulls play above the ferry. I continued my story taking both my part and Chris's.

"What's your problem, Chris?

"She grabs it."

44

"So, what's the problem?"

"That's the problem!"

"That's a problem? I thought to myself. This was my idol, my designated master in the amorous arts telling me this kind of problem? Joanie grabs his dick and that's a problem? What had she been doing before this? And hadn't any of his other grand conquests grabbed for his dick?" JoAnn laughed. Grabbing my dick is one of her favorite pastimes.

September 22, 1965.

Started work at the medical records department of Beth Israel Hospital last night. Working five to nine in the evening pulling charts for the next day's clinics and being available for emergency needs in the evening hours after the regular staff has left for the day. Medical Records is a giant file room with the charts of hospital patients, past and present. The manila folder files are in open shelves, filed numerically.

Let's say that tomorrow's Skin Clinic has 25 patients scheduled. We get a sheet of paper with the patients' names and file numbers. We pull the charts for the clinic by number and check against the name. The new files are bright tan manila folders, starched and prim. The older folders for the patients who have been seen at the hospital for years are darkened, ragged, frayed and full of old staples waiting to snag us.

I'm working with another college student named Bill. The work does not look very exciting, but I need the money for my apartment, food, and other such necessities. At least the work is better than the job as a store clerk at Jack's Delicatessen on 87th Street and Third Avenue. Seems strange: one year I pull cans and jars from shelves, the next I pull files. See the progress?

Another good thing about working at Beth Israel Hospital is its proximity to my apartment. I can walk the dozen blocks from my place on Union Square over to First Avenue in about ten minutes. Or on afternoons when I have a late lab at NYU, I can walk over to First or Second Avenue and then head uptown at a good clip. Last year the trip by subway to Jack's Deli took me almost to JoAnn's apartment.

Speaking of JoAnn, she was at my place tonight waiting for me after work. First I grabbed some Pennsylvania Dutch hard pretzels from the box I store in the cabinet above my miniscule stove, and a glass of milk. We chatted about my new job. Although she asked questions at the right places, her eyes wandered. She

45

had something else on her mind. The milk back in the refrigerator, the closet door closed, she started in with a long talk. She did most of the talking.

She sat under the window at my desk or walked in circles around the small apartment gesturing with her hands in short choppy motions. I was seated cross-legged on the bed (still made up as a couch, with my mother's corduroy cover. Mom would have of approved of the arrangements.) I pulled one of the bolsters to the side and leaned my back against the plaster wall. Listening posture. Prepared for standard weekly litany about her parents and moving out on her own. Speeches 206 and 207.

"Hank, I have been thinking all day and I've come to the realization essential to my actions." Hand chop. Her hair was down tonight, held back from her face with a pair of tortoise shell berets. "What I've concluded is that I cannot change my parent's way of thinking. I can't change their ideals for me and their plans for my life. Nor can I ever show them, by any means, that I merit living apart in my own place. Like you live in yours."

"They really don't want you independent of them," I added on cue. She continued pacing. There isn't much room to walk in the apartment, even if you march through the bathroom door and around the tub. Of course she didn't do anything like that. She just walked from the desk to the kitchen closet and back again, talking to the gold rug or to me.

"I know that. But that's not what's on my mind today. You see, the problem is not them. Don't you see? It's me. The problem lies right here." She halted her pacing, tapped her chest and looked at me. I nod in recognition. That response seemed to satisfy her and she continued her marathon walk to noplace. "I am rather self-centered and a bit too egotistical to think that by a few actions I will end good relations forever between them and me. They didn't like me leaving Dickinson College and transferring to NYU. They tried to argue me out of the move, but I wanted to be here. With you. And that didn't cause a break between my parents and me."

"JoAnn, what have you done that's so bad? Become mature?"

"That's right, I have grown up this year. And last year. I know so much more about my self and my wants and my likes. They don't want to see that. Oh, why speculate about this at all? It's for them to decide whether or not they will reconcile themselves to this new maturity in me."

"Haven't they pretty much decided that already?"

She stopped walking in circles and sat down in the chair again. Good thing she ended the great wildebeest migration. I was becoming dizzy. "Yes, Hank, they have made that decision. They have stated their opinions."

"Lots of times."

"Right, lots." She sat quietly sucking on her lower lip.

"So now what?" I asked. I wanted her to end the discussion. The hour was late, and I could use some sex before she headed uptown. These talks always end that way. I just wanted her to move on through the standard agenda.

"So now its up to me. I have to act either according to their desires the way they've expressed them, or I have to lead out on my own." A minute ago the situation was up to them. Now it was up to her. It seemed to me that this was just so much senseless circular talk. She watched me. Probably knew what I was thinking. Great, now I was in trouble.

"Do you know how much I admire you, Hank?"

The question caught me off guard. I never expected her to say something like that. "Why" I asked.

"Because you act on things. Decisively. Wham. Done. For a long time these ideas about moving out on my own have been fluttering about my head. I'm afraid to act. That's the simple truth. I'm afraid to be out on my own like you. I talk and talk and you just sit there and listen to me. Hank, it's so warm in my mother's womb. I can't give up comforts the way you would. That's why I admire you. You think something through, then you act. No hesitation. My own thoughts keep me from acting."

She sighed deeply. Something about her last sentence rang a bell with me. Reminded me of a line from a Shakespearean sonnet. Can't place it. Anyhow, that's part of JoAnn's verbalizing: she incorporates lines from other people and threads them through her own patchwork to create a quilt not quite them and very much her.

"For the moment I only have a few actions that can proceed from all my thinking. The first necessity is to be frugal."

"Frugal?" Somehow frugal and Park Avenue JoAnn don't quite fit together.

"Yes, frugal. It hurts to say this but if my parents wish to maintain the attitude of 'buttered bread' towards me, an attitude designed to buy me off, then I will have to get out of them whatever I can now. I'll have to save up what they give me. Store it for leaner times."

She looked at me for reassurance, encouragement. I said nothing, hoping she would give up and sit down next to me. No luck. She resumed her walking.

"Perhaps I can find a roommate at NYU, someone to share a small apartment. That way my expenses will be low. I don't see how I could live in an apartment alone like you do without parental support. And I don't want to be so dependent on my parents. Maybe I could make a business deal with you."

She looked straight into my eyes. There's a meaning here that I was missing. "What kind of business deal?" I asked.

"No, that's not a good idea. This has to be my problem and my solution."

"Whatever."

"No, Hank, that's not right. 'Whatever' is not right. I would rather not bring you into this part at all. The problem is between me and them."

Finally, at last long, she came over and sat down next to me. Not touching me yet. But the great migration across the Nebraska plains was complete. The bison herd rested. "Do you know how tempting it is to sit back and admire you."

"Admire me?" That was the second time tonight she talked about admiring me.

"Sometimes you don't see anything, do you?" She had her warm hand on my knee.

"See what?" She had me confused. Was she still on her parental dilemma speech or was this the long postponed journey from knee to crotch?

"How do I say this right?" She was not really asking me.

"Just spit it out."

She took her hand away. Trouble. "It's just that lately there's been a feeling of 'habit' after we've gone to bed. I'm not saying I'm unhappy. It's always great to be with you."

"Then what?" I added. My body stiffened in negative anticipation. How did we go from her usual weekly discussion of moving out on her own to bedroom complaints?

"There's this feeling of usualness whenever we go to bed. Usualness with a capital U, a feeling of Usualness that's become a pattern of what we do in bed. Our lovemaking lacks brightness. For you there's no sense of conquest. For me no real spiritual gratification. Do you understand?" She looked flat into my eyes again. No deviation. She wants an answer.

"Spiritual gratification seems a funny goal in bed."

"I'm not talking so much about me. I want to know about you."

"I never really expect any spiritual gratification. That stuff is…"

"OK, OK, forget I ever said it." She broke off the stare and crossed her arms over her chest. Good bye sex tonight; hello cold shower.

"No, JoAnn, what I mean is…"

"Forget it, forget it, forget it!" She was back on her feet. "This is really very important to me and you're not listening."

"Of course I'm listening. What else could I do?'

"I know that you haven't felt much in bed with me lately."

I started to answer. She put her hand up. "Don't interrupt me and put me off track. I know you haven't. And this feeling of habit must be broken. It must." She was back to staring at me full face.

"OK," I answered. What else can I say? "We'll find a way to break it." Please don't ask me how.

She let out a great sigh. She was wearing one of her silk blouses that show off her large breasts. Not much chance of becoming better acquainted with them tonight. What set her off? I started to wonder if it was close to period time for her. No, that was two weeks ago. Something else must have her upset.

She fell back into the chair on the other side of the room. Back to an hour ago. "Unlike you, hank, I'm not attracted to anyone else sexually."

"I never said I was attracted to anyone else." I de-emphasized the word "said," even though it's the most important word in the sentence.

"Are you?'

"Am I what?' Maybe I could deflect the question.

"OK, OK! Don't answer the question. Why can't I have a conversation with you on something this important to us?"

"I did answer the question. You're the one who keeps asking it over and over. And then you don't accept the answer when I give it. Maybe you'll answer it in reverse. Are you attracted to anyone else sexually?" Since she had just told me that she wasn't, I figured this was a safe question and a way to wriggle out of hers. That direction would only lead to a direct lie. There are a dozen girls at school I'm attracted to everyday, and half a dozen, I would like to ask out if I could only find a good way to approach them.

"Not really. Maybe only Arnie, but that not very much. You're the only person I really want to go to bed with."

"Arnie Who's Arnie?" Suddenly I was all ears.

"No one, no one important. No one who means anything. I'm sorry I even mentioned it."

"He must be someone."

"He's no one, just a fellow in English class. You don't know him."

I could picture him Arnie. Tall, handsome, rich. Probably with small, dark rimmed glasses. Pre-law. Another Murphy. Talking to JoAnn. Looking at her boobs. Undressing her. And she's smiling because there's no "Usualness."

JoAnn didn't want to talk anymore. I wanted to go to bed with her, but she just shook her head no and didn't give a reason. It was late when we left my place and took a taxi uptown. She insisted on paying which is good because I don't have any extra money.

She invited me in. The front door to her apartment building was already locked for the night and we had to ring for the doorman. At that hour he's also the elevator operator. He greeted JoAnn by name and nodded to me. Upstairs the spacious apartment was quiet and dark except for a single table lamp that spread an hourglass of light in the hall. The tile floor had an illuminated circle that tapered up the wall and closed to a sharp point at the shaded lamp. Then the cone of light opened up again on as it moved up the wall and became a large circle once more on the plaster ceiling.

Her parents had already retired. We tiptoed down the long black and white tiled hallway past their bedroom door, JoAnn's bedroom door, and through to the kitchen in the back. I snapped on a fluorescent overhead light that bathed the room in harsh brilliance. The old white porcelain table was neatly set with a solitary bowl, plate and silverware for her father's breakfast.

In the refrigerator we found half a chocolate cake and a quart of milk. JoAnn took a pair of white ceramic plates from the cabinet and set them at the other end of the table from her father's clean and empty breakfast plates. As she set them on the table they made a noise like a minor earthquake in the quiet apartment. The perfect parental trap to tell when kids are in the kitchen: heavy plates on steel-enamel tables. The forks and milk glasses sounded like a snare drum when we set them down. Even napkins didn't help much. No one came in screaming at us to quiet down, so maybe the level of noise was more in our imaginations than anywhere else.

We chatted a bit more in the night's quiet. This time about school and my latest disaster in Organic Chemistry lab. What I really wanted to do was to lie down on her living room rug and neck like we used to. But if I didn't succeed with my charms downtown, I certainly wouldn't here with her father two rooms away.

A few minutes after midnight I finished my cake and milk, and said I have to leave. My head ached from the long day as I rose from the table. JoAnn kissed me sweetly on the lips. "I don't think I ever wanted you as much as I did tonight. But somehow it wasn't right. Sleep well. I love you."

I left her apartment by the back stairs to avoid the hallway and walked down 96th Street past the UFO Research Center to the subway. Flying saucers made more sense than the events of this evening. My balls ached already.

The subway station was empty, filled only with that flat, almost acidic smell of humid subway air and the ubiquitous buzz of faulty fluorescent lights. The man in the token booth had his eyes closed and seemed more off his stool than on. When I passed him a dollar and asked for one token, his finger tips moved across the rows of tokens and he passed at least a dozen through the wooden bowl. His eyes never opened. Only his body swayed slightly. I shouted at him that I only wanted one token. His fingers moved to his change pile and he passed me a dozen quarters and dimes. His eyes still remained closed. Once again I was about to object when I heard the distant rumble of an approaching subway. I shrugged my shoulders. I had attempted to correct him. What more could I do? Quickly I took both the tokens and the change. Maybe that wasn't right. To relieve my conscience I told myself if I didn't take them, someone else would.

I returned to my apartment house in time to catch the last elevator. The old man was tidying up, preparing to leave for the night and transform my apartment into a nine floor walk up. I wondered if Andre had made it back in time. Many nights late I hear him climbing the long, marble stairs, sometimes alone, sometimes with company.

My German assignment for the next day is waiting on my desk, homework that will have to wait.

In bed, I can't sleep; that's why I'm up writing here in this journal while the rest of the world slumbers peacefully. Their sexual play free of Usualness.

I need to get out of the city for a few days. Maybe I'll call Chris tomorrow and see if he and Joanie would like a house guest for the weekend.

September 27, 1965.

Spent the weekend at Chris and Joanie's in Cazenovia, New York. I always thought that the town was well named for Chris. I borrowed JoAnn's car and made the long drive starting early Saturday morning so that I could arrive by lunchtime. I drove north on the New York State Thruway in mental discussions with Chris, telling him about my problems with JoAnn and asking for his much needed advice. Past Poughkeepsie, Catskill, Albany, Schenectady, Utica—a long ride with long questions.

When I called him earlier in the week, he was delighted and eager to have me visit. But he certainly didn't make me feel very welcome when I got there. Not a good weekend. Not by any measure. September 25. 9/25. 9+2+5=16. 1+6=7. Seven. Not one of my good numbers.

I told him I would arrive in time for lunch, and yet when I finally found his apartment (he gave me lousy directions), no one answered the doorbell. I checked the mailbox to make sure I had the right apartment, rang the bell again and listened with my ear pressed to the cold door to make sure the bell worked; I rapped my car keys on the living room window in case they didn't hear the ring. Finally I returned to the car and sat behind the wheel with the sun flashing off the windshield into my face. After half an hour or so, Chris, Joanie and their little girl drove up: they had just come back from lunch at a restaurant in town.

Chris slapped me on the back, Joanie hugged me hello with one arm. The baby in her other arm pressed against me and I smelled her wonderful wholesomeness. Joanie gave me a kiss full on the lips and the baby stuck her hand right between us. Jealousy so young. I laughed along with the others, but there was a knot growing in me, a sense of dis-equilibrium as we went in to the apartment.

"I thought we were going to meet for lunch," I asked taking off my coat.

"Lunch?" said Joanie with a stern look at Chris. "Didn't you…"

"Hank, we always eat lunch in town on Saturday," interrupted Chris. "You should have been here earlier and we could have all gone out."

Joanie concocted a ham sandwich and a glass of milk for me while Chris unwrapped the baby from its fall clothing bundles.

"Phew!" said Chris. "This one needs changing."

"Let me do that," Joanie responded in an automatic tone.

"I can change Laurie."

"Of course you can, Chris. Who doubts that? You spend time with your guest; I'll tend to the baby." She snatched the baby from Chris before he could say anything else, and headed for the living room floor with a fresh diaper. "Hmm, Laurie's have a present for mommies? Babies want a nap? Hmm?" She straddled the baby, leaning back and forward, talking, making faces, burying her face in Laurie's little tummy and making explosive sounds in the baby's flesh.

While Joanie prattled the baby, Chris and I were in the kitchen. Slowly I escaped my black mood and started feeling warm and close to everything around me. Joanie carried the changed baby down the hall for a nap. Then Chris told me that Saturdays after lunch they always take a nap too. Joanie heard the comment from the baby's room and returned to the kitchen. She was carrying the soiled diaper. Her bundle matched my returned feelings.

"We can't do that today Chris."

"Of course we can, Hank understands."

He winked, grabbed a reluctant Joanie by the waist, and led her upstairs. She looked back at me for just a moment and then smiled at Chris. That left me with a half-eaten sandwich in the kitchen. There I was two hundred miles from home for a relaxing, talky weekend, and I was alone in one part of the house, while my so-called friends were having sex in another.

I finished my sandwich and glass of milk, and washed off my dishes. Once the noise of running water and the clicking of wet dishes had ended, the small, neat kitchen was very empty and very lonely. I opened the back door quietly and closed it behind me with hardly any more than a dull click. Why was I worried about disturbing them? I had this picture of Chris yelling at me if I made too much noise.

Sitting in my car, I didn't see the wonderful colors of a rural fall afternoon in upstate New York. That's odd because fall has always been my favorite time of year: the texture of autumn sunlight; the yellows and oranges of leaves and weeds; the faint, musty aroma of distant burning leaves; the nakedness of fallow, cold ground. I experienced none of this. I just sat behind the wheel, looking at their apartment. My suitcase and pillow were still in the back seat. I wondered how I could leave now and keep my friendship with Chris and Joanie. If you could call this a friendship.

And I had left a jacket thrown across a chair in the living room. I was convinced that I couldn't leave without the jacket. Chris would see it and not understand I had left. He and Joanie would wonder and worry where I had gone without the jacket.

After an hour or so, Chris came out, and looked around and finally saw me sitting in the car. He walked over, his footsteps emphasized by the crunching of the stiff oak leaves. He apologized profusely to me and told me that wasn't a nice way to treat a guest. The words didn't help. The weekend never really perked up. I couldn't wait to leave on Sunday. We talked about this and that, nothing was said about the problems that were bothering me so much. Theatre and city talk. I didn't even mention Rusty. The drive home past the same cities and towns was just long.

I stopped in Catskill for dinner and couldn't find anything open. The whole town was closed on Sunday evening. Damn country hicks.

Drove straight to JoAnn's apartment so she could park her car in her parents' extra space underneath the building. They were off on a business trip and we had the apartment to ourselves. I was really happy to see her and gave her a huge hug and kiss as soon as the door opened.

"Wow, what's that all about!"

"Don't ask. I'm starved. Did you eat yet?"

"No, I waited for you. I knew you would be coming back tired and hungry. Maybe there's something in the fridge. Let's go see." As she turned to walk down the long hallway, I pinched her bottom. "Hey! That's for later." She smiled sweetly at me, took my hand and we sauntered down the tiled hallway to the kitchen.

Her mother had left some frozen hamburger patties (weighed out to exactly 3/8ths of a pound) which we cooked up with some peas and carrots. We ate in the kitchen sitting at the white porcelain table oblivious to the clinking and clanging of plates and forks and glasses. Annie the maid has Sundays off. We had to clean up and wash the dishes ourselves. No big deal for me, I do that everyday.

I told her how Chris behaved to me and how I almost came back Saturday night.

"Maybe its better you didn't return on Saturday. I wasn't here. I went up to Yale to visit Murphy over the weekend."

"Visit Murphy?" I asked shocked.

She walked across the kitchen to the freezer for the ice cream. That's how the world seemed to me: frozen. Murphy. My ultimate nemesis.

"My parents…"

"Meaning your father," I interrupted. She scooped out for us both full bowls of ice cream and brought them to the table before continuing.

"Yes, and my mother, too. They have been after me to see other boys, men, you know. Well, Murphy invited me up for the weekend a month ago. I said no. Then you said you were going away this weekend, and Murphy called again, and my parents…so…" She looked at me over her spoon.

"So." I said, my body frozen in place. Not a muscle had moved since she started talking. I was numb.

"So nothing. I took the train to New Haven on Saturday morning, stayed at a motel, and spent the weekend with him." When my face dropped, she laughed and reached for my hand across the table.

"Not that way silly. I stayed alone. Oh, Hank, don't you understand. I was

54

totally, absolutely, 100 percent bored with him. I only went to please my parents. They paid for everything. You're so sensitive."

"Sensitivity has nothing to do with it," I said with a catch in my voice.

"No? Really?" she asked. "Oh, I ate that ice cream too fast. God, what a headache. Hank, you haven't eaten any. This is vanilla-your favorite."

I forced my hand to lift the spoon to the dish. "We're both free people; we don't have any ropes and bonds." I ordered my hand to move the ice cream to my mouth. She was blind to my pain. Or maybe she liked it.

"Saturday night after we came back from a dance..."

A dance. There it was. She was rubbing it in my face. She knows I hate to dance. So she went off with Murphy to dance and then...

"He took me back to my hotel room and then wanted to come in." She looked up at me. My body was frozen again. "It was almost funny, Hank. He's so inept. I pushed off his perfunctory advances, and he seemed relieved, happy."

"Did he at least give you a bud vase?" I asked. That really cracked her up. For some unknown reason Murphy gives her a bud vase every holiday season. She has a shelf full of them. The funny part is that she never uses bud vases. Once we started laughing, everything came unfrozen inside me. The ice cream was good.

We washed and dried dishes, laughing over little things all around us. I invented a scheme about her father having hidden tape recorders and microphones spotted around the apartment. We had to counteract them by disguising our voices and talking in code. The game turned really silly as we left the kitchen saying :rerswhay hetay udbay asevay? We were still laughing as we fell into her bed. I stayed over at her place and we made love for half the night.

OCTOBER 1965

October 3, 1965; *Sunday*

Spent the weekend with JoAnn. Her parents were out of town again on a business trip and holiday. We spent Friday night here in my apartment, Saturday night at her parent's place, and then Sunday back here. That's a layered contrast like my mother's vanilla and chocolate pudding with graham crackers between the pudding layers.

JoAnn left here at five this afternoon to go uptown for dinner with her parents who had finally returned. The weekend was like last year when she would drive in from Dickinson College on a Friday night and stay until Sunday afternoon when she would leave the City and drive back. Our year half apart and half together with JoAnn driving here one weekend and me taking the train to Carlisle, Pennsylvania on another.

The long weekend was de-ja-vous from last year because this past weekend ran the same course as those did last year; Friday night good, Saturday decline, Sunday morning fiasco; Sunday afternoon last minute repair. She was burdensome throughout weekend; and I by Sunday, had become completely callous to anything, Friday night: great to see each other and talk over what we haven't had time to say during the week. And catch up on missed bedroom time. Saturday starts the problems of where shall we go and what shall we do. She keeps looking to me for answers; she keeps making suggestions of things to pleasure me.

What movie do you want to see? Do you want to tour this or that exhibit? I'll cook dinner for you if you like; do you want me to? Pressure, pressure. The demand for decisions sits on me, a huge weight, and pushes me into the ground. I want freedom and lightness in life, not smothering pressure.

Our relationship is based on an awkwardness that I'm sure she has been told many times—she is chasing me. Sometimes this assumes the form of doting on my every wish, sometimes by her not expressing her own wishes, and even by her not allowing me the opportunity to chase her. The situation becomes so burdensome. Too much unnecessary pressure.

3-10-65. 3+1+0+6+5=15; 1+5=6. No wonder today has been lousy. What good ever happened with a 6?

October 5, 1965; *Tuesday*

Regarding my last entry, perhaps someone could argue that I want my cake and I want to eat it too. Let me answer this way: when I am forced to be constricted, I become dulled. If JoAnn could see this about me, matters would smooth out considerably.

She operates under the principle that her presence is enough for me (she may not believe this, but her actions speak it). Well, her being next to me all the time is not enough! Where is the chase, the hunt? The thrill? The doubt, sorrow, longing? Where's the failure? In fact, where is anything but manufactured emotions?

Going to bed has become boring. What else is there to say? I must manufacture the desire. I perform because she wants me to. My body does the motions, allows itself to be stroked and placed. I'm callous to the whole thing. I know she's in bed to make things right, to please me.

Once again the old habits—now what to do? Talk again? Talk, talk, I'm sick of talk. Not go to bed? I t takes two to make that decision, and her inclination is to solve silences and difficulties in bed. She does little to help break the boredom by wanting to occupy every minute of my time. I am smothered in her body, in my small apartment, in boring classes and a boring job, in the fear of being drafted into this damned war.

Life is so confusing. What is there to run back to even if I could? My God! My head swims when I think of this mess.

No sooner had I walked in the door this evening after work when my mother called. Said she hadn't heard from me in awhile. "You didn't answer my last letter of a week ago." I ought to explain here that my mother writes letters. At least once a week, sometimes twice. Short, chatty letters that often say nothing. She expects you to return the same. When I was a boy scout in summer camp these letters were daily manna. Now they're just more burden.

She said she called because she wanted to make sure everything was fine with me. I said of course, everything's OK, I've been super busy. She asked about JoAnn (my mother is very fond of JoAnn); and I told her that JoAnn is doing well at NYU this year, and no, we don't have any classes together. JoAnn's major is English, mine is Biology.

"Dad has not been well this week," she said. I didn't answer her. (I don't want to discuss him, not even here. I don't want to talk to him. Let him break the ice he created with Rusty. I know more than two years have flowed over that dam; but some things you don't forget.) After a minute of silence she continued: "You know, it's his birthday on Saturday. We're going to celebrate it on Sunday so that Rose can come. It would be nice to have you there too."

"I'll try. I'm really busy with school right now."

A ten second eternity of silence. "Well, you do what you think is right. He is your father, you know. Fell free to bring JoAnn if you decide to come."" Before I could comment on that, she said she loved me and hung up. More pressure.

Andre and I were talking the other evening. I didn't have anything else to do, so I called him up (to make sure he wasn't occupied) and walked down the hall to his place. We sat in his small kitchen over a glass of wine. I rambled on about my mixed-up feelings toward JoAnn.

When I paused for breath, Andre shook his head. "She must really like you. You're a very difficult person, Hankie. Rewarding to be with, I think. But very difficult.'

'That's easy for you to say, Andre. Your experience with women isn't quite the same as mine."

"Oh, really? Well, Hankie, I hate to tell you this, to intrude into your opinions with some little snippets of fact. I've been married, don't you know?"

Now that surprised me. Although Andre is polished and polite with JoAnn and other ladies, sexually I only think of him with men and boys.

"Why are your cute black eyebrows going up, Hankie? You think I never tried women? I'm not like you. I try everything before I make my choices." He gave me his phony charm smile. His wrinkles and evening shadow beard ruined the effect. "Of course I was very young. And anywho, if you really must know, we were only married for a few years. That was enough."

"What went wrong?"

"Wrong? Hankie, how quaint your thinking is. Nothing was wrong. Everything stayed the same. I found the positions as ridiculous as ever. Especially the ones she liked. And as fond of her as I was—and am—let me tell you living with a woman isn't my cup of tea. Now that I've told you this great secret about my young life, when are you going to tell me about this mysterious Rusty you bring up now and then from your dark past. She seems to be a hidden Faustian force behind your relationships."

"Oh, I've mentioned her?"

"Just when things are going good in your life and you need to cloud them over."

"Yes, Rusty is certainly a cloud over.'

"Your obfuscation is so cute Hankie. And so transparent. Why hide anything? Just put it out in the open and show it, as we girls like to say. That's always the easiest way with any problem."

"I can't do that. I just can't." My palms started to sweat.

"Listen to me, my dear friend. Until you face this problem directly, that power you have created and given to Rusty's image will never stop haunting you, not in real life or in your dreams."

I left wishing I had never told him any of my problems. Maybe I'll avoid him for a while.

October 7, 1965; *Thursday*

Fireworks day in Organic Chemistry lab. My own fireworks. First, I should say that Chemistry and Biology courses at NYU are nothing like Dickinson. At Dickinson the classes are small and the labs are taught by the professors. Here, the professor lectures in a large hall to over a hundred students and the labs are supervised by grad students who believe they have far more important things to do than be bothered by undergraduates. At least that's the attitude of our instructor, Dave.

Our lecture professor reigns in the classroom. An arrogant, pompous prick of a professor. The same man who wrote the textbook. He enters the classroom two minutes after the start of the period, and locks the door to prevent latecomers. He slams his books down and looks for written questions that have to be left on the front lecture table before he enters.

Often he'll read the question out loud and then look out over the sea of ignorant Untermenschen: "The answer to this question is in the text. And I explained it better in the book than I can ever explain in class." Crumple paper, throw away question, on to the next. When he finishes with the written missives, he asks: "Any other questions? No? Then next week you'll be responsible for the next chapter and the problems at the end." He picks up his books, unlocks the door and leaves. That's lecture. Sink or swim in your own in the vast ocean of organic slop.

At Dickinson the chemistry labs were clean, well lit and very modern. Here our lab must be in the oldest, darkest part of the building. Everything is grimy black and ages old. If there are any windows, I've never located them, although some vague shapes on the wall next to me indicate the possible presence of one-time sources of light and ventilation.

Our lab consists of thirty-two students arranged in four islands of eight. Each island is made of two facing rows of four lab spaces separated by a running drain with shelves for glassware and with plumbing lines for gas, water and vacuum. My particular station lies at the up-river end of a middle island.

Today we performed a sulfuric acid reflux which is where my problems began. My experiments ran late due to my usual ineptitude. During the first two extraction attempts, I lost the sample in one of the middle steps. Instructor Dave bellowed his usual unhelpful comments: "Change the pH! The sample has to be there!"

My material wasn't there; the unprecipitated sample had long since vanished down the drain in some earlier extraction step. Where does this drain go? Pounds of pretty awful stuff have washed down that center drain this year. If there really are alligators in the New York City sewers, my Organic Chemistry class will keep their population in check.

This afternoon the reflux tube was attached to the upper lip of the boiling flask. The reflux tube looked like a glass and rubber hose Christmas tree that rose well over my head. The gas burner under the flask generated a massive flame, so high that the acid solution was bumping rather than boiling in spite of the double dose of boiling chips. I also had the reflux tube water jacket as hot as possible to promote faster boiling. Anything to get that liquid out.

That water jacket running hot became root cause of my problems. Ideally, the jacket needs to be as cold as possible. That promotes an efficient condensation back into the boiling flask for a "reflux." My immediate concern was not the proper maintenance of my experimental apparatus, but rather the swift-footed clock. I didn't need efficiency; I needed speed in my reflux. There was no way to change the temperature of the cold water line to the reflux tube, so I cut back the effluent flow until the effluent line steamed. Dave would have had a cow if he had seen that. Of course he didn't see it. He's always so busy with his own experiments that he never looks at ours, unless we go up and beg him for a few precious minutes.

At four-fifteen the hands on the clock were screaming at me. I had already lost most of the afternoon in repeated failures. My boss at Beth Israel Hospital does not like us showing up late for work, and time would not slow down to accommodate me.

Then my mental clouds parted and a ray of hope showed through: a saving idea, a eureka, worthy of Archimedes: Liquids can be made hotter under pressure. What a marvelous idea! And what better way is there to add pressure to a reflux system than to cork the top of the tube! I had to climb up on a chair to implement my brainstorm. ("Brainstorm": Excellent choice of a word considering the events that followed). Within seconds the system seemed to be operating better. The damn experiment could be completed and I could be out of there on my way to my job in half an hour.

Totally pleased with myself, I made a final note in my stained and grimy notebook about changing the pH (that would please Dave no end). My smile faded like a spring breeze behind an accelerating Third Avenue bus when I heard an explosive sound above me. The newly placed cork had blown off the top of the reflux tube. This was no champagne cork; this was a volcanic eruption, my personal Etna.

Hot sulfuric acid rained down on the entire lab, across every island of struggling students. Small steaming spots appeared on my shirt as hot acid ate through textile. I could hear the hissing of droplets in my hair; my nose scrunched at the unmistakable odor of burning protein. I ran for the water spigot to wash the acid off my face and hands. By that point others had begun to react to the acid deluge; the lab was full of shouts, curses and chaos.

Dave ran out of his office demanding to know what was happening. Somehow, luckily, no one noticed that I had caused the problem. I sneaked back to my place and pretended to be in the final stages of my reflux. In fact, except for some lingering boiling chips, the flask was empty. I'll have to go in some extra afternoon next week and repeat the process. Damn,

Thinking back on it, corking the reflux tube wasn't very smart. But that's Organic Chemistry. I'm tired tonight or I would tell the story of how my partner across the island set everyone's experiment on fire by running acetone down the long central drain. Now there was a blaze to remember!

October 8, 1965; *Friday*

Up early this morning. No reason, just restless. Gives me time to catch up on my lagging homework. Beautiful morning outside my window. The street sounds of delivery trucks and cabs around Union Square seem right in place. This old apartment building with its marble entrance way was probably an elegant residence last century. Theodore Roosevelt's family had a house on the south side of Union Square when he was growing up. That was a time when Union Square held greater grandeur than a hangout for bums, prostitutes, weirdoes and transient students.

The early morning sun flashes and glitters off the windows on the opposite side of the park from my small flat. A walking morning. My ten block sojourn to Washington Square will be a pleasure.

I hope it doesn't sound as if all my feelings about JoAnn are negative. In spite of myself, I love her deeply and am enmeshed in everything she does. In general I admire her actions as regards her parents. Perhaps this admiration leads me to anger when she does not live up to my expectations of her in other ways.

Sometimes I feel that I cannot be at rest with JoAnn until I am at rest with myself. And that peace and acceptance always seems just slightly beyond my reach. JoAnn has told me many times that she loves me; and yet I cannot say those simple words back to her. She doesn't demand the statement from me; nevertheless, its absence hangs limp in the air between us. I never could say those words to Rusty, either. Although with her, she said it more than enough for the both of us.

The other night after we had gone to bed, JoAnn curled up next to me and told me about a fight she had with her father the week before. "About you as usual, Hank. Only more intense this time. My parents really blame you for my many changes this year. That's not right."

"Makes life easier for them," I said into her ear. Stray hairs tickled my nose.

She took my fingers in her hand and kissed them one by one. "Right. Well, after dinner I said I was going downtown to spend time with you. That touched off the scene.

"'You can't go,' said my father. 'Your main responsibility is your schoolwork. That's why we pay your tuition'.

"I told them that my homework is caught up for the week.

"'Weekends are for socializing, not school nights,' he shot back.

"'What did you think we did at Dickinson on school nights? Twiddle our thumbs? I'm not in high school any more, dad.'

"'You are living in our house and you will follow our rules. You're not going out tonight!' he shouted.

"I thought I was listening to a grade B movie. The lines were so predictable. Well, you're not going to believe what happened next. My father stormed out of the dining room, stomped down the hall, and started piling furniture in front of the door. The hall table and two upholstered chairs were first. Then he dragged the sofa out of the living room and added that to the stack.

"'I can't believe you're doing this to me. What did I do?' I answered, probably hysterical at this point. I remember a lot of crying.

"While my father was dragging furniture though the house, my mother was giving me dagger eyes. Then she started in on me.

"'Don't you see what you're doing to my life? This is the hell I have to live with. Why can't you compromise with your father? Why do you put me in the middle?'

"That wasn't fair of her. I'm the one in the middle, not her. All I'm trying to do is be myself. What's wrong with that? How can I do that with a possessive father? What kind of a life do I have locked in the house like a hamster?"

JoAnn's parents are always polite to me when I visit for dinner. Yet I believe her story. So there must be more sides to her parents than they have ever shown me. Not that I feel the need to see every side.

I can commiserate with JoAnn. I know plenty about problems with fathers. Three years ago my father took my world apart. And Rusty's. Maybe he was right. Maybe we were too young to marry. But that doesn't give him the right to call me "Sir Galahad the White Knight trying to save the world." And why does he think this cloud between us is going to dissipate if he simply avoids it?

Maybe he thinks this strain between us is part of a *phase*. How many times have I heard that I'm *just going through a phase*? Every problem in my life was part of a phase. As long as your kids go though phases you don't have to deal with the real people in front of you and relate to them in the present tense. You only have to wait. The phase will pass.

On the night of my 14th birthday I thought dad was going to come upstairs to my room and talk to me about boys and girls. I was certain he would. He had to. That's what fathers are supposed to do. He never did. Not a word. Not then, not ever. Every night throughout the winter, spring and summer of my 14th year I waited for him after supper to call me into his office. Instead night after night he rose from the table, walked outside to his garage and loaded his truck for the next day's work.

He never said anything to me. So now I don't talk to him. Let him see how it feels. Let him cure this disease he created.

October 12, 1965; *Tuesday*

I have to write a term paper for English 210. The topic is "Abandon All Hope Ye Who Enter Here," the sign above the entrance to Dante's hell.

All hope of what? All hope of leaving hell and all hope of seeing God? The problem with that idea is that no one in Dante's hell expresses any desire to join the other crew up above who sit around and sing songs for eternity to the Man in White. Like me, Dante's characters find the traditional idea of good times in heaven deadly boring.

Dante's hope must mean something more closely associated with his own century and to the return to ancient themes and beliefs that abounded in the start of that marvelous century, the 1300s.

Let's start way back with some classical references. Aeschylus says that Prometheus gave man blind hopes when he took away foresight. Prometheus, who possesses this foresight even when chained to his rock and tortured forever, has no hope. He has total knowledge and total despair. There can be no hope for anything better when you know everything that you are now and ever can be. Hope exists only where the future lies in shadows.

When man had foresight, he was without hope of anything new or different; he was a poor creature, moody and fretful. Why try for anything better when you already know the results? When everything is foreknown, there is no freshness in life.

With hope, man raised himself to cultural accomplishments and lived without the fear of death. That is one of the messages of the play *Prometheus*.

The knowledge and despair of Prometheus are shared by the souls in Dante's hell. They cannot mask the knowledge of their eternal plight, of what will happen to them now and forever. Hell holds no hope of freshness or accomplishment. Dante's fallen souls can never rise above what they know will be.

Thinking about the paper has left me with questions about myself. What would my life be like if I knew exactly what will happen for the next twenty years? Or if I knew for certain that I could never be anything other than what I am now? Supposing I know that no woman over 5'6" will ever be attracted to me because I'm too short. How would that constricting knowledge change my life? Would I think less of myself? Would I feel trapped in a body that will forever exclude me from potential pleasures?

Or supposing I know that Murphy will always be smarter and more successful than I? Would that alter how I relate to JoAnn?

October 13, 1965; *Wednesday*

I walked up Second Avenue after class this morning. Usually I go up Broadway, but today I wanted to check out a used book store at Second Avenue and 12th Street. The buildings on Second have a wonderful ornateness that I enjoy so my mind only minimally on where I was going.

"Hey, you, mister," said a gravelly voice. I dropped my gaze to a large Gypsy woman seated on a low stool propped against a brick building. She wore a red and black paisley tent dress with sequins, small round mirrors, and beads. Her hair was bound up in a scarf of the same material as her dress. Although she looked about 35 from the lines on her face, I had the feeling she was much older. "Yes, you, mister. Come here."

I stopped. Big mistake. I've lived in New York City long enough to know you don't stop when someone calls to you. I walked over to where she was sitting. In for a nickel, in for a dollar.

"You're college boy. I see you walk here often. You want I read your future? Tell you about life? Girlfriends? Come inside." She stood and motioned me to a doorway next to her. The door was ajar and there was a cascade of bead strands behind it. Behind her was a shop window also covered in beads and red paisley cloth. A sign in the window announced: *MOTHER SELENA. PALM READINGS.*

I hesitated. Something didn't seem right to me. "No, be afraid," she said reaching for my arm. Her grip was dry and cool, her skin weathered. Not the smooth warmth of JoAnn's hand. "Plenty college boys come here. I tell them about love, future. You come too." By then she was pulling me in through the beads.

The room was small, stuffy, defined by dark fabric hung from the walls and covering the ceiling. Maroon sunlight filtered through the fabric from the street. The room, bathed in seraglio surrealism, was bare of furniture except for a round table and two ladder-back chairs set in the center under a tasseled light fixture. The table was covered in a black, pleated cloth.

"Sit down," she said. I obeyed. She sat opposite. "Put out hand." I placed my right hand palm up on the table. She took it in both of hers, opened my fingers slowly and stroked the lines and curves. "OK. Good hand. Good future. First, five dollars to read. Put money on table."

"I don't have five dollars."

She snorted. "College boys always have five dollars. Show the table your money."

"I have three dollars in my wallet. Sorry." I started to pull my hand away and leave the table. She gripped my hand tightly. "OK. Three dollars. For first time college boy. Put money on table."

I took out my wallet and extracted my last three dollars. These I placed in the center of the table, hoping this was worth the trouble. Actually I was wishing I could find a way out of the situation. The three dollars could have bought me a book by Mary Renault or a new Vivaldi concerto.

"Three dollar fortune. What your sign?"

"Sign?" I respond.

"Your zodiac sign."

"I don't know."

"College boy," she said with contempt. I thought she was going to spit on the floor. "What is date of birth?"

"November 11."

"November. That makes you Scorpio. Good sign, strong, masculine. Sign of the sex organs. Passion." She looked right into my eyes. Even though the light was poor, I noticed for the first time that some of her hair had escaped her head covering. The strands were gray and brown, scraggly. Her eyes dropped to my hand where her fingers were tracing my palm lines. "This line is life: strong, but not too long. These lines, they represent women: there are many of them in your life. They love you, but you will not make them happy. This is your home line: tangled, you never settle down. This line is for wealth: weak. You spend your money now." She closed my hand. "That what I see in college boy hand for three dollars."

"Estelle!" she shouted while still holding my hand firmly in hers. The back curtains parted and out came a younger version of my palm reader. Same kind of billowy dressing that showed off an ample bosom. The girl had long black tresses that were not contained by a scarf. She stood rock still, smiling like a Cretan Kouros.

"College boy want to see my daughter dance? Five dollars. Dance naked— ten dollars. You like that. She pretty girl. Put money on table." The girl started with sinewy gyrations. She was smiling at me.

"You took all my money." I snatched my hand back, grabbed my books and bolted out the door toward the street. The beads smacked my face as I ran through them. I raced up Second Avenue, dodging people and crates of merchandise.

"Hey, college boy! Come back!" the woman shouted at me. I turned to see her running after me, her dress billowing in her wake. No way was I stopping this time. I turned on the juice and hurled forward a few blocks.

When I called JoAnn tonight and described the scene, she thought it was hilarious. "Yeah, but I lost three dollars. That's the last time I walk that part of Second Avenue." But I wonder about her predictions.

October 17, 1965; *Sunday*

JoAnn left about 5pm to head uptown for her regular Sunday dinner with parents. She soared in great spirits this weekend. She believes that she's worked out a living arrangement with a girl from my Classics class whom I introduced her to a few weeks back. Before class one day I heard Sara talking about how she wanted to move out of her college dorm and into town if she could locate a roommate. I told Sara about JoAnn and they met. They've been looking for an apartment in the West Village area. JoAnn feels positive about the girl and about moving out of her parents' place.

Speaking of meeting girls in class, I went on a date Friday night with a girl named Judy. Of all places, we went to a disc-o-tek in the East Village on Dom Street. I met her in English class. She's physically smaller than JoAnn, and I was instantly attracted to her wide smile and bright eyes.

I never know what to say to open a conversation with a girl. As luck would have it, on the way out of class on Thursday, she asked me to explain a comment I made in class about the Fool in Shakespeare's *As You Like It.* An easy topic for me since I did the play with Chris two years ago at Dickinson. When I saw that she was actually interested in what I was saying, I asked her if she had time for a cup of tea.

At the coffee shop I wasn't ever relaxed. My regular waitress was absent, and I had this premonition, this stark fear, that JoAnn was going to walk in the door at any moment and see me with Judy. What would I do?

In any case, I have to start dating other girls, I have to live a freer life. Judy and I spent half an hour talking about this and that in class, nothing important. She stirred her coffee, I sipped my tea. I'm thinking to myself: *How do I ask this girl out? Should I do it now? Is this a good point? Time's running out! I have to do it now!* Finally, I grit my internal teeth, such as they are: "Are you free to go out Friday night?"

"Are you asking me for a date?" She stopped clinking her spoon in her white coffee cup. I knew she was about to tell me to fuck off. She has this huge boyfriend, and I was merely someone she wanted to ask a question. Not be hit on.

"Yes, I guess I am," I answer with sweat forming across my forehead.

"OK," she answered simply. "Where do you want to go?"

"Uh. Um. I don't know." A real manly response.

"What do you usually do on Friday nights?" She waited for a moment while I fumbled with my tongue and stepped on my dick. How can I tell her that on Friday nights I usually meet JoAnn, turn Dr Jeckle couch into Mr Hyde bed, and screw for several hours? Fortunately, she answered her own question: "Hey, how about we go dancing at the Dom? It's a few blocks from here and real cool. You'll like it. I sure do."

Dancing. Me at my most self-conscious. Always the sickening knowledge that people are watching me and shaking their heads in disgust. Always that acute sense of my height compared to others on the dance floor. Always the tangible belief that the girl I'm with would rather be with someone taller, better looking, and more experienced on his feet. Feelings that go back to grammar school and dancing lessons.

Judy proved a strange girl and the date was even stranger. The Dom is weird. You're there with a room full of people and yet you're alone. You can't talk for the noise. The flashing multi-colored lights and blasting music would make a perfect aspirin commercial. Judy didn't care if I danced like Fred Astaire or Fred Flintstone. She was on the floor to dance. We stayed for several hours. She had a good time.

Clearly she has far more experience dating that I do. She controlled the evening. I was Prince Phillip to her Queen Elizabeth. Never once did she look to me to make a decision the way JoAnn does. She met me at the front door to the hospital right after work. She was dressed for her comfort and pleasure; and her make-up was designed to fit in with the East Village: wild blue eye shadow, gold sequined shawl, and a red paisley dress (shades of my Gypsy nightmare woman!). She didn't care one whit that I was in jacket, shirt and slacks. My choice. If that's how I felt comfortable dancing, fine with her.

At the end of our evening at the front door to her brownstone, she thanked me for a nice evening and promptly let herself in, closing the door behind her. No hesitation, no doubts about what's next.

I told JoAnn Friday afternoon that I had to work on an English theme paper this weekend. "So why don't I knock it out Friday evening and see you Saturday?" She agreed with the plan. The good news is my ploy for Friday night succeeded. The bad news is I really do have a paper due on Tuesday. Now I have to start it tonight even though I'm dead tired.

Later.

JoAnn just called. Very emotional, nervous, upset. Told me she had an awful battle with her parents. She told them over dinner that she has found a girl she would like to room with. "They hit the ceiling. Both of them started yelling at me. At the same time. It was like an explosion."

"Welcome to the world of parents. "

"I might as well tell you what they said. It was awful. First, they objected to Sara. How can they object to her when they don't even know her! Mostly they objected because you recommended her. What has that got to do with it! I made my own decisions about Sara."

"Apparently it has quite an effect on your parent's beliefs."

"Then they said that I can't just go off and *poof!* room with someone I hardly know and they don't know at all. I should wait several months, MONTHS, maybe until January or February until I know her better. Then I got hit with the usual lines about how I'll get an apartment and then I'll leave school, how my grades aren't good enough for an apartment, and finally the usual crap about how I don't talk to them enough."

"They certainly don't see you as very mature. Anything else?"

"Yeah, lots more. There was a tirade, my father was screaming at me about how I'm lowering myself, lowering my morals, and an apartment will ruin me socially. I think my mother told him I'm on the pill. I made her promise she wouldn't tell anyone, but I think she did. When my father was screaming at me about my low morals, I looked over at her. She had her head down. She broke her promise to me and told him. Damn."

"So what was the bottom line on all this yelling?"

"My father told me he wouldn't help me if I moved out before February. Help me financially. Then my mother threw her big punch: My nonsense was ruining the relationship between the three of us."

"What relationship is that?"

"I don't know what to do. I have to keep at least a speaking relationship with my parents. I can't cut the cord and walk away. I dislike their views; I disagree with them. Living at home has been intolerable this year. I thought it would be so easy to move back into my old room from living at a dorm in Dickinson. Easy? It's been total hell! Why do they think I'm still a little girl? They send me away to grow up, I do that, and then they don't like it. That's not fair!" There was silence for a minute as she quieted down. "I guess I have to do what they want me to do. What other choice is there?"

"You know you're only postponing the inevitable. You're telling your parents that you accept their values and plans and you're telling everyone else that you don't."

"My mother told me that they never should have let me transfer out of Dickinson to New York University. 'All these problems would have never happened if you had stayed with the original plan.'

"Damn. This has been such a great weekend. Sometimes I think my parents don't see me as an independent person. I'm like an object to them, a piece of art work that they fashioned for their own pleasure. Except I'm not behaving the way they designed me to and they're angry at the object." Silence on the line. "Can I see you tomorrow after work? I'll cook dinner for you. I'll have it ready when you get back from the hospital. Please?"

How could I say no to her request even though I need to. With an English paper due on Tuesday morning that I told her I was staying home on Friday night to write, that means I have to burn the midnight oil tonight. Or set the alarm for early tomorrow morning. Or both. Damn.

October 21, 1965; *Thursday*
Terrible dreams last night. Monsters and ghosts. I woke several times from a bad dream, only to fall asleep to a worse. By this morning I was covered in sweat and wrapped in the sheets. I know what caused the dreams.

After Organic Chemistry class today I decided to run up the four flights of stairs to Physiology. Never enough exercise in the City. When I turned the corner on the last flight, I saw her walking down the hall. Total freeze on my body parts. Rusty. Same small size, same tight walk, and the hair: that intense red. Only the hair-do was wrong. This Rusty had hers in a puffed permanent; my old Rusty kept her hair long, sometimes with a lock that fell over one shoulder and sometimes twisted up in a bun. Never a short perm. Plus Rusty wouldn't be in school here. And this girl was too young.

She was Rusty and yet at the same time I knew this couldn't be her. I wanted to shout, or hide, or grab for her, or melt down into the floor. And my body was frozen. I couldn't do anything. Finally the crush of people started pushing me from behind; the same people I had forced my way past up the stairs were now bumping against me. As she walked away, she became swallowed in the hundreds of shapes in the hallway. I could occasionally see a spot of red between taller heads and thicker shoulders until even the slightest indication of her electric presence vanished as though nothing had ever happened.

The event occupied less than five seconds in real time, but my mind was a kaleidoscope of fragmented images, past and present, for the rest of the day. Holding, touching each other on my red and black blanket on a vaporous spring day; a bronze sun reveling in his strength, we seemed a twin that sun and I; a picnic high above the Cumberland Valley on a rock outcrop. Then on the floor of Professor Graffman's office early on a Sunday morning, dressed for church but stealing time for love; Rusty had the key to his office for part-time work. Walking hand in hand through a snow-quiet campus, the trees with their naked arms raised to the dark sky. Pennsylvania Dutch country snow, heavy and dull, we a counterpoint with the lightness of lovers.

With these images through the day is there any wonder that my mind stayed locked in troubles through the night? Why didn't my dreams show the bright side of our time together? We did bask in joy if only for a little while.

In one dream I was in a house talking with three fellows. A strange house with people I've never seen before. The conversation was pleasant, interesting, even though nothing important was being discussed. For some reason I walked away from them in the kitchen and left the house though a glass garage door. A car partially covered in snow was parked in the garage. In a corner of my mind I knew that in an earlier dream I had covered the car with snow myself in order to hide from someone who was chasing me. I had an acute sense that the car was in the garage because of me, but I couldn't remember driving it to the house. The engine was running but no one was in the car. Had I left the engine on?

I turned to go back into the house telling myself that the car and the snow weren't my problem any more. Through the glass door to the kitchen I saw Rusty. She was inside waiting for me. She wore a large, heavy dress that showed quite plainly that she was very pregnant—ready to be delivered. A shiny pink bow covered the outermost bulge of the dress. She had on black leather gloves and her fingers were long and thin. We reached the door at the same time, I from the garage side, she from the kitchen, and we fought over opening it. She pushed hard on the door to get into the garage while I held the door closed with my shoulder. I was in a panic. I didn't want her in the garage. All that time I was watching that pink bow and strange movements it was making. The baby moving inside her.

I looked up from her stomach to her face. She caught my eye. I was transfixed by the clearest image I've ever had of her face in a dream. My resistance dissolved. She said "Hank" and pushed the door open. Her left hand reached out and grabbed my shirt. I told her: "You don't have to be so cold." Then she swept her gloved right hand up above her head as if she had a knife in it to stab me. But it wasn't a knife she aimed at me. It was my genital organ. I woke greatly afraid.

When am I going to get over that abortion mess and free myself from these hauntings? And who is this apparition at school? Rusty had a younger sister, but she was taller and thinner. Maybe I'll look closer next time. If I see her again. Was she real? Or a daytime extension of my nightly mental wanderings?

October 24, 1965; *Sunday*

Yesterday JoAnn and I went on a picnic in Central Park with Janice and Johnny, my married friends from school. We had a great time. The weather was cool and brisk, piles of leaves inviting us to jump in and romp though like we were kids. Our Frisbee soared high and far in the cool Canadian air. Even JoAnn and Janice joined in the Frisbee tossing, though like any time that girls play baseball or toss Frisbees, we men had more fun watching their contortions, bumblings and gigglings than in the toss and catch.

The season had long past when we could rent a rowboat for the lake in Central park. The water had a sickly green cast; but we enjoyed the wavelets and ducks. We explored the castle and rocks that overlook the lake like a medieval defensive fortification. On a massive stone slab I declared scoured flat by ancient glaciers, we ate our sandwiches and salads.

Such a great couple. JoAnn was as impressed as I by their vitality and fun. Both of them work and go to school. Janice takes classes at NYU in Social Science; Johnny is studying for a graduate degree in Accounting. They live in a small apartment on Jones Street in the West Village.

I met Janice last year in a Psychology class. I liked her immediately and asked her out to lunch. She looked at me with shock in her eyes. "Hey! You see this gold ring? I mean, I'm flattered and all that. And you sound real sweet. But I'm married, as in very married." Nonetheless, we did have lunch and she quickly introduced me to Johnny.

What I learned yesterday is that they are first cousins. They married secretly and scandalized the family. We were sitting on a tattered old blanket, relaxing after lunch in the golden sunshine.

"Well, actually we didn't marry right away. Right, Johnny?"

"No, I wouldn't say right away. Especially if you consider two years a little more than right away."

"Two years? Yeah, that's right! Well, there you have it. You see," Janice said to JoAnn and I, "We would go home to North Carolina for Christmas. I stayed with my parents and Johnny stayed with his parents. It took us a while to build up the nerve to tell everyone that we were married."

"What Janice isn't telling you is that our families are very religious. Church of Christ. You don't know that church, do you? I didn't think so. They don't have many congregations up North. Yet. Thank God for that. We knew being married as first cousins would upset everyone. Actually, marriage didn't bother us. Not a bit. We've always been in love with each other. Tying the Gordian knot was the easiest thing I've ever done."

"What happened when the news finally broke?" I asked.

They looked at each other and laughed. "We finally told them last Christmas," Janice said. "Johnny said he had enough of this separate bed stuff for the whole week. So right after Christmas dinner, when everyone was still seated at the table, Johnny announced…"

Johnny stood up and raised his coke bottle to the lake. "I have an announcement to make. I hope no one is upset about this. I've been secretly married for two years!"

"Well," continued Janice, "Some of our folks are into declaring for Jesus every Sunday, so public announcements in a loud voice have a familiar style. It was the content that kind of threw them off. Johnny purposely made it sound like a confession of sin."

Johnny flopped down and lay on his back looking up at the sky. "Did not."

"Did to."

"Did not."

"I said—did to!" Janice punched him on the arm.

"Oops. Defeat by greater forces."

"Just tell the story," said Janice with a raised fist.

"Yes, I obey, oh One With Mighty Fist. My mother, Janice's aunt, started crying. 'How could you! You're only a baby!' I was twenty-four and she still referred to me as a baby. 'And why didn't you tell us you were seeing a girl? Two years! Who is she?'"

"That's when the fun started," said Janice. "Because I said: 'Aunt Betty, I know who she is.'"

"'Oh, child, you do? And you didn't do anything to stop him?'"

"'Stop him? Why should I do that? Johnny married me!'"

Johnny rolled over on his side and faced us. "Janice and I had a pretty rough time of it for the rest of the evening. We were both over twenty-one when we married so they couldn't do much about annulling the union unless they were willing to travel to New York and start some kind of legal claim about blood relations. So they sent the kids out of the room and started in on us about monsters and deformities. Gruesome stuff."

"But Johnny and I don't want babies, so that talk went nowhere. After an hour they gave up. Except we still weren't allowed to sleep together. Neither my mother nor Johnny's was willing to let us sleep in the same bed in her house. So after all that to-do we still had to sleep apart. We're in a bind about what to do this Christmas. Johnny wants to avoid everything and go to the Bahamas. I don't know what to do. It's such a mess."

The afternoon was loads of fun and the wonderful feeling lasted through the rest of the weekend. JoAnn and I walked back through the park hand in hand as the sun set behind the Central Park West rooftops. Janice and Johnny headed downtown. We went to a Bergman movie and ended the evening turning the covers down on Dr Jeckle couch.

October 28, 1965; *Thursday*

A few lines here before I turn out the lights.

I've looked every day on the sixth floor before Physiology. Today I saw her again. She walked down the hall straight toward me. My feet turned to concrete and I had to will myself to move forward: left foot, right foot. I walked right up to her and said: "Hi." I'm never that direct with a girl. Never, ever.

She's looked up from her books straight into my eyes and gave me a strained smile. We're exactly the same height. "Hi," she answered and then continued straight down the hall and into a classroom door. She didn't look back.

The green eyes and thin smile were almost a double for Rusty. And the hair! That same amber halo of an October sunset. The face is thinner than Rusty, the flesh more tightly drawn, the features more angular. Rusty had a softness my mystery girl lacks. And my mystery girl has a more attractive figure: thin, muscular, and a bit more chesty. Although neither one would win a race with JoAnn in that department.

But at last I've sent the ghost back to the Netherworld. The girl is not Rusty.

Who is she? How can I introduce myself to her? Should I? How will I meet her again? Hang around the hallway and look like a fool?

10-28-65. 2+8+1+0+6+5=22. 2+2=4. A 4 day. One of my lucky numbers.

JoAnn was waiting for me when I came back from work tonight. She was in a playful mood and followed me into the bathroom when I went to take a piss.

"Go on," she said when I hesitated unzipping my pants. "I want to watch." That seemed like a strange request, but whatever.

Down went the zipper and out came my friend. I stared into the bowl, relaxed and let the water flow through. JoAnn pressed against my back. Her hands came around me and grabbed my dickie. "Let me," she said moving my hands away. "Ooh, this is fun." She poked her head around my left side to watch. She moved my dickie from side to side so that the stream fell first in one side of the bowl and then the other. After a minute I ran out of water. "Now what?" she asked.

"Shake it gently." She slammed it around. "Gently, I said!" She ignored my request and bounced the hose up and down, then back and forth, and accompanied the shake down cruise with several grunts of satisfaction. The drops splashed on my pants, on the floor, on the wall, on my shoes. Not one drop fell in the bowl. Of course none fell on her either since she was behind me.

"Do you have this much fun every time you pee?" she asked still pressing against me and holding on to my sausage.

"Right. Lots of fun. One of life's great pleasures. Ranks up there with blowing my nose and not getting snot on my shirt."

"Don't be vulgar." She didn't let go, and my friend began to show some interest in her touch. "Umm, what's this?" she asked. "Well, I know what to do with that."

October 31, 1965; *Sunday*

Halloween has always been a special time for me as a young boy growing up in New Jersey. The costumes, the black night, tick or treat, bags of candy. Last night JoAnn and I bought a small, a very small, pumpkin at D'Agostino's Market. With some old oil paints we created a grotesque face in reds, blacks and whites. Then we attached a wire to the stem and suspended the pumpkin on the outside of my apartment door.

This afternoon we came back from a trip to the Museum of Natural History. The pumpkin was missing from the door. Only a dangling wire remained, cut clean. What a city! Who would steal a little pumpkin? What would he do with it? "Hi, mom, how do you like my little pumpkin? I stole this painted beauty just for you."

JoAnn did lots of talking this weekend about having her own apartment with Sara. A rehash of what I've heard for the past several months. Same lines, same hopes, same problems. No resolution. In the middle of one long monologue the thought crossed my mind that I haven't been able to shake loose, a prospect that JoAnn and I may be rooming together soon. If her parents kick her out and if she and Sara do not get along well, then the door is open for me. And neither of these ifs is improbable.

My problem is that I'm not completely sure how I feel about this possibility. Living with JoAnn has certain advantages. But it also means that I can't date other girls. Here are the two dilemmas: loneliness vs companionship and independence vs being tied down and smothered.

NOVEMBER 1965

November 4, 1965; *Thursday*

The NYU chorus will perform Bach Cantata #67 this fall. Bach is so wonderful to sing. The choruses shimmer. You want to sing them over and over. Our director, a mild-mannered, limp-wrist creature, asked for soloists. Auditions were held this afternoon; no scheduled times—show up when you can. For me that was before chemistry lab.

The director sat at an upright piano in a small, cluttered music room. Metal chairs and heavy black music stands scattered as if players had pushed them out of the way and left in a hurry. He was playing duets with another limp-wrist soul. It was a cacophonous modern piece that assaulted my ears with cascades of unrelated notes. Noise disguised as music. They finished in a burst of two and four hand keyboard stompings and smiled at each other like lovers wrapped in mutual orgasmic ecstasy. Give me a break.

Finally he noticed me and called me over to the piano. His companion slipped from the bench and silently slithered away. We reviewed the tenor solo (actually part of a quartet in *Mein Jesu Ist Verstanden Alein*). I miscounted and stumbled through the notes as if I had never seen a music score before. Mercifully, he took me through the part three times; then surprisingly he awarded me the part.

My day for unexpected surprises. I got a phone call late this evening from Dancing Judy. She invited me for dinner and pumpkin pie making at her place tomorrow night. I told her I couldn't come until after work, about nine. "That's fine with me. You remember where my brownstone is—facing Irving Park close to your hospital?" I'm very nervous and looking forward to the evening. Maybe I'm excited?

Letter from my sister Rose. She says brother Anthony joined a fraternity. I'm not surprised. He will fit in well. Always the party and fun; he never did like hard work.

Anthony would ask dad how much time he expected us to take to wire a house or finish it with plugs and switches. If dad said take half a day to do the job, Anthony would nod and wait for dad to drive off in his smoke-filled truck. Then he would find an empty room to sleep before starting work. Stretch out on the plaster-spattered plywood floor with his jacket under his head and conk out.

One day last year, a Saturday in September after Anthony had left for his first year in college, I was working with dad. One of our tasks that day was to check on a finished house. The general contractor had phoned the night before to complain that nothing in the house worked—not a plug or light. The inspector would not approve the job; the house could not close; the general contractor could not collect his check.

The house was situated on a wooded lot landscaped beautifully by the Mexican crew. The pleasant scene reflected my relief. I recognized the house as one I had done the rough wiring on earlier in the summer. Anthony had finished the house with plugs and switches after the sheetrock had been installed and mudded.

Dad and I started our search for the problem in the garage where the power entered the house at the meter board. Needless to say, the meter and main breaker box were properly wired. I do good work. My father set the blue steel box cover back in place over the circuit breakers and screwed it down tight. He looked at me through the corner of his eye. "I recognize your wiring, Hank. Did you install the plugs and switches?"

I told him what he already suspected: "Anthony installed the plugs, switches and fixtures."

His face sagged and he muttered one of his run-on curses: *Goddamnsonofabitch.* A low grade curse like a low grade fever. Hardly worth a mention.

We progressed through the house room by room trying plugs and lights: nothing worked. Finally we could no longer avoid the obvious. Deep down we know the nature of the problem. At least I did. He removed the cover from a plug and unscrewed the device out of the wall box. No wires were attached. The wires had been pushed back into the box unstripped and untouched. Then the plug had been pushed into place and screwed down tight, followed by the cover plate.

This time my father raged and delivered one of his favorites: *Goddamnitalltohell!* A quality curse that rang through the empty house. A real 104 degree fever curse. Fortunately the blast wasn't directed at me. In any case, we put the house to rights in an hour. Everything worked. It should. I wired it.

Perhaps Anthony slept too long and woke knowing that he could never finish the job before dad returned. So he unpacked the plugs and switches, pushed the wires back into the box and then put in the plug and added its cover plate. Or maybe he was only half awake when he did the job. Nah. He knew what he was doing. And he knew that he would be long gone to college before the problem was discovered.

Dad never mentioned the incident after that and neither did Anthony. I'm certain dad never brought it up to Anthony because he would have groused to me if the old man had said anything to him. That's typical of issues in our family: Nothing is ever discussed or brought out into the open. Anthony will only know about dad's annoyance if I tell him. When I was growing up, my mother maintained a position as the conduit of information about my father's thoughts and feelings. They certainly never came directly from the source.

My skin has been terribly itching and I've been scratching badly all week. Nervousness? Excess sexual energy? Diet? Bad soap? My whole life I've been plagued with this eczema. My father said he had it as a boy and burned it off with acid. That doesn't sound like a good solution to me, although on nights like this anything would be better than scratching myself to death. My mother used to tie socks on my hands at night when I was a child so that I would not bloody the sheets. Maybe I should visit the skin clinic at the hospital. I pull enough charts for that clinic to merit a trip there.

November 6; *Saturday*
Judy's father was out for the evening. The elegant apartment with a grand piano and shelves of books was silent and comfortable. We had a nice evening making pumpkin pies. She planned to use a can mix, but I convinced her to add some fresh pumpkin scraped from the inside of a jack-o-lantern left over from Halloween. She hadn't put her pumpkin outside the door for someone to steal. Or maybe the thief was content with raiding apartments around Union Square.

I felt awkward during the evening, unsure what to say or comment on. Some women have that effect on me, while with others like JoAnn I am completely at ease.

JoAnn will be over soon, so I only have a few minutes to write here. Andre wants us over for dinner this evening. He's a good cook and always has some "cute" story. Then JoAnn and I will probably go out to a movie. Home to Jersey for a visit tomorrow. Time to bring my laundry and make my mother feel wanted.

November 9, 1965; *Tuesday*

A few minutes here before I walk east along Fifteenth Street to Beth Israel Hospital and my exciting job as one of Tootie's medical records minions. Tootie is my name for our boss.

Rainy day today. New York City rain that never feels clean, that streaks the windows in classrooms high above Washington Square, that swirls the garbage down the sides of Lower Broadway. Not pouring rain today that requires rubber overshoes, and yet enough to leave pants, shoes, socks and feet wet. An umbrella rain. A rain cold enough for a jacket and warm enough to leave you sweaty from walking. Fortunately the rain tapered off by this afternoon, and it looks like I can walk to work in dry shoes.

Yesterday I cut German to go to the hospital's Skin Clinic. German: the one class I don't need to cut. I have never been able to score well in foreign languages. I constantly miss an ending or an umlaut. But my scratching and itching have been so severe that there wasn't much choice. The clinics are held in open rooms that are more like expanded hallways. Rows of folding chairs are set out on the tiled floors. A nurse presides up front seated at a metal desk. She writes down the patient information and reads off names from a list. The doctor sees the patients in a small room behind the nurse's desk. Reminds me of waiting for confession in church. Doctors and priests, nurses and nuns. One authoritarian world parallels the other.

I pulled the charts for Skin Clinic the night before, so I knew there would be 32 people in the clinic. I also organized the stack with my name on top. Maybe the nurse would leave the stack in that order and call me first. Give me a small chance to make half of German class. No such luck. The nurse had rearranged the charts in alphabetical order. That meant 12 people ahead of me. I timed the first two people called: six minutes each. Assume two no-shows and six minutes each for the next eight patients: 48 minutes total. German class was out of the question.

Clinics were created for local residents who cannot afford a regular private physician. The room and the people in it reflected that situation. Overdressed in layers, disheveled, unwashed, unshaven, faces full of sores. People on the edge of survival. Obese colored women overflowing their chairs; thin, vacant colored girls with moon-eyed babies; bag ladies clutching their treasured possessions; haggard, ancient Jewish men sitting woodenly in frayed suits under shiny yarmulkes; tall, empty-faced men shuffling feet and swaying their bodies from one side to another. Noisy people: grumbling, belching, coughing, muttering. A current of bitter resignation and dark anger.

There was nothing for me to do and I was glad I brought a book to read. I'm still with Sigrid Undset in the fourteenth century. *Kristin Lavransdatter* contains as many pages as the New York City phone directory. And it's much better reading.

After half an hour only five patients had been in and out of the examination room. Nature called for me to take a leak. A tall, musty smelling colored man left the bathroom as I entered. The room possessed a veneer of standard institution clean and disinfectant under fluorescent lights hid behind opaque grids in the ceiling. As I stepped up to the urinal I noticed rivulets of blood laced through the water staining the Florentine cake. I backed away thinking: I have to tell someone about this. That man is really sick. But who do I tell? What do I say?

Nurse, you see that man over there? He pissed blood into the urinal.

So?

Well, he belongs in a hospital.

This is a hospital, son. And why is this any of your business? Are you a doctor?

I exited the bathroom without pissing. The man had vanished from the clinic room. Would I recognize him if I ever saw him again?

Dr Silver asked me a few questions and shook his head when I told him about years of salt water baths, various ointments, reduced acidic food intake. Then he quickly wrote me a prescription for hydrocortisone. He had dry, firm hands that transmitted complete confidence. No personal questions or communication. I thanked him and he nodded; he was already reviewing the next chart before I left the room. Six minutes. Maybe I should have said something about the blood in the urinal, but the situation never opened up enough for any kind of talk other than the exact problem at hand.

Tootie had my prescription ready for me when I came in to work. She asked me a few questions and I gave her back the proper polite responses. Then off to the bathroom to apply the cream to the inside of my elbows and knees. When I returned, I told her about the blood in the urinal.

"Hank, Who do you think goes to these clinics? Look at the charts. These people have multiple problems. We help them every way we can at no cost to them and plenty of cost to us. That's not a complaint. It's part of our mission. Blood in the urine is not a huge problem in the general scheme of things at this hospital."

Perhaps I should explain how Tootie got her name. When Bill and I first met, we both remarked on her general shape like a matzo ball with legs, on her waddling walk with the click-click of her odd low-heel shoes, and on her huff-huff breathing when she walks fast down the hallway or across the room. "You know what, Hank?" said Bill. "She looks like a little steam engine chugging down the tracks."

"Maybe she needs is an air horn announcing her entrance," I added.

"That's it! She's a Tootie!"

November 10. *Wednesday*

Whoever expected last night! And am I ever dead tired!

When I arrived at the medical records room last night, Tootie was off on some errand and Doris was working with two doctors who were completing their chart dictation. She can have that job. The residents and interns are always pissed-off when they have to update charts. "Goddamn waste of my time," is the common complaint that can be written in polite society.

Tootie sees final chart documentation as a major focus of patient care (whether the patient lived or died, whether he came in for heart surgery or a hangnail). When necessary she employs the ultimate weapon: suspension of hospital privileges. That brings the tardy docs in. As I said, Doris can have the job of working with angry young doctors who see no point in detailing the clinical progress of a dead patient.

Bill arrived on time for a change. He goes to school at Pratt Institute and has a longer commute than I do. We donned our buff colored BIH jackets and perused the lists of charts we had to pull for tomorrow's clinics. About 5:30 we were working our way along the stacks, pushing the rolling ladder ahead and scaling up and down to reach the high charts when the lights flickered and dimmed. For just a second. Enough to catch our attention. "Oops," said Bill from the next row of stacks, "there goes another heart patient!" We both laughed and continued our work.

"Hank," said Doris standing in the doorway, her full black face centered in the upturned collar of her fleecy coat, "I'm going home. Have a nice evening." I answered good evening back and returned to my work. Her shoes echoed on the tile floors as she walked away.

Maybe I was born that way, or maybe I like being outside; in any case, I'm a window looker. And what I saw, or rather what I didn't see outside when I worked my way to the end of the stack left me confused. "Bill," I said loudly, "something's wrong outside. Take a look." I couldn't figure out what looked wrong.

He rounded the corner carrying an armload of charts for OB Clinic. "What did you say? What's wrong?"

"Look out the window. There's something odd going on." Outside we saw the lighted windows of the back wing of the hospital and the darkened brownstones on 17th Street. The street had its usual traffic of scurrying pedestrians and cars with their headlights on. Then the oddment struck me. "The houses are dark. Why don't they have lights in the windows?"

Bill dropped his charts to the floor, they spread out like viscous liquid. He ran down the main aisle to another bank of windows farther back. You can see the top of the Empire State Building from those windows. His face was pressed against the glass when I caught up with him. "Dark," he whispered. "Everything is dark. Even the big buildings. It's a power failure. At rush hour."

"When the lights flickered..." I began

"That's when the power failed," he finished the sentence. "The hospital generator kicked in. That's why we have power. I wonder if the phones still work."

Up front in Tootie's office area I tried calling JoAnn and reached her on the first ring. "Hello?" she answered in a small, frightened voice.

"JoAnn?"

"Yes! Is that you, Hank? Everything went black here. I thought my desk lamp blew out, but when I went out into the hall, those lights were out too. I guess we blew a fuse. I found a flashlight in the kitchen and I looked in the fuse box, but I can't find what's wrong."

"JoAnn," I said softly to calm her down. "Where are you now?"

"I told you! I'm in the kitchen staring at the fuse box. Just tell me how to fix this thing."

"Can you go back through the apartment to the front windows?"

"The windows are fine. What are you talking about?"

"I know the windows are fine. Please do as I say. OK? Put the phone down, go to the windows facing Park Avenue, look out across the street and tell me what you see. I'll wait on the line for you."

"This sounds stupid to me," she said as she put down the receiver with a decided thud. I heard the kitchen door slam. A minute later I heard the click of another phone extension. "There's nothing out the front windows. Everything's dark. It's very scary here. What's going on?"

"Everything is dark downtown too. This has got to be a power outage. Must be all over Manhattan. The lights are on here at the hospital. We have a backup generator. Maybe I can…"

"Wait a minute. Someone's knocking at the front door. I'll be right back. God, I wish someone were here with me. Don't hang up. I'll be right back."

I looked up from the phone. Doris stood in the doorway with a confused expression. "I can't get home. Nothing's working. The power's out. The subway's closed. The street lights are off, traffic is a mess, buses can't move. How am I going to get home? What about my kids?"

"Try the phones. They're still working."

She tried one. "No dial tone!"

"Try it again. The lines must be jammed. Mine is working." I thought to myself: I was lucky with this call and I had better keep the line open.

JoAnn came back on the line. "That was the doorman. Checking on the apartments to make sure we have flashlights and candles. He's got a portable radio. There are one or two stations still broadcasting. The doorman says he heard that there's a power blackout all across the City. Everything's out. My parents are in Connecticut for a business meeting. I wonder how long this will last."

"Can't be long," I said. "How much time does it take to reset a relay?"

"Can you come up here?"

"I doubt it. We still have a lot of work to do. We just started pulling charts. And our lights are on. I'll try to call you when we finish work and let you know."

"Please."

"If the power's still out, how will I get uptown?"

"Please."

"OK. Listen, I'll try. Call you later."

Doris was talking on the phone to her kids. She must have found an open line that rang through. Bill was on the phone to someone.

A security guard appeared at the door. He had a walkie-talkie in one hand and was wearing a holstered gun. Both were out of the ordinary. "Any problems?" he asked.

I shook my head in the negative and asked: "Do you know what's happening."

90

"Only that there's a blackout and our generator kicked in. We have enough fuel oil for three days, so that's no worry. You'll have to hold down the outside calls. We need those lines clear for emergencies." He waited for me to nod an agreement, gave the place a final look, spoke a few cryptic comments into his walkie-talkie, and then moved on down the hall.

Doris slammed the phone down. "My kids are frightened. My husband's not home. I know he's caught in a subway. I'm down here in this goddamned hospital. What am I going to do?"

I felt totally hopeless. I didn't know what to say to ease her pain. Bill was still on the phone trying to explain to some girl why he couldn't leave. And even if he did, how would he ever get to Queens? From his tone I had the impression that he was losing the argument.

"Oh! Oh!" The unmistakable puffs of the Tootie! Our flawless leader bounced and waddled her way through the door. "What's going on? Why aren't you working? This is an emergency! Off, off the phone Bill. Quick, everyone back to work! Oh, Doris, I'm so glad you're here! Such a relief to have someone from my regular staff that I can depend on."

"Yes, M'am," said Doris in her submissive voice. She slowly removed her fleecy coat and slumped it over a chair. Both she and the coat sagged in weary resignation under the weight of fate.

Tootie picked up the phone. "Put me through to Dr Bernstein." We all looked at her. Bernstein, the chief administrator. A true God. "Dr Bernstein? This is Medical Records. I want you to know we have a small staff here and we will be able to meet any need." A great smile cleaved her turnip face. "Thank you, Dr Bernstein. Yes, we certainly can do that." She slowly lowed the receiver into its cradle. Then she noticed that we were looking at her. "Well, let's not stand around. You two boys have charts to pull. Doris, come with me to the Admissions Desk. Oh, you don't know how lucky I am to have you here with me, Doris."

Tootie exited with a bow-headed Doris three steps behind. Bill and I returned to the stacks, any hope we had of leaving early trampled under Tootie's tiny feet.

At nine o'clock Tootie was away from the office on some errand around the hospital. Doris was slumped dejectedly at a desk biting her fingernails. Bill and I seized our golden moment and escaped before Tootie could enlist us in her after-hours Elite Corps of Emergency Stormtroopers. Doris watched us leave with envious cow eyes.

We stepped outside into a foreign world. No street lights, no house lights. The visual world gelded. The streets appeared larger, the sky higher. The trees no longer defined the street's canopy, their bottom branches normally lit by street lights while their tops were draped in Stygian darkness. Tonight the trees stood in a full chorus of leafed arms stretching upwards to the starry skies. Stars! Above Manhattan!

These changes in the visual were not matched by an audio subtlety. The air was filled with horn blaring and angry voices. Oh well, too much to hope that serenity would ever settle here.

I crossed Second Avenue at Sixteenth Street and encountered my first shock: A man directing traffic with a flashlight. Not a cop, just an average fellow. Waving at cars and stopping them with a light beam in their windshields. That's not the most surprising part. People standing in the middle of Second Avenue making strange gestures is hardly unusual. The true oddity resided in the drivers complying with his directions.

The traffic was nearly in a complete jam. Like one of those hand-held puzzles with the little white squares with numbers and a single open space. You have to move the tiles around to bring the numbers into proper sequence. That's how traffic flowed on Second Avenue. One small space here and there for a car to squeeze into and create an equally small space behind it for another car to move into.

I looked north up Second Avenue into a vast river of red tail lights, an endless shoal of Red Blinking Gooney Fish. At regular intervals marking intersections were the flickerings of flashlights like tiny lighthouses. What fun for the legions of frustrated would-be policemen. A once in a lifetime great opportunity.

Across Third Avenue was another flashlight soldier. More obedient cars and cabs. Then I noticed that the cabs and private cars were full, people packed into front and back seats. Not one car with a solitary driver.

The sidewalks were crammed with executive types in dark suits and leather briefcases marching uptown. What were they doing in this part of town? Then I realized that they had been walking all the way from Wall Street. Hours of walking. And they were making better time in their buffalo migration that the people in the cars.

Once inside the marble entrance to my apartment house, I was surprised by the sight of our elderly elevator operator sitting in a chair. His lined face was illuminated by two flickering candles set on the hall table. "Hello, Leon," I said.

He squinted at me and then nodded in recognition. "Not much sense to ask if the elevator's operating?"

"No way. I was lucky, is for sure. Power gone out right after I come down from the 7th floor. I coulda been stuck in this old thing hung tween floors. So I'll sit right here for my shift. Don't give a damn if the power don't never start up again."

"Could be the best evening shift you've had this year."

"Yes, sir. Could be," he said with a smile.

The stairway up looked awfully dark. There wasn't much of a choice: Climb the stair or nothing. And for some reason I felt a strong need to check my apartment.

The first flight of white marble steps were visible in Leon's candlelight. But as I turned the corner for the second flight, only gray-black shadows indicated the steps. This second flight consisted of darker marble steps anyway. On the third flight the steps changed from marble to age-darkened, unwashed steel; these were completely invisible in the darkness. I climbed with one hand outstretched and counting the steps so that I had some idea when the final step was near. Anything to avoid that awful feeling of stepping up into air. For some reason our stairway has no emergency lights. Saved the owner a dollar, I suppose.

On the fifth flight I saw a candle flickering at the top of the stairs. No one there, no doors open down the hallway. Placed by someone on this floor who had stumbled and groped up the steps the way I had? Why would a New Yorker care? *I'm up safely. The next person has his own problems.* Isn't that the City way?

Candles on the seventh, eighth, and my own ninth floors. Was I in the right building? There was a light from an open door opposite my apartment. Mrs Keller's apartment. The slight illumination seemed like a flood of heavenly light that filled my eyes as I looked in and knocked on her open door.

"Oh, Mr Intili. There you are. I was worried about you." Mrs Keller sat, as usual, in her oak Morris chair surrounded by books and magazines. But she was not alone. The other chairs were cleared of books; three people, two men and a lady, sat politely with tea cups and saucers balanced on their knees. I recognized them as neighbors from the few times I had met them passing in the hall.

A massive, flowery oil lamp dominated Mrs Keller's apartment. The frosted glass emitted a pale warmth that mellowed the room. I perched on the window sill. "Now, Mr Intili, let me make the introductions. This is Mr Ames and his wife. They live in the large front apartment."

"Please call us Jack and Beverly," he said as he stood to shake my hand. His wife didn't offer hers. Instead she smiled bleakly at me from tired eyes. "Mrs Keller is always so formal with us."

"And please call me Hank."

"There is not one thing wrong with proper formality. I was brought up with civil manners. I'm comfortable with these old fashioned rules of etiquette and I taught them assiduously to my children. That they haven't continued the tradition is to their own detriment. The world is a sadder place for it. Now, Mr Intili, you must stay for a cup of tea. The lights may be out but the stove gas is still on. We can boil water so all is not lost. You're not in a rush are you? You just sit there and let me find you a cup in this mess." I didn't move a muscle. I wouldn't have dreamed of interrupting her party. She made a whole ceremony out of pouring me a simple cup of tea.

"Oh, now, I forgot to introduce you to Mr..." Mrs Keller held her head to one side trying to remember the other man's name.

"Cranbeau. Roger Cranbeau." He stood to shake my hand. His grip was limp and pasty. An older man, maybe 55, overweight and trying to look younger in what he probably thought were stylish clothes. The yellow cravat and open silk shirt only looked affected.

"Yes. Mr Cradbeau. He lives on the tenth floor and came down to see if everyone is all right," Mrs Keller said as she passed me a tea cup. She had already added two lumps of sugar. Nothing wrong with her memory.

"No, no, my name in Cranbeau. Not Cradbeau," he whined. We looked at him. What difference did it make? And what was he doing on our floor? Looking for another pumpkin to steal off a door? "What an awful day," he said, his hand waving in the air. "This blackout has ruined my plans. The world immobilized by some fool in Podunk."

"Surely it's not that bad, Mr Cran-beau," she said slitting his name. "I grew up in a world without electricity. We did well. Our small town in Illinois was electrified after the Great War. I never noticed any harm to draw water by hand, heat with wood, and see at night with oil and candles. Now aren't you glad I kept this old oil lamp? Finally found a use for it other than decoration. Mr Intili, were you caught in the blackout?"

"No. I was working tonight at the hospital. The lights flickered and the back-up power generator clicked on. We hardly noticed anything."

"Well, you were lucky," said Jack whom I've never spoken more than two words to in a year. "I was working in my office off Canal Street. We usually work to six. That way we can take late calls from the west coast. When the lights went off and didn't come back on, it damned near…"

"Mr Ames. Could we please watch our language?"

"Sorry. It darned near caused a panic until people started flicking their Bics. Finding our way out of the building was contained panic, but better than being caught in the subway I should imagine. Four of us shared a cab going uptown. Fortunately one man had a small bottle of brandy in his briefcase. Most expensive drink I've ever had considering what the cabbie charged us."

"Well," said his wife, "I only work a few blocks from here. That's why we rented our apartment. So I could be near work. Well, at first no one knew what happened. Lights out and all that. There had been a birthday a few days ago and one of the office girls had saved a coupled of candles. Those stubs provided enough light for us to close the office and head home. What a walk! I certainly wouldn't want to live in a big city without lights. No thank you. Then I had to walk up the stairs in this wretched building in my heels. Yes, Jack, wretched. There, I've said it and I mean it. This proves it. Walking upstairs in that dreadful, frightening black stairway. That miserable, lecherous old doorman was no help at all. Wouldn't leave his chair for anything. Wouldn't let me borrow a candle to find my way up the dark stairs. Wait until I report him to the owner."

"People have put candles near the stairs now on some of the floors," I said.

"Weren't you lucky," she said with a bite in her voice. "I came up half scared to death in the total blackness. Anyone could have been on those stairs and who could have seen him? Fortunately Mrs Keller had her lamp lit and her door open. A true Christian angel. Otherwise I would have never found my way down the hall and into our apartment. Our landlord keeps the hallways dark enough as it is."

I excused myself and crossed the hall to my own room. Enough light filtered in from the large window for me to see that nothing was disturbed. I tried the phone. No dial tone. I stayed on the line for a full minute. Finally a dial tone. I called JoAnn.

"Hello?" she answered.

"Hi, Sweets. It's me. If you want some company, I'll try to make it uptown."

"I would love to see you. It's very lonely here. My parents finally called. Connecticut is without power, too. How long will it take for you to get up here?"

"The streets are jammed with traffic."

"Not here. Park Avenue is just average. Everything is moving."

"Well, then, maybe not too long. See you then."

I took my toothbrush from the bathroom and gazed across an eerie Union Square. A full moon had risen, flooding the treetops with milky light. Nice weather and a full moon. What better time for a blackout?

Across the hall, I told everyone I was going to visit my girlfriend uptown. "Are you sure you should try that tonight?" asked Mrs Keller. Her question had a strained inflection as if she was showing concern with a moderate casting of moral judgment. In any case, my mind resided elsewhere. I said goodnight to everyone.

Before I started down the long, dark staircase, I knocked on Andre's door. Corky answered with a burst of barking that settled into a whine. Like Mr Crapbeau. Corky was huddled against the door. No one home. No one to take him for his evening walk.

Going down the black stairs between the seventh and second floors was worse than climbing up. Always the fear of tripping and falling. I said goodnight to the elevator man who looked at me as if I had lost what little sense I once possessed. What was outside on a night like tonight?

I crossed 15th Street to Third Avenue and then started walking uptown with the rest of the bison. A total traffic snarl for forty blocks (about two miles). In the 40's the street intersections had real policemen. Maybe that's why the congestion was worse there than in my part of town. I never met a cop who could direct traffic without causing a jam.

After 50th Street the traffic thinned and I caught a bus with standing room only. No one was talking. The riders weren't the usual working class folks. Instead this bus was full of business types with long faces. The hour was past eleven and they were past talking or even grumbling. The bus discharged the men in suits in the 70's and 80's and picked up the usual night people. By the low 90's only a few people were left on the bus and the traffic was no different from a regular evening.

With the exception of a few scraggly looking whites, the bus was filled with black faces when I disembarked at 94th Street. On the East Side of Manhattan 96th Street is a true demarcation between black and white populations. The trains from Grand Central Station emerge from the tunnels at 96th Street and Park Avenue. The City changes. JoAnn's parents live in one of the last fine apartment buildings.

It was midnight when I finally reached JoAnn's. The moonlight cast the square, squat apartment houses into dreamlike characters in a graveyard play. Here and there a golden candle in a window broke the milk white and slate gray facades. An urban forest of Arden.

I had to pound on the front door for five minutes before the regular night doorman appeared. He shined a flashlight through the glass and into my face and held it there for some time. He must have recognized me right away; the delay was his revenge for rousting him out of whatever he was doing. Probably sleeping. He looked as if he were about to ask me who I was visiting, but that would have been a step too far. Reluctantly he unlocked the big metal and glass door and let me in. We walked in tandem to the stairway. I took out my own small flashlight and told him I could find my way upstairs.

He hesitated for a moment. He probably should have accompanied me since I am only a visitor and not a resident. But he shrugged his shoulders and left me on my own. Maybe he was tired; maybe he had climbed too many stairs already that night; or maybe he plain didn't give a damn.

JoAnn was pleased to see me. Very pleased by the way she hugged me hello. She had candles lit in the hallway, bedroom and kitchen. I hadn't eaten, so we sat at the white porcelain kitchen table and snacked on bagels and vanilla ice cream while I told her of my adventures for the evening. Ah, she loved me for the dangers that I passed, and I loved her that she did pity me.

She had the trundle bed pulled out and made up with fresh, crisp sheets and fluffy blankets. Linen and covers perfectly neat and cornered. Looked almost too good to mess. But we did, energetically, for an hour. She got on top and pumped me dry.

We slept for a while and woke at four. The beds lay close together, in the dark room with its solitary candle we could barely see each other's outlines bunched under our covers with only our heads poked out. For some strange reason we spoke in whispers.

"Your birthday is in two days," she said. "My parents will be back by Thursday so I can't stay over and give you something extra special on your 21st birthday. I can see you that evening, but not for the whole night. You know what I mean. That will have to wait for the weekend. Then you can have your choice of the menu, ala carte. So for Thursday is there anything in particular you want to do? A movie or a dinner at a fancy restaurant?"

"I don't enjoy fancy restaurants."

"OK. Then what else?"

"What else?"

"For your birthday."

"Whatever."

"Why are you being like this? All I want to do is find out how to give you a great 21st birthday, and you're being evasive. Don't you want me around?"

"I'm not being evasive." I turned away and looked at the ceiling. I couldn't tell her about my birthday and Rusty. I couldn't figure out how to resolve the problem. I don't even know if I can explain it here in this journal. JoAnn said nothing more and we both drifted off to sleep.

The radio woke me up. And the lights. The whole apartment sprang to life. Everything JoAnn had tried to turn on and had failed to turn off was now reacting to the original command. We both hauled out of bed and went around the apartment turning off lights, radios and even the electric mixer in the kitchen. I didn't ask about the mixer.

I showered, dressed and headed downtown. JoAnn kissed me goodbye at the door. "Thank you," she said sweetly. Down in the street, the morning was like any other.

At school no one talked about anything except who was where and what happened. When I arrived at work this evening, Tootie told Bill and I that she was proud of how well we had managed the difficult evening. Doris only passed us a sullen look. Our exiting at nine must have ensured that she was there for the rest of the night. Where would she have gone anyway with the subways out? I'll have to ask her about the kids and husband next opportunity.

I guess I ought to write about Rusty. Half of everything I write has her in the text or in the margin. I wish I could get her out of my life, she weighs me down like an anchor, like a drag chain. Maybe like Morley's chain. Do you think I can exorcise her ghost by writing her out?

My first semester at Dickinson College I tried out for the annual musical: Gilbert and Sullivan's *HMS Pinafore*. I've always been in singing groups through church and school. But I was really surprised when I got the lead tenor role: Raphe Rackstraw. All the other leads were seniors who had been doing college musicals for years. I sang in high school, but I certainly wasn't a lead. Never saw myself that way.

Sometime during early rehearsals I noticed a senior girl with brilliant, long red hair and wonderful hazel eyes looking at me. I can't remember how we started talking, maybe about my part and hers (Cousin Phoebe). It turns out that we were both singing in the College Chorale, me as a first tenor, she as a second soprano.

She had an odd way of talking. You asked her a question, and she answered like she was quoting from a poem or a novel by Dickens. The words didn't flow like normal speech. In fact she did write poetry, a lot of it. One evening she showed me a whole book of her poems. "Can I borrow these?" I asked.

"My poems are my companions. They don't stray from my side."

"Just for tonight. So I can read them in depth. I promise I'll have them back to you before class tomorrow."

"For you, my own love, one night."

I stayed up through night and copied the poems into a spiral notebook. Somehow managed to stagger to 8am Biology class. Which I then proceeded to sleep through. When I returned Rusty's poems, I didn't tell her that I had copied them.

The book is now in my desk drawer next to my notebook of dreams. What is most striking about the poems is their mix of frankness and airy wording. One minute she's completely open and personal; the next line is as obscure as a mountain in mist.

Rusty worked for Dr Graffman in the psychology department. He had the four rooms in the top floor of an old converted house. Rusty had the keys to his office and the back door. Somehow we figured out that if we met in his testing room on Sunday mornings, no one would bother us. That ended any chance Father Ryan had of getting me to church. Late Saturday nights were also good times, although we were almost discovered twice.

One night we were lying on a blanket on the floor behind a desk under the dormer window that looks out over the president's house. The lights in the room were out. We were clad only in our underwear. I was still uninitiated in sexual intercourse. We heard heavy footsteps on the stairs, a key in the lock and the door opened. We froze, breathless. Whoever was there stood in the doorway for a moment, then closed the door and went back downstairs. Had he come forward even one step into the room, he would have seen us. Expulsion would have been a certainty.

The other time was actually pretty innocent. Late one evening on a school day Rusty was grading papers for Graffman. I was seated at his desk studying for a German test. Probably a waste of time knowing my inability to soak up anything in that language. We heard someone bounding up the steps two at a time and in burst Graffman. Apparently he thought we were doing something unnatural. Not that I didn't always have that on my mind. But this was one night when we were there for a legitimate purpose. He mumbled something or other. We answered that we only planned to be there until Rusty finished his work. Then, mustering what dignity he could, he said good night and went back down the stairs.

Of course huggy-kissy in underwear on a blanket could only last so long. I wish I could say that I was merely bumbly and inept. We were also very stupid with the usual results. Maybe I should have known better Although in my feeble defense it could be said that sex was a taboo subject in our house. I can't remember a single time either of my parents talked about sex. Another big nothing from my father.

I can't write any more about this tonight. How do I free myself from this curse?

November 11, 1965; *Thursday*

This diary has seen much emotion from my pen—anger, happiness, frustration. But tonight I'm crying. Today is my birthday, I'm 21 years old, and I'm crying.

Today is the day Rusty promised to visit me again. For how long have I imagined what I would do if forced to choose between her and JoAnn? What would happen if JoAnn was with me in the apartment and Rusty knocked at the door? Who would I ask to leave? Would I turn to JoAnn and say: *This is deeper and more ancient than you. I need time with Rusty.* Or would I stand there with the door open and tell Rusty: *Life moves on and I can't let you in anymore.*

But the reality! JoAnn isn't here and Rusty didn't come.

That bit about Rusty at the door—that was always fantasy. She's married and has obligations elsewhere. She started the fantasy. She promised to seek me out on my 21st birthday, a promise she made on our last day together.

Months after the abortion we saw each other again. She came to visit me at Dickinson College on a vaporous Saturday in September. The air was warm and heavy with moisture, the sun golden through the brown and russet leaves of horse chestnut, oak and sycamore. And like the vanished high summer sun, the enchanted, magical feelings that had overpowered me a year before were gone. I only wanted out and away from her. And I told here that.

We were seated on a rock rim high above the Conidaguinet Creek in Carlisle. The same flat, warm stone slabs we had kissed and caressed on in the November afternoons of the year before. Rusty sat with her arms around her knees, her head bowed forward. I stood beside her throwing pebbles in great arches over the treetops into the stream far below. Throwing stones and telling her that I didn't want to be with her anymore.

"Hank, what can I tell you? That for me the sky is lighted when you're there? That the earth is flushed warm green? That I imagine the touch of your body as I walk at night?" Rusty and her fancy, stilted language.

"Sure," I responded as I tossed another stone into the hazy air and watched the distant speck silently splash into the slate blue water far below.

"I don't regret the all of myself that I've given to you. I know that without you timelessness is gone and too present is the here and now." I felt her looking at me with those deep green eyes that snared me a year ago from the other side of the crowded rehearsal room. The first eyes that ever laughed at me in pleasure. Eyes that I knew without looking had the doleful pleading of a young puppy. I didn't want either the laughter or the begging. They would only drag me back into the swamp.

"Christ Almighty, Rusty, what do you want from me?" My stomach churned and shuddered. I was angry. I picked up a thin, flat stone and flung it away with a snap of my elbow.

"I want a life made full by more than one. I want the best I know is in you." Her soft soprano voice had a slight huskiness as if there was a catch in her throat.

"This kind of talk is juvenile crap."

"Perhaps I mistake the need for love on your part for love itself." She spoke so quietly I could barely hear her. The cry of a kingfisher sailing through the air above the creek was more audible. Rusty was quoting from one of her poems. Most of what she said that afternoon were lines from her poems. Well, that's how she talked. The lyrical speech was a central part of her recondite fascination. It could also be damned annoying when you wanted to communicate a simple message like *go away*.

My shoulder hurt from throwing stones and the activity seemed pointless. Finally I looked down on her. As I suspected, he begging eyes were on me. The golden, dappled sunshine highlighted her red hair with a medieval halo.

"I can't be with you anymore. I just can't."

"All right, Hank. I was hoping the two of us would be there to help and heal us both. One love can never heal the vacant love of another. But I see now that healing cannot, will not, be. So I want you to know this: On your 21st birthday, wherever you are, whoever you're with—and I know as sure as there is a God that you will never be without a woman; there's so much power in you—on that night I will visit you again and make love to you with the full force of my love. I won't ask anything from you. I won't stay. That will be my gift."

I left her seated on the rock over Conidaguinet Creek and walked the two miles back to the college. I fell in bed and slept for the rest of the afternoon. I never saw or heard from her again. That was four years ago. Rusty doesn't know where I am. How could she find me? Who would she call to locate me? Silly fantasy.

But JoAnn! How little does it take to spend some time with me tonight on my birthday? On my 21st birthday.

This morning she caught up with me in the coffee shop after English class. I was seated at the counter having my usual pot of hot tea with a corn muffin. She sat down beside me and gave me a kiss. "Here you are. Happy birthday!"

"Is this his birthday?" my favorite waitress asked JoAnn as she placed a cup of coffee down in front of her. She smiled at us with her whole face. It's sea of freckles moved on tides of genuine joy. The waitress likes JoAnn. Everyone likes JoAnn.

"Yes. And did you know he's 21 today?"

"Twenty-one." The waitress shooed a fly away with the back of her hand. She has a hard, angular face with crow's feet already appearing at the corners of her eyes. "So damn young. How does anyone get to be that young? Well, happy birthday. You're a lucky fellow."

"Lucky?" I ask.

"Of course you're lucky. Look at this lovely girl you have."

"Lovely girl? Oh, you mean JoAnn?" I said in imitation of an old joke. No one laughed. "That's an old joke line," I explained.

""Doesn't sound funny to me," said the waitress. JoAnn said nothing. She sipped her steaming coffee. The waitress turned her back on me and walked down the counter to speak with someone else.

"That wasn't a very nice thing to say to me. It wasn't funny."

"Why are you taking it so seriously? Can't we just kid around now and then? Does everything have to be serious? To have deep meanings?"

"Not everything. Just some things. And people's feelings are one of the things that you shouldn't play around with like checkers."

"Now I'm guilty of playing checkers?"

"Why are you being like this? You've been mean to me for days. No one can talk to you, no one can get close to you. Nothing." She returned to her coffee. Probably to think up some new nastiness to throw at me. But what she finally did say caught me completely off guard. "I bought you a record for your birthday." Her voice was markedly less cheerful than when she first came in. "The Telemon trumpet concertos I know you've been looking for."

"A record?" I was so surprised so lower jaw dropped to my navel.

"I'll give you the present now because I'll be too busy studying to see you tonight. I have a big test tomorrow."

My body turned into a pillar of salt. We sat quietly on the stools for a while. She sipped her coffee, I stirred more sugar in my tea. I didn't say anything. It was her move. Let her talk.

"And you haven't sounded very much like you wanted to have me around you tonight."

"I haven't sounded that way? You're the one doing the talking."

"Now I am. You haven't said anything to me whenever I ask you what you want to do on your birthday."

"You asked me?"

She didn't answer my question. "Are you seeing someone else tonight?" she asked her cup of coffee.

"When did you ask me what I wanted to do?"

"Hank, I'm not going to play your insulting word games. Here's your record. I'm sorry you don't want me close to you tonight. I had some special treats planned for you."

She plopped a dollar down on the counter and left. My waitress was watching me with molten lead in her eyes. Somehow I've done something wrong to JoAnn and everyone is pissed at me. What have I done wrong? It's my birthday, not hers. But, as I said, everyone likes JoAnn.

Later tonight after work I treated myself to dinner at Gloria's Restaurant on East 26th Street. I found the place last year on one of my exploratory wanderings. I go to this basement eatery now and then alone for dinner. I mentioned the place to Andre one night. He said he knew about the restaurant and quickly changed the subject. I don't know what his gripe is. The food is very good, there are only ten tables, and the prices are low. You bring your own wine. Tonight the cellar atmosphere with only a few occupied tables seemed just right for my mood and the occasion.

The waiter sensed something was wrong when he came over to bring me a salad. "Are you OK tonight?"

"Yes, of course," I croaked. I couldn't look up. He would see water in my eyes.

"I don't mean to pry into your personal life, but you're a regular customer. One of our smiley people. I've never seen you so quiet and down in the dumps."

"I usually smile?"

"Yes. That's how we all know you. Our smiling student."

Something shifted inside me. I wanted to talk to someone. "Well, you see, today is my birthday, and…"

"You're birthday! You're such a pussycat! Why didn't you tell us?"

Another twinkie. I should have known. No wonder Andre knows about the place. No doubt Andre's gripe has something to do with the waiter. Maybe he was "too cute" or too naïve the way I was two months ago. In any case, the waiter sauntered back through the nearly dark room lit with tiny Christmas lights and flickering table candles. He entered the kitchen area that is only partly disconnected from the dining room.

"Gloria!" I heard him shout.

"We ain't deaf, Todd," came a scratchy, high-pitched response. I recognized this disembodied voice. Everyone else did, too. The constant kitchen banter is one of the restaurant's main attractions. I don't know the people in the kitchen apart from an occasional glimpse through a picture-sized portal.

"Yeah," said a younger woman's voice. "We certainly heard enough of his screaming from his apartment last night." That set off a cascade of hidden laughter.

"Watch it!" answered the waiter whose name must be Todd. "For your information we have a birthday out here tonight."

"What!" said a growling female voice. "Whose birthday? No one told me about any birthday. In my restaurant? Who would do such a thing?"

Two heads appeared in the portal. Their faces were set in dark shadows by the strong kitchen light behind them.

"Where?" the younger woman's voice asked.

"Table two," Todd answered.

"Oh. It's our student," the young woman's voice said quietly. The heads disappeared from the window and there was more whispering that I couldn't decipher.

Todd came back out into the dining room trailed by a striking girl several years older than me. She was dressed in a plain shirt and jeans with a tomato-stained kitchen apron that she was wiping her hands on. Her eyes were direct, her face large and sensuous.

She spoke to me in a subdued, feminine voice: "Why didn't you tell us this is your birthday before you came in? We always love to prepare something special for our regular customers. Table two. Let me think. You ordered a simple spaghetti dish. I'll change that and make you a veal scaloppini or chicken parmigiana. Whichever one you want."

"No, I couldn't do that."

"It's no trouble. Gloria won't mind."

"There really is a Gloria?"

"Of course! This is her restaurant. Is there a Gloria? What a question. I know what we'll do. Let's go back to the kitchen and you'll meet the real Gloria."

I started to object. But before I could say anything, she had her hand under my arm and was pulling me up from my chair and dragging me down the narrow aisle. "Birthday Boy coming through!" she shouted to the other customers. Everyone laughed.

The kitchen was nothing like I imagined. More like an old home kitchen than a New York restaurant. No more than twelve foot by six foot with home-style appliances: a four-burner gas stove, regular refrigerator, double sink. How do they manage to cook with a full house?

Then there were the people. Two large, older women, one at the sink with a great toothless grin, the other sitting on a stool under a phone on the wall. She was wearing a nondescript tent dress and ripped slippers. Strings of pearls hung down from her neck, her hands were positioned on massive hips and she was staring at me. Her steel gray eyes were like a Captain Video Space Ray Gun punching a particle beam right through me.

My guide pulled me in. "Mama, this is the birthday boy. He didn't think there was a Gloria."

"Of course there's a Gloria," answered the large woman with the pearls and gray eyes. "Who else do you think I was?"

She posed me a question that I couldn't avoid. But the query didn't make any sense. "I love your restaurant," I answered. "I come here whenever I can." I was praying that my red, teary eyes weren't showing. I couldn't bear the embarrassment.

"Oh, what a lovely thing to say," Gloria responded. One hand moved to her pearls. Her face softened. "My daughter does the cooking." She pointed to my guide. "She started a few months ago. The recipes are mine."

"Mama, don't start; not now."

"Not start what?"

"You know I've been working here since I was fourteen."

"Fourteen? Impossible. You started cooking when you finally left that sailor bum. That wasn't fourteen. Fourteen was something else."

"Mama, please. Let's not go into that. And I started here at fourteen making salads and helping Sissie at the sink."

"That's right, Gloria," said the baggy lady with soapy arms standing next to the sink. She had a mushy face, sunken in around the mouth, puffed out in the cheeks and jowls.

"Impossible. Absurd. Who could believe such a thing? Todd knows better than that." Gloria held her ground, but I couldn't follow her thinking. Todd didn't respond or didn't have the chance to answer.

"And this," continued my guide ignoring her mother, "is Sissie, our dishwasher and everything else."

The toothless lady cackled and nearly curtsied. "Nice to meet ya!"

"And you already know Todd the waiter."

"Doesn't everyone?" cackled Sissie.

"Watch it!" said Todd without any rancor.

"And I'm Yvonne. Now, what's your name?" Her soft gray eyes were looking flat into mine. We're about the same height. "So we can sing *Happy Birthday*." I noticed her breasts were small and very nice. Or so it seemed through the shirt. Lucky shirt. I told her my name.

They did sing to me, they did cook me a special dinner, and I did feel much better. Until I walked up the steps out of the restaurant into the cold, empty street. Then my black feelings returned.

Back in my apartment, I opened my closet kitchen, and from my pint-sized refrigerator I took out the birthday cupcake my mother gave me last Sunday. My mother for whom birthdays are always the most special days. Maybe that's what I enjoyed so much about the restaurant: the ancient feeling of being extra special on my birthday. Maybe that's what brought me out of my black mood for half an hour. I placed a single candle on top of the white cupcake and sang Happy Birthday to myself softly. I imagined that I wasn't alone, that my bed wouldn't be cold and empty. And Rusty thought I would have someone else with me! Ha!

November 16, 1965; *Tuesday night*
Reading again from Sigrid Undset's *The Master of Hestvigen*. Left me thoughtful and contemplative tonight.

Happiness and knowledge are not only for another time, but also for this hour. Not only for another place, but also for this place. The truth and the beauty in the story of the love of Ingunn and Olav have meaning only if they strike a chord of unison within us, and if we take this unison, this compassion, and build it into the structure of our own lives. Happiness and knowledge are not gifts from the gods; they are the results of our own work and energy.

The truths that matter in the Universe are the truths of our own existence. These truths we must find for ourselves, fight for, and then be proud in their possession. The only beauty in the Universe is the beauty we see with the mind's eye, the beauty we feel. And this beauty belongs to those who, when touched by it, take pride in it.

Ours is a Universe of flux, change, and Plato's cave-black loneliness. From the prison of a womb we have come into the unspeakable and incommunicable prison of this Earth. In the time of our lives we must live. We must work and fight and love for that which gives meaning to our lives, for those flashes of truth and beauty from which, with the energy within us, we can create happiness and knowledge.

I have interwoven some ideas from Wolfe and Saroyan which seem congruent with the whole content. Olav too has the problem of Wolfe: Who can look into his brother's heart and who can know his father? Olav knows Ingunn loves him, yet he cannot see into her heart, nor can he understand how she could lay with another man. Her bonds to him cannot be broken even by her betrayal. Nor can he see into his own heart. When she dies, he begins the lifelong search to understand the actions of a single year.

Because Olav doesn't live in the time of his life, because he spends that time searching for a door, a lost lane end, he never fully lives his life. As an old man no one understands or knows him. He's merely the old ogre, the invalid against the wall. Olav admires his ancestor Torgils who fought Death with the axe to prevent the Grim Reaper from taking his beloved. But Olav, though he admires

Torgils, does not live his own life with a similar intensity and directness. He hides his shame, Ingunn's shame, his crime, his feelings for the bastard boy and his own daughter. Everything hidden. He never really lives. There are no stories passed on after him that show him as a hero the way he saw his ancestor Torgils.

November 21; *Sunday*
Can't sleep tonight. Too much on the brain. I am very discouraged about school and love life and work and myself. My marks are poor this term and my attitude worse. I'm wasting life away in this City. College is a joke—you learn more outside of school than in. But if you leave school, the army gets you. And that's worse.

All my good intentions towards JoAnn have petered out. As a person, she fails to excite me. She remains crushed under her parents and her social training, even though she admits to knowing there is another, better way to live. She still has no apartment, still goes home every Sunday for dinner, and still comes alive only behind her parents' backs. I have no more hopes that she will ever rise above her upbringing—she may want to, but when faced with the need for action, she won't do anything but talk. I only wish I did not have the emotional attachment for her that I have.

She tells me that she feels torn in different directions by different, difficult people. By that I suppose she means me. In any case, this week I'm going to be nasty. This duplicity of hers nauseates me. But what can be done that doesn't backfire on me? For unless I am willing to undergo discomfort for my convictions, I am no better than she.

November 22, 1965
Today standing in the hall before German waiting for the earlier class to end, I was lost in some foggy realm of thought. Don't remember what I was thinking, what lofty thoughts were vaporizing my mind.

"Hello," said a high-pitched, raspy voice. *Her* voice. She stood right next to me, looking into me with her clear eyes.

"Uh, hello," I stammered.

"Do you often stand around the halls without noticing anything?" Her lips stretched thin across her mouth in what seemed a cross between a smile and a grimace. Up close I could see that her red hair in its tight perm had highlights of blond or gray. It lacked the purity and freedom of Rusty's. Her eyes squinted a little and her voice had a splash of pixieness. "Or is it just the sixth floor you hang around every afternoon?"

"Hang around? No, I have German here in a few minutes," I said tripping over my leaden tongue. She put me on the defensive. I needed to ask her name, needed to ask her out for a cup of coffee. My tongue stayed glued to the top of my mouth.

"Right. Well, see you again." She flashed her smile and walked away sharply. No hesitation, no slow moves, no feminine smoothness. Her body seemed to lack any softness, everything in tight movement.

Slowly my feet freed from their concrete overshoes. I ran after her and caught up a dozen steps later. "Wait!" I shouted. She didn't stop but did move her head in my direction. We were striding side by side down the hall away from my German class.

"Yes?" she asked.

"I don't know your name."

"And I don't know yours. Maybe next time." She turned on a dime and entered a classroom.

November 25, 1965; *Thanksgiving*

This has always been my favorite holiday. Christmas is so commercialized, so pressured with presents and demands; Easter is religious and who cares about bunnies and eggs; Fourth of July is parades, military speeches and fireworks. Thanksgiving stands like a Doric column: simple, direct, satisfying. Not ostentatious like an Ionian column, not monolithic like a Minoan. Thanksgiving is family, friends, dinner, maybe a football game at the local high school. No unreasonable demands or expectations. Thanksgiving has the orange and yellow light of autumn, light jackets and scarves.

And turkey is something so simple even my mother can cook it. The stuffing you buy in a store; cranberry sauce comes in a can; potatoes, sweet potatoes, and pies you ask your guests to bring. A manageable holiday.

JoAnn and I were concerned about how to handle Thanksgiving this year. Whose house? Last year we spent the afternoon with my family and the evening with hers. Two dinners. Too bad Alka-Seltzer didn't ask us to do a commercial. We would have won an award. Signed huge contracts. Made millions on our protruding pot bellies.

This year JoAnn's parents solved our problem by deciding to spend the holiday in Bermuda. They asked JoAnn to accompany them, although *ask* may be too mild a word. She told me about her parents' demands on Monday night.

"When I came home for dinner on Sunday, they let me have it both barrels of the proverbial shotgun. Nagged me for an hour about going with them. I thought the torture would never end. They asked me endless questions: What would I do all week? Could I quote behave unquote on my own for a week? Where would I go on Thanksgiving? Why didn't I want to be with them? Endless verbiage.

"Actually a trip to Bermuda for a week sounds great. But I could tell them honestly that I can't miss this week of school. Two tests on Tuesday and an English paper due Wednesday. In fact that hardly gives me time to see you. Well, they left today, and I'm here in New York."

My mother called on Tuesday night after I returned from work. "I want to make sure you'll be here for Thanksgiving. Rose and Carl are coming around noon, and Anthony will be here if he stays home long enough for us to see him. Your Uncle John and Aunt Bea will be here too. So everyone is expecting you."

"Yes, mother, I'll be there. Did you want me to bring anything from the City? My usual bottle of wine? Or some pastries from Venerio's?"

"No, you don't have to bring anything unless you want to. The important thing is that you come. I don't mean to be pushy with my son, but I need to plan. Is JoAnn coming with you? You know she's always welcome. Everyone loves to see her. I'm only asking because we need to know how many people to set the table for."

"Yes, mother, JoAnn will be with me. Her parents are away for the week, so we don't need to rush back to the City like last year." I added to myself: *Unless dad pulls one of his scenes again.*

"Oh? Did you want to stay over? We can make up an extra bed for JoAnn. You know she's always welcome to spend the night here. And since her parents aren't home, maybe they'll appreciate it more if they know where she is at night."

"Mother, I can assure you that they know where she is most nights. They may not like it, but they have a pretty good idea."

"Well, I think you know how I feel about that." Silence. My mother's deadliest weapon unsheathed. And victorious.

"Would you like us there early to help you cook?" I had to say something to give her a reason to declare an armistice. "I may not be a great chef, but I like to make a mess. And with JoAnn along I have someone to clean up behind me." Mother laughed. Truce.

Actually we had a delightful time today. Uncle John put my father in a good mood. This has been a year with minimal family feuds. The great fight three years ago over my grandmother's death and who took what property and who showed what lack of respect has been plastered over, or at least papered over. And since both dad and Uncle John aren't talking to their two sisters related to the funeral games, they have that in common.

Late in the afternoon, dinner served, my mother went out with Aunt Bea, Uncle John and Carl to the grocery store to buy ice cream. As usual my mother had forgotten dessert. Anthony had long since departed for a party and would not make a second appearance this day. Rose, JoAnn and I were seated at the cherry dining room table with my father chatting about this or that. Mostly family stuff. Dad was still in a remarkably good mood. The wine JoAnn and I had brought from the City helped.

"Hank told me that he has two aunts, your sisters," JoAnn commented to my father. Not a statement really, and not the force of a question either. More a polite probe. JoAnn's backdoor way of asking things.

"Sore subject," I piped up.

"Old and sore," added Rose.

My father dragged on his Kent cigarette and looked out the large picture window before answering. "I have two sisters, one older, one younger," he said to JoAnn. He likes to talk to JoAnn. Everyone likes to talk to JoAnn. He was wearing a clean shirt today and didn't have his usual workman smell. Maybe he took his weekly Sunday bath a few days early. My father firmly believes that bathing is bad for you. "It washes off the natural protecting oils," he explained to me once. Sunday morning when everyone else is at church is his standard bath time. I wonder what threats and inducements my mother had to use to bring his skin in contact with soap and water today. Maybe he can now look forward to a ten day stretch without disturbing his precious protective oils. In summer by Friday morning you need the truck windows open when you drive to work with him. Not to mention the afternoon.

His wavy, almost curly pepper hair was combed back. His dark, parchment complexion made him a handsome man in a rugged way. He flicked the ashes into his half-full coffee cup. (He doesn't have to clean it out. Cleaning cups is mother's job. He bought the cup. That's the bargain, isn't it?) One more drag and he told his story.

"Josie is my older sister. She was what you would call a willful child. My mother regularly called her a lot of other things. It was no picnic growing up in a poor household where we spoke only Italian until we went to school. Then our classmates beat up on us until we learned English without an accent. My mother had her share of problems with her own sister and that one's boy friends. The last thing she needed was a daughter who was man-crazy. Well, no one can make children be what they're not; it all comes out. Who knows where Josie is now? Another year, another man. Last we heard she was wandering around the South with several gentlemen in tow paying the bills."

"Has she called you this year?" asked Rose. My father shook his head and lit another Kent. "JoAnn," Rose continued, "There was a time when Aunt Josie would call up every year dead broke or in trouble and ask dad or Uncle John to bail her out. Literally. Or ask them to send her traveling money. We know about Aunt Josie."

"What about Aunt Angie?" I asked. I wanted to change the talk from sex problems to money. The talk about Josie was cutting too close to my own bones.

He coughed deeply, over and over, then cleared his throat with a deep drag on his cigarette. My father is the only smoker in the family. "We haven't spoken since my mother's death. John doesn't speak to her either. Josie may be difficult and costly now and then, but my younger sister Angie is past understanding. Greed is her problem. What that one did would fill a book." He turned to JoAnn and addressed her directly. "You need to understand that my mother was not an easy woman to live with. When I told her that I wanted to marry a girl from Newark, a girl from a broken home, a broken Neopolitan home, she started screaming at me. My father stood there a helpless horse while my mother cursed me and called my girlfriend every vile name she could think of. And my mother knew a book full. I wouldn't give in and she wouldn't back down. She didn't talk to my wife for seven years. Not until my oldest son, Hank, was born did she visit our home. She was a difficult woman.

"To be fair, she didn't have a happy marriage. She didn't love my father. He was sixteen years older and it was an arranged marriage. She was forced to leave Sicily as a young girl of fifteen and travel to America to marry a man twice her age. She could read and write, she was shrewd and calculating. He was a quiet, gentle man happy to work as a driver and mason. It was not a good match.

"Let me tell you a story about my sister Angie and my mother. So you can see what I'm talking about. Understand? My mother was in constant trouble with Internal Revenue. Every year she had a new scheme to make money and she was determined that the government wasn't going to take a penny more of it away from her than she wanted to give. She believed that you pay the government a share. Not much of a share. In fact as little as possible. Needless to say, every few years they would audit her.

"On goes this big poverty act with her dragging my father along to the IRS office for him to be himself: a big, burly, uneducated, illiterate immigrant peasant. A real show. One year in the late 40s things must have become very serious because she approached her daughter Angie and told her she had to buy the family house and rent it back to them. That way my mother didn't have any major assets. She didn't come to John or me, which I don't understand. Well, John I understand because at that time they were fighting over the ownership of another piece of property across the street, the first house John bought, he thought with his mother's help. My mother believed she purchased the house and was taking rent from John, not mortgage payments. A complex story.

"So she couldn't go to John for help. She could have come to me, but she didn't. Who knows why? She went to our sister Angie, and Angie agreed. They visited the local Italian lawyer who knew my mother, with all her various deals and troubles, quite well by this time. But he had never met Angie. Big fancy office, dark furniture, poor lighting. They sign the papers transferring ownership of the land and house, and my mother pays Angie rent every month with a check to make it look up and up. Three, four years pass. The IRS problem is resolved and my mother wants the house transferred back. She tells Angie the time has come to return to the lawyer's office. Angie says *No.*"

"She what?" I asked. I couldn't have heard right. How can you tell your mother that you won't return her house?

"Angie says: *No. You gave the house to me, and the house is mine.* Naturally that starts a big fight. Feud of the year. That's how much of the story John and I know for sure because we heard about it every time we spoke to our mother. Her ungrateful daughter this, the whore that. Usual family stuff in our house. The rest of the story only came out last year when my mother died.

"After Angie said *No,* my mother called in a favor from an old lady in the neighborhood. Sometime in the past my mother had written a letter for her, forged might be a better description, a letter that saved her marriage. Don't ask. The woman had a daughter remarkably similar in appearance to Angie."

"Short and squat," I interrupted.

"Hank, please. My mother dressed the girl in Angie's clothes, and they went

113

to visit the lawyer in his office. He passed them papers to sign and my mother said her eyes were hurting her. Could she take the papers home to read and sign them there? The lawyer shrugged his shoulders. Why not? Everything looked fine to him. He had no reason to suspect the other woman wasn't Angie. He had only seen her once, several years earlier. And who lies about her own daughter?

"She brought the papers home, thanked the girl and paid her a few dollars. She forged Angie's signature on the papers and returned them the next day to the lawyer. Then she said nothing. Through the years she kept her silence. My father died. He was an old, sick man. Then two years later my mother died. With the secret. It came out when the lawyer read the will.

"I was present, John was there, Angie was there. John and Angie sat on opposite sides of the room. They had almost reached a breaking point over items in the house. Josie we couldn't locate. The same Italian lawyer reads the will. When he gets to the part about the house, Angie throws her arms over her head and screams: *It's mine, at last. It's all mine!* I was there. I saw this. The lawyer gives Angie an indignant, questioning look. 'What are you talking about? You sat in this office in front of me and signed the house back to your mother. It's joint property' Angie was furious, abusive, and totally beside herself. That was quite a scene"

"The lawyer must have known at that point that he had been fooled," said Rose.

"Of course he knew. But what could he say? Could he admit that with his diamond pinky ring and gold watch he had been fooled by this little old lady in black? Your grandmother had her revenge. A last laugh at her daughter from the grave.

"Angie tried to horse trade our shares of the house. That's when John dug in his heels. Angie had already taken several bankbooks and emptied the contents (that's another story), and he felt enough was enough. I agreed, reluctantly agreed. We haven't spoken to Angie since. Maybe it was inevitable anyway, knowing the people."

"See, JoAnn," said Rose. "This is the kind of family we have. Who would ever think it from quiet New Jersey?"

November 28, 1965; *Sunday*
Spent the weekend with JoAnn. The weekend was supposed to be devoted to writing a paper. It wasn't even started. Neither was the German or Greek

Classics. We had friends over, went to the movies, had Sunday brunch with Andre. No schoolwork.

I spoke to Andre Wednesday night after work about my problems with JoAnn, Judy and the mystery girl. He looked at me with amusement. "Hankie, you're so young and cute. Why don't you relax and enjoy some carnal pleasure? That's what the girls are there for. You're all young. That's what you should be doing."

But I can't simply do that. There has to be more there. My Catholic upbringing.

We had lunch today with Andre at a local Irish pub. He was at his most effusive. We met him at his apartment at half past noon. He opened the door in his jockey shorts. Nothing else except a gold chain. He stood there looking at us, one leg bent, one arm thrown out to the door frame.

"Hankie and Jo, what are you doing here at this hour?" He really does have a very tight, muscular, hirsute body. Corky was underneath him between his legs. Odd how closely they resemble each other.

"You said to come by at half past twelve for brunch."

"Come in, come in, both of you. Don't argue, Down the hall. Wait for me in the living room. Play with Corky." He closed the door and marched behind us. "My dear young friends, no one arrives on time for a brunch date. Ever. It isn't done. Half an hour is fashionably late. Always."

"We can wait down the hall in Hank's apartment," said JoAnn. She was half smiling. Maybe she found the situation as much amusing as embarrassing.

"No, no. You're here now. You'll just have to wait for me to finish my coiffure." Andre brushed his hand through his hair.

"I think you may need to do a bit more than brush your hair," I said to our nearly naked host. He was still posturing his body. Who was the show for? JoAnn? Me? Corky?

At brunch we chatted about movies and music. Then Andre hinted about a new love, but he refused to supply any details. "This could be The One for me. Stay tuned."

Rose called this afternoon. Thanksgiving was a momentary illusion of tranquility on the parental home front. She says the parents are arguing again. What else is new? Life there is always a battle. I was smart enough in high school to figure out how to avoid the battles and to move away from it when I was old enough. The old man is really sick—mentally. Was he always this way and I didn't notice?

I never saw my parents affectionate together. Only a good-bye peck on the cheek to my mother in the morning that dad would emphasize with a pat on her behind with his right hand. The left held his lunchbox. Always the same routine, never a deviation, never a sense of deep affection. No hugging or kissing or laughing.

The fights I remember as long as I've had memory. Loud ones with my father threatening to send my mother to the "funny farm" or to call for the men "in the white coats with the nets" to take her away. My mother responding with silent fights, days where she wouldn't talk, the house filled with tension and anger more palpable than blasting words or slaps.

Other homes have parents that cooperate in raising their children and where they enjoy their lives together; homes that are a joint venture with a richness wholly missing from my upbringing. Even JoAnn's parents seem more a team than mine. I can't say I like their life style or the way they treat JoAnn, but they are together in their actions towards her. I grew up in an inter-parental vacuum.

Several weekends ago when I was home for a day, I had the chance to talk with Ralph, my parent's next door neighbor. Ralph is a history professor at the local college. He and I used to talk late into the night, many nights, during that awful summer after my freshman year in college and Rusty's pregnancy. We never talked about that, I'm not even sure Ralph knew. But we covered most every other topic we could think of. On that afternoon the talk turned to my father and our impressions of him. I spoke about his work and energy. Ralph painted with a larger brush.

"Your father is a man of incalculable common sense, stability and know-how. A man of basic knowledges: about homes, construction, gardens, plants, business and people. A man who cannot be stampeded into poor decisions or deluded by easy answers. When I had a termite problem and thought the house was about to collapse on my head along with my small savings account, your father went down the cellar with me. He jabbed a screwdriver into a beam here, a joist there. 'No problem,' he said. 'I know a carpenter who can fix this in a few hours.' And the man did.

"See those bushes by the rail fence? I couldn't get those things to grow for love or money. Your father took one look and said: 'No problem. I know where there's some good, acidic dirt, well-composted. It's right up in the woods behind your house. Grab a shovel. I'll get my wheelbarrow. You'll have those roses blooming in a month.' And they were."

Ralph's view certainly has validity if we examine my father's rock hard determination that I would not be a teenage father, that I would not fulfill my wish to be "Sir Galahad on a white horse" as he explained my attitude about Rusty's pregnancy. Unfortunately his method of saving me from becoming Sir Galahad did not address what I saw as right, or our relationship, or anything except his view. The pregnancy was terminated and so was the relationship between father and son.

Wrote to Chris a week ago and have received no reply. I cannot fathom what is going on with him. Does he really want to avoid me? I feel the problem lies somewhere in me, but I don't know where. JoAnn asked me if Chris is really a true friend. I changed the subject; I didn't know how to answer her.

DECEMBER 1965

December 1, 1965 Wednesday

The New York Times wrote an article today about Mikhail Sholokov who won the Nobel Prize in literature. The writer of the piece cited Sholokov's *And Quiet Flows The Don*. This writer is not a Sholokov reader or he would have known that *And Quiet Flows The Don* is one half of a larger work called *The Silent Don*. The second part is *The Don Flows Home To The Sea*.

The books tell the story of the Cossacks, the White Russians, and the finally victorious Reds. The book is written from the perspective of the Cossacks not the Communists. I read somewhere that Sholokov is married to the daughter of a high Soviet official which has saved him from being purged. Certainly his later book on the collectivization of the late 1920s would have won him a place in the Lubyanka. This last book says nothing nice about the Soviet organizers, their methods or their results.

In case my prejudice doesn't show, let me be plain: I like Sholokov. I read some of his work in high school and the rest a year ago. He's not a Dostoyevski; but who is?

December 2. Thursday

JoAnn left a few minutes ago to go uptown. A nice sex surprise for me when I came back from work pulling charts for Tootie. A welcome surprise since I've been damned horny today. Cock felt as heavy as a brautwurst from Jack's Deli.

Michail Quill and the Transit Union broke off bargaining talks with our Mayor-elect, John Vleet Lindsay. A certain transit strike is coming. What a nice way to greet his new term in office starting in January. Unbelievable. Maybe I can bring my bicycle in from New Jersey if the strike does happen and the weather doesn't turn awful.

December 4. Saturday.

Went out in the cool, crisp morning to buy a paper. That looks to be the high excitement on a lazy day ahead. Tried to call Judy yesterday afternoon, but there was no answer. Just looking for someone to go out with to break the monotony.

New York Times has a lead story on the Viola Gregg Liuzzo trial in Alabama. Incredibly, the jury convicted the clansmen. Maybe there's hope for the South after all. Viola Liuzzo. I wonder if anyone will remember her name twenty years from now. Or recall her story. Or empathize with her cause.

Another story in the paper says that Bob McNamara will intensify the air strikes on the coastal supply lines. This after the Vietcong blew up the US billet in Saigon. What kind of rocks occupy heads in the Administration? For God's sakes the army can't even protect its own buildings in the middle of the capital city! What are we doing in this obscene, insane war? Has reason departed?

We can't win in VietNam. This is a civil war fought for internal reasons, a war with roots back in the Japanese occupancy. Even if we bomb the North into submission, we can't win because we can't occupy the land. Hell, we can't even occupy and hold Saigon! Who's going to occupy Hanoi? General Ky? Pure craziness.

Are American boys, specifically meaning me, supposed to go on fighting in an undeclared, illegal, immoral war? What are we fighting for? Who asked us there? And what's worse: I voted for this Administration! The bastard promised he wouldn't send American boys to Asia.

There's supposed to be a big rally in front of the Selective Service Induction Center next week. Maybe I'll go.

Last night (Friday) JoAnn and I had Janice and Johnny over to my place. We cooked dinner in my closet kitchen and ate around the card table. Spaghetti and meat balls with my mother's secret recipe. No one was concerned about the lack of space. After dinner we put the folding table and chairs away behind the bathtub and sat on the floor playing Monopoly until one in the morning. We changed the rules a bit and added more money so that no one went broke. You collect $500 every time you pass GO. You play the game for the fun of it because it's nearly impossible to run out of money. The new rules even allow you to borrow money from another player (at usurious rates) if you do run out. The game continued until we all agreed that the night had grown too old. Janice and Johnny were in their usual wonderful form. We asked them about Christmas.

"Johnny made plans to take us to Bermuda for the holidays. The situation at home didn't look very good. But then this week…Oh, you tell them, Johnny."

"Me? You forgot how to tell stories?"

"Johnny, quit being so difficult. Or you'll sleep on the couch for a week."

"Uh, oh. Big guns out tonight. Battleship in the water. Yes, mam-sahib, white slaver, faithful servant obeys your every wish. Let me bow down and caress your tender knee cap."

"Johnny, you're so silly. Why don't you just tell them the story. OK, be like that. I'll tell the story. And don't you interrupt me."

Johnny raised his hands to heaven in supplication. "Lord, help us to understand women. Or at least just one."

Janice jabbed him in the side. "Don't you make faces at me. These people only want to hear what happened. And since you won't tell them, I have to." She turned away and looked at us. Johnny rolled his eyes at her. "One day last week," she said, "Wednesday, I think…"

"It was Tuesday."

"Oh, this is too much." Janice swung around with a haymaker and punched Johnny full in the chest. However, since we were seated Indian style, there wasn't any power behind the hit. He rolled backwards anyway, clutching his chest and groaning. "Who's telling this story?" she demanded with her fist still raised.

"You, you, oh mighty Cassius Clay in disguise."

"One day last week," she began again and looked at him. He smiled but made no response. "Wednesday," she said with snake eyes.

"Anything you say, dear."

"Wednesday. My mother called. She said the family (meaning my mother and her sister) had discussed the situation and decided that everyone belongs together on Christmas. That whatever our differences, they were less important than being together. That sounded good, but it didn't solve our problem. So I asked the important question: What about sleeping arrangements? Mom hemmed and hawed and finally, grudgingly conceded that we could stay together at her place. So it's home for Christmas."

"So it's goodbye Bermuda," said Johnny.

December 9. Thursday.

Organic Chemistry Lab today with its daily allotment of disasters. Fortunately none with my name on it. We were engaged in a series of chlorination and nitration steps. The usual smelly, incomprehensible concoctions that eluded me and probably ended up with the alligators in the sewers.

Dave warned us not to let the flasks boil to dryness. No explanation, only the usual preemptory orders before he disappeared into his own cubicle to work on his grad project that seems infinitely more important to him than our peon pursuits. No one in the class knows (or cares) what project he's working on. For the sake of the City I hope it's an antidote to what we regularly send down the drain.

Not that Dave had to worry about me dehydrating my stinky mixture. I alternately add so much acid and base to my experiments trying to adjust the pH in vain hopes of saving my samples that they never go to dryness.

In our class, far in the back corner, lurk a few budding Pasteurs who can actually perform a successful titration or distillation or degradation or any of the other—ations. These dedicated bastards drag the rest of our scores down with their successes. If the class as a whole would fail to create a final result that even faintly resembled the desired product, maybe we could secure a lab instructor who actually instructs. Instead, these few pointy heads doom the rest of us to non-supervision and constant harangues about our incompetence.

Well, today we had the great pay-back, the cosmic equalizing. We were at least two hours into lab and I had already lost my sample twice in some step or other. Who knows where it went. One minute it was bubbling in lovely colors, the next there was only milky soup, its active ingredients floating off into the air or down the drain. Not much difference that I could discern. Then from the far back of the room, from the genius corner, came a miracle.

"Hey, Dave!" shouted a raspy future chemist voice. "What did you say about dryness?"

That brought Dave out of his cubicle in a New York second. "What?"

"What did you say happens if the flask boils to dryness? I ask because that's the general state of ours."

"Holy Shit!!" screamed Dave as he ran back through the various bubbling experiments cursing and screaming at one of his usual pet students. Oh, what a lovely day. Why can't we be blessed with more of these?

"You dumb fuck! I told you not to let the experiment dry out! Oh, you did it! You damn sonofabitch! Don't touch it! Now everyone listen up! Shut up over there and listen! Turn off your experiments. Don't grumble at me, just do it. Turn off the gas, water, gather your books and leave. Now. No, goddamnit, I don't know when you can come back to clean up and I don't give a rat's ass. Don't you dummies know anything? Why do you think I told you not to let your toluene experiments go to dryness? Christ, just what I need on my record: a flask of hot Tri-Nitro-Toluene."

That caught our attention. I was packed and vamoosed out of the lab in three seconds. Several others had me beat. A few of the duller types took a while before they understood the initials. The college police arrived in less than five minutes to evacuate the whole sixth floor. Then the seventh, then the fifth. Half an hour later the New York City Bomb Squad removed the flask in a massive armored box. I hope Dave throws the offending genius out of class. Maybe have him incarcerated for the rest of the semester. That would give the rest of us a chance to pass lab this semester.

After the cops left, and students were let back into the building, I had just enough time to clean out my flasks and beakers before I had to head uptown to Tootie. I hope we won't be held responsible to make up the experiment. A fanciful hope. I'll probably be spending an extra afternoon here next week repeating my weekly failure.

December 10. Friday.
Yesterday I asked Judy out to Carnegie Hall for the Boston Symphony playing Brahms Symphony #1 on Saturday night. She accepted. Then she called me early this morning and nixed the whole thing. Said *no* without a real reason. In fact she was extra cold to me after being real warm the day before. Scramble. Left me with only JoAnn to ask when I wanted to date someone else for a change.

Then I saw her again in the hall. She walked towards me. Her eye caught mine and her face slowly transformed into a tight smile. This time I was ready. "Good morning," I said cheerfully, easily.

"Well, good morning." She started to laugh.

"What's so funny?"

"Took you long enough to say hello like a normal person. I better not wait for you to make introductions. That could take years. My name is Martha." She stuck her hand out from under a pile of books she was carrying. Her grip was strong, bony, very assured. Not like so many girls who practice having a handshake like a soft dishrag.

"My name is Hank. Do you have time for a cup of coffee?"

"How about after this class?"

We talked through the rest of the morning at my usual coffee shop. Can't remember exactly what we discussed: classes, school, life in the Big City, nothing very deep. My favorite waitress winked at me approvingly. Finally I built up the nerve and asked her out to the symphony. "Sure. Why not. Sounds great. But only if we can do dinner first. Dutch treat. Then the concert. OK?"

About Judy saying no after saying yes. She's a strange girl who won't loosen her grip on herself and let go. The status quo is fine, so why disturb it with uncertainty? I would like to try to melt her, but she won't meet me half way. Can't figure out why she backed out.

Tootie, the Queen of Medical Records, threatened to fire me on Wednesday. She claimed that I'm not working up to par. I believed her in earnest until tonight when she threatened to fire Bill because he had car trouble and couldn't get in last night. Maybe she wants both of us fired, or maybe she's being bitchy for her own reasons.

Wrote to Chris. A cheerful letter that forces him to move or be acted on. Let's see what's up.

Home for Christmas in less than two weeks. I'll buy mother a large long-neck bottle of wine as a present. Sister Rose wrote me that she and Carl plan to be there. Maybe everything won't be a total disaster. I had written Rose about some of my troubles with Chris. She had some odd comments in return. Here's part of her letter:

> *Dear Hank,*
>
> *We were hoping that you would come to mom and dad's anniversary and then your letter arrived saying you would. That's great.*
>
> *I'm sorry I woke you up the other morning, but assumed you would be awake by then. Not everyone stays out until four in the morning and leading a life of sin and disgrace...*
>
> *Your letter also surprised me because I thought a man of your worldliness would have already learned a bitter lesson of life that certainly applies to your friend Chris: Friends are friends in name only. The world is full of so-called friends. Real friends exist only in novels and short stories. They are imaginary figures and only a few people are privileged to find them. My only true friends are my husband Carl and my family. The less we expect from people, the better off our own lives are in the end.*
>
> *Carl's moving into a new store in Salem (NJ) this weekend so I'll probably be a widow for a while. Plan to come visit us some weekend with JoAnn. We love to see you both.*
>
> *Love, Rose*

December 13. Monday.

Still no word from Chris. I was sure he would send me a letter by now. Maybe I should overcome my feeling of awkwardness and call him to find out what's wrong. How would I start the conversation? What would I say?

Date with Martha was fabulous. She really knows how to handle herself.

JoAnn spent Saturday together at my place doing homework mixed with a little sex. I told her I had to go home Saturday night and Sunday. "Do you want to borrow my car for the trip? The weather is miserably cold and rainy. You'll have a hard time with the train." I readily agreed. Took my small suitcase, loaded it with a few clothes, drove us uptown, and dropped JoAnn off at her parents' place, leading her to believe that I was going home to Jersey. That may have been a devious act, but she did offer me the car.

Rained something awful when I drove to 77th Street to pick up Martha. Glad I had the car. We would never have caught a taxi, her apartment house is blocks east of the subway, and who wants to take a date on the bus?

We decided on dinner at The House of Milan. Driving there she asked me: "Where did you get the car? I know you don't own one."

"I've owned a few cars. My first was an old green bomb, a '47 Dodge. Then I owned a huge '56 Pontiac."

"Right. But not this one." She punched me lightly in the arm.

"I borrowed it from a friend," I said defensively. God, how this girl can put me off balance.

She gave me a tight, wide smile. "I don't believe you." That smile and her short laugh are remarkable features—they penetrate. Then she lit up a Marlboro. That's her one trait that I don't like: she smokes.

"I started smoking as soon as I got out of that prison boarding school. But that's another story. So, tell me about your friend who loans you a car with blotted Kleenexes on the floor."

I invented a story. Can't recall what I said, but I do remember her response: "Yeah, right. You're such a liar."

Eric Leinsdorf (Old Chrome Dome) directed the Boston Symphony Orchestra in Brahms' First Symphony. At the end he was beating whole measures rather than single notes. I thought the orchestra would fly apart into chaos. Instead, at the last possible second, at its farthest point, the separate instruments merged precisely in a great rush. The effect had my hair standing on end; it was wonderful.

We drove back uptown to Martha's apartment. Actually she shares a place with three other girls. A three bedroom apartment in an expensive, modern building. The rooms are bright although they lack the charm of JoAnn's place. No molding, no heavy doors or frames, no fancy paned windows. We thought the place would be ours, but one of her roommates had returned early. The three of us sat in her living room and chatted for a while. When I left, we kissed goodnight at the door.

What about JoAnn? Well…what? She is so laden down with problems it seems she will never rise up. She's a nice, sweet girl. Period. I must and will make her just someone else to date. As a "wife" she only annoys me. I guess I should be sorry for this egotistical view.

December 16. Thursday.

God, what a depressing day.

Cut German class (the class I least need to cut) to see the Chairman of the English Department. The most detestable man I've ever met.

I transferred from Dickinson with fine grades in English, and I aced both of my English courses here last year. Nevertheless, NYU informed me last month that transfer students are required to take a Freshman English Equivalency Test. You must pass this test to be excused from freshman level English classes. Letter really pissed me off. They accepted my courses and grades; then they say that they don't accept the validity of those grades. Colleges must be the stupidest places on Earth.

The Equivalency test was given two weeks ago. It consisted of two paragraphs that were widely different stylistically. One I recognized as being from a novel by James Fennimore Cooper, the other was new to me. We were instructed to compare the writings on the basis of rhetoric. No explanation beyond that.

Yesterday the results were posted on the bulletin board in front of the English Department. My name was not on the pass list. I read and reread the list thinking I misunderstood. Unbelievable! I had failed an English test! I tossed and turned in anger last night—hardly slept a wink. This morning I marched into the office of the chairman of the English Department.

His secretary greeted me with typical New York neutrality. "Yes?"

"I want to see the department chairman."

"Do you have an appointment?" she asked in standard response 14A to an undergraduate request. She could have been passing out gilded checks for all I cared this morning.

"No, I don't. And that doesn't change the fact that I want to see him." My voice quivered with heat.

For the first time her eyes focused on me. I had gone off script. Students are supposed to be meek and obsequious. We aren't supposed to demand a dollar's worth of service for the dollar we spend. She was middle-aged, a bit stout from sitting in her chair most of the day, and dressed in muted brown colors to match her brown existence.

"Yes, you're making that quite plain," she answered in a firm voice, a shade less neutral. She lowered her pen to the desk, never taking her eyes off me. "What do you want to see him about?"

"My visit concerns his so-called English Proficiency Test. And I want to see him now." My voice had risen ten decibels. Her eyebrows raised an inch and a door opened behind her.

Professor Pseudo English stood in the doorway. Dark tweed jacket, cream color shirt, brown knitted tie with just a ghost of a design, black pants with a stiff crease. Complete with a pipe in the corner of his mouth and carefully disarrayed hair. Medium height, medium build. Arrogant, sneery British lips and eyes. "Shirley?" he asked without removing his pipe so that the vowels slurred. Ha! His first misdirection. A true Englishman would have removed his pipe and held it six inches from his face before talking. Anyone who watches movies knows that. He hadn't studied his role very well.

"This student wants to see you about…"

"…Your stupid English Proficiency Test," I interrupted to complete her sentence. I absolutely refused to play by their script. That would have led me no place. Their script with its goddamned test created the mess in the first place. My stomach began to ripple and knot. Fear and anger. "We need to discuss it. Now."

He looked at his secretary, then at me. His eyes were light colored and with as much luster as the slimy lake in Central Park. Finally he removed the pipe from his mouth. "I'll give you one minute." He turned around and walked back into his office. Zeus was granting a mere mortal in audience in his throne room on Mt Olympus.

I entered his office and closed the door behind me. His eyebrows raised a notch. The mortal had not been granted permission to do that. Mere students enter his sanctuary with reverence, with groveling. They certainly don't close the door and stand toe to toe with the god as if they paid for the place, paid Zeus's salary and were here to demand an accounting of his actions.

The office was of a piece with the man. Mahogany book shelves neatly stacked with eclectic volumes in vellum and shiny dust jackets. Huge dark wood desk with papers properly lined up on the right side waiting for the god's perusal. Behind the desk a huge window with an unobstructed view of Washington Square and Arch. And of course a whole wall covered with framed parchment documents with fancy lettering and red seals.

"Good morning, professor," I said calmly, trying my best to directly contrast my voice with how I actually felt. "I asked for this meeting to discuss the Proficiency Test."

"Yes, you announced that quite plainly. I assume you did not earn a passing grade." He was standing, facing me directly. He was a few inches taller than me. His demeanor flat; not the slightest show of anything below the surface. Complete disinterest.

"I transferred at the beginning of last year. I have already taken two English courses and earned a grade of A in each class."

"English courses have nothing to do with the Proficiency Test. I made that quite clear in my cover letter last month. All students are required to take this test. Had you bothered to read the letter, you would have known that."

"Do you mean that the grades your English professors give out have nothing to do with English proficiency? Two professors last year and my professor this year have consistently graded my work with their highest marks. How could that not indicate proficiency in English?"

"There is no discussion here about proficiency. The matter is one of your failure. The rules are quite explicit: You must take the freshman courses and then, after that, you must retake the Proficiency Test. And I think that about says it all. So good morning." Pipe back in the mouth. Zeus dismissing the petitioner. Pompous prick.

I didn't leave. I didn't even shuffle my feet. "Who graded the tests? I think I'll start with that person."

"Totally unnecessary. I personally graded the tests. Now if you will excuse…"

"You graded them yourself? Why didn't you say so? That makes things easier. Pull mine out and let's review it. Let's discover how I failed an English test when three professors from your own department judge my work consistently at the A level."

"That's impossible. The papers were graded and then discarded." For the first time he looked at me directly, eye to eye. Not a look that peered through me to the wall behind, not a look over my left shoulder, not a contemptuous condescension. No, this was real eye contact. He was telling me a lie. He knew it was a lie and I knew it was a lie. Zeus had been caught with his hand in the cookie jar.

"You threw out a test paper of this importance on the comparison of two quotations based on rhetorical style without giving a student the opportunity to review?" I asked the question in the general sense. "You destroy papers of this importance less than one day after grades are posted? Who the hell do you think you are?"

"Who the hell I am, young man, is chairman of this department!" He slammed his pipe down on the desk. His English affectation had departed. The language and style were pure New York City.

"Oh yeah? Well, Mr. Chairman, where's your degree in Rhetoric?" I stomped across his office to the wall with the framed documents. "Let's see. Here's a big one with fancy lettering and seals for a PhD in English. Here's a little one for Early English Literature. Here's a prize for a dissertation on Spencer. But where's the degree in Rhetoric?" I turned and faced him. His face was red, his eyes burning. "You asked for a comparison based on rhetoric. Where are your credentials to judge my competence in English writing based on rhetoric?"

"There is no such degree and no such degree is necessary. And I'll be goddamned if I'm going to be talked to like this by an undergraduate in my own office!"

"Right! We don't belong talking in your office!" I was pissed beyond all bounds. "We belong in the office of the Dean of Academic Affairs. In fact, I'll tell you what: You produce my test paper graded by a competent individual, degreed in Rhetoric, or by God I'm going to the Dean's office right now. And I'm going to demand a review of this whole shoddy process. And if the Dean doesn't want to talk to me, if he shares your arrogance for students, then I'll sue this University and you personally to produce that test and show where you're competent to judge rhetorical style and I failed!!"

The walls rang with my last shout. The ensuing silence was deafening, infuriating. Maybe a minute passed where neither of us moved a muscle. Obnoxious pig eyes boring into me. Then, a miracle: He looked away and reached for his pipe. He spoke to the desktop. "I'll review your test."

"And I'll be back in an hour to check the board."

On the way out of his office, as I passed his secretary, I though she had the slightest hint of a smile before she returned to her typing.

The confrontation really upset me. I called sister Rose tonight and told her the story. "Well, brother, I can't say I think your approach was too smart. You could have used other, less confrontational means to your goal, if you know what I mean. You have to remember that in our childhood upbringing there were few direct disagreements with dad. Discipline was supplied by mother. What this means to us is that we have poor conflict management skills, especially with authoritarian male figures."

That may be. But who needs this kind of conflict? What was I supposed to do—go in there and plead on my knees to mighty Zeus and his framed icons? Then there's this additional point: In truth, when I was taking the test, I didn't have the least idea what they wanted from me or how to compare the two passages based on "rhetoric," whatever that is. So Professor Pompous Prick may actually have been right in his grading. In any case, I don't have to take a stupid freshman English course or repeat the test.

When I spoke to JoAnn tonight, she was very negative about my actions at the English Department. "Do you have to burn your bridges to complete ashes and then stomp on them?" I didn't have an answer.

12/16/65. 3+7+11. 21. 2+1 = 3. A three day. Not a great number, but not a disaster either. Can't expect much from a three day, even if one of the numbers is my lucky eleven.

Oh, by the way, my name was inserted in the pass list.

Our New York University Chorus concert on Tuesday night went surprisingly well. The Bach piece was a gem. Such a pleasure to sing the choruses. JoAnn came to hear us. I shook in fear as I always do before a performance. JoAnn said my short solo sounded fine. I thought my voice was strained. In the spring we plan to perform Mozart's Idimeneo in concert form.

A few short comments on JoAnn. Although she has wanted to, I have not let her sleep over here on school nights when her parents are in town. She says she'll tell them she's sleeping over at a girlfriend's apartment. Sounds to me like high school tricks. Seems to me she should realize that she is living in her parents' home; and until she moves out on her own, she should obey their rules, or at least not wave a red flag of insult in their faces.

December 23, 1965. Thursday.

JoAnn and I drove to New Jersey after midnight last night to find a Christmas tree. The City was quiet with a crisp, clear air. We drove down Seventh Avenue and then through the Holland Tunnel and out along Route 22 for thirty miles or more. Drove through that vast billboard, neon-light, huckster strip of road that becomes uglier each year. Someplace past Plainfield we turned off Route 22 and scouted for trees. A mile into a suburban area with red, green, yellow and white lights decorating every home, we found a dark divided road with small fir trees in the median.

Watching to make sure there were no cars in either direction, I stopped the car, quickly jumped out with my handsaw while JoAnn scooted over to the driver's seat. She drove off with instructions to meet me in five minutes on the other side of the median.

The night seemed colder here than in Manhattan. My breath smoked in the still air. A light dusting of snow covered the road. The grass in the median was filled with clumps of ice that crunched under my feet. I picked out a small, full evergreen no taller than my chest and cut it off at ground level.

I hid among the other small fir trees by lying on the icy ground and waited for JoAnn to return. She took forever. Finally I saw the lights of a car that I hoped was hers. That ground was getting mighty cold. I couldn't stand up and wave my arms until I was sure it was her car. When I saw the car slow down, I took a chance and jumped in the air without the saw or the tree just in case it wasn't her. No need for worry. I opened the back seat door, stuffed in the tree and saw, and off we drove. We laughed through our nervous tension, constantly looking in the rear view mirror of the red flashing lights of a cop car until we were back in the Holland Tunnel.

Bad news: We returned to my apartment building after 1:30 am and had to walk up the nine flights of stairs with the tree and hand saw. I never expected our grand caper would take us later than 1 am and the last elevator. We were a strange pair trudging up the stairs with a tree. JoAnn in front holding the top, me in back with the sticky stub in one hand and a Craftsman saw in the other.

Back at the apartment we were wide awake. So we opened the closet-kitchen and popped popcorn. We ate some and threaded the rest to decorate our tree. The scraggly green thing looked very Christmas-like and filled the apartment with a wonderful smell. We turned the couch into a bed sometime after three. JoAnn's parents were away on business/pleasure, so she slept over.

This morning we were up by ten. Well, I was up and JoAnn made use of the situation. After lunch we took out the paint cans and brushes and changed the color of my walls from bare white to cream. Looks much better, especially with the blue-green Christmas tree. JoAnn took off to her place a few minutes ago to change clothes and check up on everything. I was glad to have some time to myself to scribble in this book. Her parents won't be back until tomorrow, so she'll probably spend tonight here too.

Yesterday evening before our tree raid, Andre knocked on our door. He had Corky in tow. "Just taking the doggie down to do his duty and meet some new friends."

"The dog meet friends or you?" I asked.

"Maybe both," he smiled. "It's happened before." Andre was wearing his shearling jacket. Corky loped up and down the hall, obviously eager to go outside. "Corky, behave!" Andre snapped. The dog stopped instantly, sat on his tailless butt, flicked his ears left to right and waited. "Now, kids, listen. I'm having a Christmas party tomorrow night. Just a few friends. Very informal. And you two would certainly brighten the evening. And," he peered around me to talk directly to JoAnn, "I could use some straight friends to keep the evening respectable. Could you fill that role?"

I looked at JoAnn. She nodded yes. What else could she do to one of Andre's elegant *yes* questions?

"We would love to come. What time?" I asked.

"Hankie, Christmas parties start at eight. How could someone so smart be so lacking in social knowledge? Dress casual. You do know what that means? Or must JoAnn instruct you? No, don't answer that. The answer is obvious. Good. And I promise JoAnn there will be other ladies. Anywho, half the boys there will be girls."

So we're going down the hall to Andre's tonight at eight.

JoAnn's parents want us at their apartment tomorrow night (24th) so that we can exchange some presents. Christmas eve with a Jewish family exchanging gifts around their Christmas tree. Certainly better than New Jersey and that mess.

I promised my mother that JoAnn and I would go to New Jersey on Christmas morning.

December 25, 1965. Saturday.

Christmas day. Cold and clear. The City lies quiet this morning. I hear the pigeons flapping their wings as they fly around the naked trees in Union Square.

We had a fun time at Andre's party Thursday night. He was right about a mixed bag of guests: straight, gay and undecided, bisexuals and trisexuals ("try anything sexual" as Andre would say). There were several Wall Street types and even one college student who stayed close to Andre during the evening. His new, hidden boyfriend that he's hinted about for the past month? The fellow was nothing spectacular to look at: average height, weight and complexion. Looked a bit young for Andre who is certainly old enough to be his father.

In spite of myself I enjoyed dinner at JoAnn's last night. Her parents' bright mood was enhanced by the rum-spiked eggnog. Her mother had spent the afternoon decorating a perfectly shaped, full, long needle fir Christmas tree with hundreds of lights and ornaments. We exchanged presents. They enjoyed the books I gave them and I'm a few shirts and ties richer. Clothes I actually need badly. There was also a Verdi *La Traviata* for me that JoAnn's parents slipped under the tree. I gave JoAnn a pair of blue and red earrings from a vendor near school who makes them by hand. How I envy his craft and freedom.

After presents and dinner, JoAnn and I rode a quiet Second Avenue bus filled with late shoppers downtown for a Christmas Eve concert at the church fronting Gramarcy Park. Right next to Judy's brownstone, although I stayed mum on that subject. E. Power Biggs played the baroque organ and the Manhattan Brass Quartet accompanied him in a series of splendid pieces. What a rich combination of sounds filled every part of the church! The deep undertones of a pedal organ with the clean, polished notes of trumpets and trombones far above. The music put JoAnn in the mood to polish my organ for an hour or two before she returned uptown.

As I write this I'm waiting for JoAnn to pick me up so that we can drive out to New Jersey to celebrate Christmas there. Rose and Carl arrived last night from South Jersey. Maybe their presence will make the day better. Dad has always been partial to his oldest daughter, the way most fathers are. He certainly hasn't been very partial to me.

By and large this has been a good Christmas season. Especially compared to the last few that have been tight and demanding. Not that Christmas has ever been a bowl of cherries for me.

Growing up I cannot recall a Christmas without a scene over the tree. Dad always waited until the last day to buy a tree in order to get a "good deal." Then he purchased a scrawny, misshapen el-cheapo that he remedied by cutting off and re-attaching various branches. He would drag the tree into the back garage, hook up his electric drill and bore one inch holes into the trunk where the foliage was bare. Then we cut branches off from the back of the tree and inserted the amputated limbs into the newly drilled holes. As a final step, this arboreal Frankenstein was nailed to a board and brought into the parlor to be decorated and to start its terminal drying process.

My sister always self-appoints herself master of the tree decorating committee of one. That begins a battle with the rest of us over who will decorate the tree with what items and in what sequence. My mother who collects tree ornaments and never discards anything insists that whole boxes of mismatched lights and bulbs be added to the tree. Where and how the addition is made is not important to her; their presence someplace is the critical issue. Anthony and I have no problem with mom's approach to tree ornamentation. And with only one day allocated to work on the tree, I don't see how you can be too fussy. However, older sisters, highly sensitive to the opinions of friends who may happen to see the prize exhibit, impose a higher level of style and appearance.

The angel at the top of the tree always tops the argument. Over the years my mother has collected several angels. A large plastic angel in white and blue had always been my favorite. Huge, veined, clear plastic wings distribute the soft light from a single bulb inside her torso. Sister Rose likes a metallic angel with aluminized wings a bright, bare bulb in the back. Over the years various trees have suffered two fates. Either Rose's metallic angel won out through her sheer persistence, or Anthony and I won out with the plastic angel because Rose had to leave for a party.

What bothers me most about the Christmas season is December 26th. Tomorrow the weeks of Christmas carols will be gone, the stores will quickly dismantle their displays, and the built up energy and goodness will vanish as if it never happened. I wonder if all life is like that: In the end everything vanishes without a trace or remembrance. Twenty years from now will I remember the events of this day? Or will anyone remember what we talked about or laughed about? Do I write these lines so that in some small measure I can relive the day?

Do I really think Christmas is just another day? Why can't we free ourselves from Morley's chains that we fashion in our own lives? Are we also condemned to wander aimlessly weighted down with our own past actions and remembrances? Life must have more Free Will than that. It must! And yet every time I step back into a family situation, there I am with my chain behind me. I make predetermined responses and statements like I'm reading from an old script. Nothing is real or spontaneous.

December 26, 1965. Sunday.

Grudgingly I had a good time at home. Rose had festooned the tree in better than average fashion. As she explained to me when we were alone: "As you can imagine, when Carl and I arrived yesterday afternoon, Christmas Eve, dad hadn't bought a tree yet. He had the outside lights draped on the bushes, and mom had the mantle decorated with a manger. But no tree. I'm not saying he was waiting for his usual last minute price reduction. No, I'm not. Maybe he was waiting for one of us to go out with him to his favorite tree lot. Maybe. Then again, the last minute price reduction didn't hurt. So Carl and I went out with him to pick a tree.

"Of course we ended up at the usual place where his 'friend' sells Christmas trees. Some friend. Sells us trash every year. Who needs that kind of friend? Well, they shook hands, shuffled feet and blew cigarette smoke in each other's face. Usual greeting among old friends.

"Maybe Carl being there helped. I refused to look at anything except the full, long needle trees. I found a beauty in this forest of rejects. Dad walked over with a disinterested frown, took the price tag in his two nicotine-stained fingers and rolled the stiff paper over. With a smoke-filled grunt he walked over to some scraggly, half-dead twig with fuzz pasted on. A true candidate for his smile. A tree with assets too hidden for my taste. Dad asked Carl what he thought. Carl moved one shoulder a manly inch and grunted. Dad nodded his head slightly in a recondite male-only language and moved on to the next withered, dying leftover. Cave man communication.

"Well, I stood by the tree I wanted and said so. Dad came over again and fingered the price tag like the paper proclaimed the tree was sin incarnate. He mumbled: 'Let's look at another.' Carl fingered the price tag and grunted. Must have been coated with special male molecules. I opened my purse and took out my wallet. That got a reaction. Shamed dad into buying my tree after the obligatory haggle with his friend. Ha! A decent tree for a change. How about that!"

JoAnn had knit a new sweater for my mother. Mom oohed and aahed and wore the bulky wool creation around the house for the rest of the day. Looked funny having a gray and white full lumpy sweater over her red Christmas dress. But mom seemed to enjoy the gift. She couldn't stop saying: "Look at this beautiful sweater JoAnn made for me. Just what I need for the cold winter nights." Rose joined in the accolades for the sweater. "Hank, do you realize that sweater is 100% mohair? The yarn alone must have cost JoAnn a fortune. This is a very valuable sweater." Then JoAnn surprised me with a half-sweater cable knit that fit perfectly. So I wore that around the house all day. Like mother, like son. One more sweater in the house and we would have looked like a Sherpa village.

I brought my mother a gallon of red wine as a Christmas present. A long neck bottle—a very long neck bottle—maybe four feet tall. The neck so long you have to tip the bottle over to pour a glass. We tipped through the afternoon.

The weather was surprisingly mild for Christmas Day. Anthony and I went out back and shot some baskets in the frayed and deserted hoop hung over the garage door. The basket was lower than regulation, not that such an infraction could possibly matter to us. At five-four neither of us is exactly cut out for playing in the NBA.

"Did you notice the gap in dad's teeth?" Anthony asked between shots. I hadn't. "Look at that wonder when you go back in. You missed the scene here two days ago. Usual big fight between him and mom. This time he accused her of bending his dental plates so they wouldn't fit right. Stupid. Really stupid. Then he stormed out of the house to the garage. Half an hour later everything was dead quiet. Mom pulled me over and asked me to check on dad. Last thing in the world I wanted to do. It was their fight. Why should I be involved?"

"What did she threaten you with?" I asked as I attempted a lay-up with the usual result. The ball bounced off the rim.

"No car that night. So I walked back here to the garage to see what's happening. He had his top plate, his dental plate, on the workbench and he was filing on it with a wood rasp. He pretended not to see me. I didn't say a word. Turned around and walked out. This place is a zoo. Glad I'm out of here and back to school in a few days."

December 28, 1965. Tuesday.

Difficult to write here. Feel I have to make an entry even though I don't want to. I don't want to do anything but crawl under a rock.

Date with Martha last night. Dinner at the Dardanelles Restaurant, then to my apartment. She sat on the couch/bed made up as a couch. I sat at my desk chair or on the floor. When she took her shoes off, she loosened up and talked about herself.

"My parents sent me to an all girl finishing school for high school. It was ghastly." She flashed her cold smile. In the subdued light from my desk lamp she was incredibly sexy. "Uniforms, rules, hair cut a certain way, four of us in a room with no real privacy. No social life, as in no boys, during the week. And everything chaperoned on the weekends. I mean everything. You never had a chance to get to know someone, much less do anything. Ghastly. Summers my parents shipped me out to a girls' camp. Orders, regimen, rules. God, I hated it.

"After high school they made me go to Sarah Lawrence. Damn good school but only girls again. Real prudes. Rich snobby types, bitches, you know, like me." Again the thin smile. "But at least we got to go out. And did I ever make up for lost time! That first year I did every boy I went out with. I tried every part of his anatomy and mine that I had spent high school and summer camp imagining. God, I can't even remember the boys' names anymore.

"Maybe I shouldn't talk like this. Not very polite and all that. But you're comfortable to be with, Hank. Well, to continue with my story, at first I didn't know what to do or what to say. I must have been awful. I remember asking my first boy: Where do I put my legs? And later to another boy: Am I biting too hard? They would look at me like I was crazy or they would just grunt. Not that anything made much difference. There was no love or affection or even warmth. No one even pretended those things. Nothing was like what the girls always talked about. Why did I do it? Partly curiosity. Partly I liked doing it.

"If he drove a car, we did it in a car: back seat, front seat, hood. Anywhere we could. Anything. If we walked, there were always bushes handy. That one year I learned about everything my parents tried to shield me from. One night I even tried it with a boy and another girl. Now that was weird!"

This sex talk from Martha turned me on something fierce. The front of my pants became mighty crowded. But that tight smile of hers and her sharp laugh put me off. I knew that I should have been undressing her, that's what she was asking me to do. And I couldn't move over to the couch.

"I transferred out of that girls' prison and came here to New York University. And one day in the hall this cute, dark fellow walks up to me and says hello. Real sexy." She smiled again, inviting me.

Only she doesn't know that I wasn't saying hello to her, but to a shadow of a memory.

When I finally built up the courage to join her on the couch, the clock showed ten minutes after two. Late! Then to make matters worse, I got cold feet, or maybe I was plain frightened of her, because I didn't do more than put my arm around her and lean back against the bolsters. In a few minutes after I failed to make the requisite moves, she fell asleep.

I covered her with a blanket and then pulled out the extra mattress from the bathroom closet and slept on the floor. I certainly didn't have a good night's sleep. When testicular pain didn't keep me awake, I tossed around under the covers terrified about the morning. JoAnn was expected for breakfast at nine.

At eight I turned on a record and started cooking eggs and bacon before Martha's eyes were open. She woke to *Three Cornered Hat*. Between mouthfuls we made a date for Wednesday.

My eyes were on the clock more than on here or the food. That damned minute hand wouldn't stop creeping up towards the nine o'clock hour. I brought her coat from the closet and almost pushed her out the door. I was in a panic that JoAnn would arrive early. Martha kept mumbling under her breath: "What's the rush?"

"I have an appointment uptown I can't be late for."

"An appointment? At this hour?"

"Right. With an insomniac doctor who keeps very early hours."

"A doctor? Is something wrong?"

Finally pushed her out the door and into the elevator at ten minutes to nine.

Tore through the apartment like a Tasmanian devil. Cleaned and washed our breakfast dishes, put the spare mattress back in the closet, and smoothed the corduroy cover on the couch. My mother would be proud that the couch maintained its Dr Jeckle personality and never transformed into Mr Hyde. (Or is it Dr Hyde and Mr Jeckle? And maybe my mother knows that a couch by any other name is still a potential bed). I checked the bathroom trash basket for female things and found a lipstick blotted tissue that waded up and threw out the window. Prayed JoAnn wasn't on the street looking up at my ninth floor window that she could see above the roof of the bank.

"Hank, did I see you throw something out the window?"

"Me throw something out the window?" I play Woody Allen and point first at myself and then at the window.

"That window above the bank is your apartment, isn't it?"

"Oh, out that window. Yes, yes, I did."

"Well, what was it?"

"Uh, nothing. My rent check. Yes, that was it. I was making a protest with my rent check. I wanted all of New York to know that paying my rent to him was like throwing money out the window."

Five minutes to nine I left the window open to dissipate any telltale odors and settled down exhausted in my desk chair. JoAnn knocked on the door exactly on time, a mere ten minutes after Martha left. That was too close. She kissed me hello, took off her fluffy coat and placed it neatly on the couch.

"Your apartment's cold this morning. Why is the window open?"

"Oh, uh, yes, well I woke up this morning and it was stifling in here. Must have forgotten to shut it. I'll close it if you're cold."

"This place stifling? That's a novelty. This place is always an ice cube."

We had a nice breakfast (my second round of bacon and eggs for the day). I was super-sweet to JoAnn, on my ultra best behavior. Maybe too good because she started giving me queer glances.

"Your apartment is really clean this morning."

"One of my days. I always have this nest cleaning instinct before my period." That was a line of Rusty's that I've used a hundred times.

"No, seriously. You're never this clean during the week."

"That's not true. I'm always neat." I started to sweat.

"Yes, you're always neat and organized. That's one of the things I like about you. But you're not known for neatness at nine o'clock in the morning." She stood and walked around the room. I watched an idea form in her mind. She planted her feet and squinted her eyes, looking at me square. "Was someone here last night? I mean, we're not married or anything. There's no rule you can't see someone else."

"JoAnn, I haven't been with anyone but you." Meaning: I haven't bed to anyone but you, although that failure may not be by design. I hoped she heard my statement in its larger context and not in its narrow meaning.

She gave the room one more distrustful perusal before starting in about her schedule. She had promised to spend the day with her mother, first to lunch, then shopping. Dinner and evening would be ours. That left almost two hours before she had to meet her mother, and we used that time to good advantage. Me especially since my balls were aching with low level lack-a-nookie pain from the night's frustration.

Spent the afternoon in much needed study. My grades are awful this term.

Andre called about four. Asked if we had had any plans for the evening. "Do you two want to go out, my treat? There's this new place on Third Avenue in the Twenties. I've heard it has the cutest waiters. I really have to try it out. Just once. And what safer way than with my straight friends." Since I'm dead broke after Christmas and still haven't scrounged together January's rent of $75, a free dinner sounded terrific.

Although the restaurant looked perfectly fine to me, Andre expressed disappointment in the waiters. He spoke to JoAnn: "Nice buns on the one near the door. On second thought, maybe a shade too flashy. See how he moves. He knows he's cute. Don't you agree?"

JoAnn nodded yes (what else?) and looked closer. "Oh, I don't know. Yes, I agree the buns are nice. I might not throw him out of bed for eating crackers." They started giggling like schoolmates. I rolled my eyes to the ceiling. "And speaking of nice things—Hank and I noticed a certain younger type person at your party. And I though I saw some interesting leers from your direction."

"Leers? At my age, darling JoAnn, any look is considered a leer. So don't be tacky or presumptuous. There may be some interest there. A few fishing lines in the water, so to speak."

Our waiter came around and poured me a second glass of red wine. He left to whispered comments between JoAnn and Andre. I hardly noticed anything. In fact, I'm not even sure what we ordered. I'm such a cheap drunk. After dinner Andre invited us to a gay bar he was going to cruise. "A little grocery shopping. Nothing serious."

"Tomatoes?" asked JoAnn.

"No, darling. Fruits. Hopefully without too many bruises."

JoAnn and I exchanged looks. I answered: "Thanks for the invite, but not tonight. We had planned on a movie. A Bergman at the Bijou."

Andre shrugged, kissed JoAnn full on the lips and wished us both a good evening. His eye had a twinkle. We hadn't fooled him.

We walked hand in hand down Third Avenue back to my apartment. I felt very close to her. I knew the evening would be a bedroom venture. No objection from me.

Later, when we were resting, and I was wondering if I could ever summon the energy for Act III today, JoAnn raised herself up on her elbow and looked down into my face. Her breast rested on my arm and her loose hair fell down over my shoulder and across my cheek. She brushed the strands away so she could see me clearly. "Hank, I want the truth. A girl was here last night."

"No," I answered firmly. "I haven't had anyone but you in this bed."

"You're playing word games with me. I know you too well for that. Now I want an honest answer. Maybe not in this bed, this exact bed in this exact spot, but there was a girl here last night. I deserve the truth from you."

Her face seemed to grow larger; I had the feeling I was looking up from the bottom of a pool into a great visage covering the whole surface of the water. I couldn't find a way around the truth. "Yes. But nothing happened. We only talked."

"Then why was this apartment so clean this morning?" Even though the room was dark, I could see her stern eyes. She pressed her breast further against me. He face continued to grow in size, and the room floated behind her. I was almost sick with claustrophobia.

"We were only talking. The suddenly she fell asleep. I didn't know what to do. So I took out the spare mattress and slept on the floor. That's all." Silence. "There was nothing more."

JoAnn sat up, planted her back on the plaster wall and crossed her arms over her chest. Trouble. I should have lied. What demon possessed me to tell the truth?

"Well, at least you told me the truth. That much I should be glad of."

"I'm telling you: nothing happened." I was possessed by cowardice. She always has this effect on me, this robbing me of manliness, this making me feel like a little boy with my mother and older sister looking down at me, belittling me.

"Then I guess it's time for me to be honest with you. Do you remember last month when I told you that I went to visit Murphy at Yale?"

Murphy! My nemesis! "Yes," I croaked. My voice had turned to powder.

"And I told you that I pushed off his advances? Well, that wasn't the whole truth. We went back to my motel room. That much was true. But I didn't send him home at the door. That part I lied about. I didn't want to hurt you. Or maybe I was frightened to tell you the whole truth. Well, no matter. This time I will tell the whole story. Here's what really happened.

"We went back to my motel room after the dance. At the door he said he wanted to come in and talk to me. We've been friends for years, so I said yes. We stood in the middle of the room. He looked right at me. 'I want to go to bed with you,' he said. 'I've always loved you and always wanted you.' That was so sweet of him, and I wanted to please him in return. But I couldn't do what he wanted. I would never have felt right about that: going to bed with Murphy while I was with you. I couldn't do that to you. And I'm not really that attracted to him. You're the only one I give myself to."

She said the words, but there was something wrong with them. A half statement? A half lie? I knew those waters well enough to sense a less than complete truth.

"So you said no to Murphy?"

"Not exactly."

"What do you mean *not exactly*?" My body stiffened.

"I felt sorry for him. So I took him to the couch and jerked him off. There wasn't much personal involvement for me. He shot off so high that his semen splashed on the wallpaper. Then I sent him home before anything else started."

Murphy beating me again. Murphy can shoot a mile. That's all I could think, over and over the phrase bounced through the corners of my brain: Murphy can shoot a mile.

"I'm telling you this because today I've taken a new look, a fresh view, of our relationship. I've decided it's not of such serious intent. Not to me and certainly not to you. Definitely not to you. So I've decided that I'm going to start dating around."

"Like your parents want."

"My parents have nothing to do with this. The decision was mine. In fact, I have a date tomorrow night. Now I'm getting dressed and I'm going home."

I sit here looking out over a dark Union Square writing my lines in this journal. My whole being is filled with shock. She means what she says about dating other men and maybe even spreading her legs for them. Well, she didn't say the last part, at least not exactly. Logic takes me there. There is a sadness that something that was once between us has died, never to be again. A specialness lost.

One thing is absolutely certain: In the future I had better be more careful about having other girls over.

30 December 1965.

It's four in the morning, I'm wide awake and pissed off mad. Sitting on the cold tile floor of my bathroom. Chris is a sleep in my bed. My spare mattress waits for me on the bedroom floor. What should have been a great night ended up a complete, total, unmitigated disaster.

Chris called me this afternoon. "Hank? This is Chris. I'm in town for a day or two visiting friends. Can I impose on you? Maybe see you for dinner and stay over. Would JoAnn mind?"

"JoAnn's out for the evening." I didn't tell him she's on a date with someone else, probably spreading her legs for someone who can shoot a mile. "Of course you're welcome. Where are you? Let me give you directions to my place."

I had already called Martha for a date after work. Dragging Chris along would cause a few complications, but not many. Anyway, I wanted him to see the situations I had been writing him about.

Chris had a bright and shining smile when I opened the door for him an hour later. He was bundled in his heavy Upstate New York sheepskin coat. I took his suitcase from him and tossed it on the couch. "Yeah, the place is small," I said. "I have an extra mattress tucked away in the closet. We'll manage. It's good to see you!"

"Of course we'll manage. Feels great to be in the City. Before you ask, everything is OK with Joanie. She wanted a few days with her mother and the baby in Connecticut. That gave me a chance to come into the City for some shopping and visiting."

He was full of shit. But I don't know how to say that to Chris. No way would Joanie just let him take off.

"I'm not interfering with your life, am I?"

"No. Not really. I have a date this evening. No problem. I would love to have you join us. Martha won't mind."

"Martha? Not JoAnn? You're still with JoAnn aren't you?"

"Of course I am. I wrote you about Martha two weeks ago. Not that you ever answer my letters. Sure JoAnn and I are still together. We're not married. Or engaged. I date other girls now and then."

"She dates other guys? Opps. Bad question. Raw nerve."

"Listen, Chris, speaking of raw nerves, there are a few complications this evening. I have to work tonight until about nine. And it's really time for me to leave for the hospital now. Can you wait that long for dinner? You can sack out here if you're tired. Or if you want to go out, there's an extra key in the top drawer of my desk. We'll head up to Martha's for dinner as soon as I get back. OK?"

I called Martha from the hospital and told her about my unexpected guest. Did she mind an additional person for dinner? "No problem," she said.

I finished work an hour early. Bill and I flew through the stacks, up and down the rolling ladders, pulling charts for the various clinics like pigeons flying in teams around Union Square. The hospital was quiet and we had no interruptions. Bill smiled as he agreed to hang around and punch us both out at nine. That means I have to hang around on New Years Eve and punch him out.

Chris was dead asleep on the couch when I returned. He didn't wake until I shook him hard and called out his name. We rode the third Avenue bus to 77th

Street. I used the time to explain that I have some intentions for the evening beyond his pleasant company. He flashed a Satyr smile. "Don't worry, Hank. Just give me a signal. Wink or shake your head. Any good stage cue and I'm off stage right to your place with an awful headache or a case of sudden-onset recurrent syphilis. Then the play is yours."

The doorman in Martha's building greeted me with a tip of his hat. "Fancy place," Chris commented as we walked down the mirrored foyer to the elevators.

"Martha shares an apartment with two other girls. They're hardly ever there. One lives with her boy friend and keeps the apartment for 'appearances sake' as Martha calls it. The other is a stewardess who's always traveling someplace. Not a bad arrangement."

Martha let us in and I made the introductions. We didn't even sit down; everyone was famished. Chris was his gallant self and helped Martha on with her coat. In the hallway I pressed the button for the elevator. It took forever. Nothing in the world is more awkward than waiting for an elevator while you try to think of something witty to say to fill up the empty space. Press the button, shuffle your feet, look at the doors that tell you nothing. Fortunately I was with Chris tonight. Chris, the Master of Charm, my mentor in the amorous arts.

Dinner at a local restaurant. Wine and laughs. A great time. Chris was in the story telling mood. "Did Hank ever tell you about his theater work at Dickinson?"

"This one is a regular sphinx on personal subjects."

"Well, let me fill you in. I saw this crazy freshman around campus, dating these senior girls, singing in musicals, and I thought: That's a prime candidate for our theater group." Chris looked at me but spoke to Martha. "Look at that baby face. Perfect for the stage." Martha laughed and lit up a Marlboro.

"At the beginning of the next year, that was my senior year and Hank's sophomore year, we had a set-building night. The director planned three Shakespeare plays for the year using the same set. So I dragged this fellow along with me to the theater. He brought his toolbox and saw. An Italian carpenter. A regular Japetto. We get to the theater and they've already started building the set. Hank doesn't even say hello to the director. He walks over, scrutinizes the set from every angle, and starts complaining: 'This is no good. This part isn't strong enough. Where are the triangles? You have to build with triangles!'

The director shoots me a look that says: Who is this madman? I shrug my shoulders. Then this crazy guy takes out his pinch bar and tears the set apart! Pulls off the boards, pulls out the nails. Doesn't ask anyone's permission!"

"Come on, Chris, I wouldn't do that."

"Like hell you wouldn't," said Martha with a poke in my ribs. "That's exactly what you would do."

"That's exactly what he did. So I start to apologize to the director for this madman and Brubaker, that's the director, says to me: 'No. Let him do it. He looks like he knows what he's doing. And that's more than I can say.'

"So, by himself, with the rest of us watching and cutting a board now and then at his direction, this crazy fellow built the set in maybe three hours. A whole two level dramatic set!"

"It was built wrong," I said defensively. "The crew had constructed the thing with squares. You needed a set that had to last for the whole year. You have to build that with triangles supporting the structure." The both started to laugh at me. "Don't laugh. This is serious. Watch." I collected spoons and forks and constructed a square and a triangle. "Now, if you build an under structure with a triangle, and, as you can see, a square with a diagonal is a double triangle, then that structure has far greater strength than just a simple square. Look." By now they were in stitches. "The hell with the both of you! This is important if you're going to understand the story."

Martha laughed so hard she started to choke. Chris wiped tears from his eyes.

"Big joke," I grunted. "The set lasted for the whole year, didn't it?"

"Lasted? We worked for a week tearing that beast down at the end of the season!"

Later when Martha left the table for the obligatory trip to the restroom that every girl makes when she's on a date at a restaurant, I comment to Chris: "Who does she remind you of?" He shook his head. "No, seriously, Chris, who?"

"She doesn't remind me of anyone we know in common."

"Of course she does. Look at the hair, the eyes. She's a dead ringer for Rusty."

"Rusty? Your Rusty? No way. Not even close. Rusty had long hair..."

"Right. Long red hair. Red, like Martha's."

"No, Hank, Martha isn't anything like Rusty. Rusty didn't smoke and Rusty wasn't nearly as hard as this girl. This Martha, she's a tough as galvanized nails. You better be damn careful with her. She'll rip your dick off."

I looked Chris in the face. He wasn't fooling. "No way, Chris. You're way off base on this one."

"Well, it's your life. I sure hope I'm wrong."

Martha returned and our discussion ended. "Got real quiet here. You boys talking about me?" she said with a thin smile. Chris and I fought over the check. He won. Good thing because I'm dead broke.

We walked back to Martha's place in the brisk air blowing from the river straight down 77ᵗʰ Street. Upstairs we sat around her living room, drinking wine and chatting. A pleasant tableau: my closest friend and my newest flame. I was about to give Chris the agreed signal when the evening started to unravel. I should have known the night was going too smoothly.

The doorbell rang at quarter to one. The three of us exchanged looks and shrugs. Chris and I certainly weren't expecting anyone. And Martha's roommates were both gone for the week. Martha crossed the living room to the door and peered out through the peep hole. Her shoulders dropped. "Oh, God," she spit out. She turned back to us smiling and pure white.

"I don't believe this. I don't believe it." She laughed without humor. "You're going to have to excuse me for a minute. Oh, shit, what am I going to do?" She unlocked the door and went out into the hallway. We heard her talking but couldn't make out the words. They didn't sound friendly.

Returning back into the room, she carefully closed the door and rested herself against it. A very dramatic pose. "How could this happen to? Why tonight? Shit! What am I going to do? Goddamn them."

Chris flashed me a nervous grin. We had been through a number of strange nighttime situations at Dickinson, and he was passing me the old look that said: *It's time to jump on the ponies and head out of Dodge.* But I didn't have any idea what to do. I wasn't there to grab my hat and run; I was there to finally score with Martha.

She marched into the kitchen. There was a clinking of glasses and ice. I followed her. Her face was as tight as I have ever seen it.

"Who are they?"

"Damn them both. I told them not to come here tonight."

"Who?" I persisted.

"They're friends of mine from France, OK?" She threw ice cubes into the two glasses. Slammed them in like a dunking basketball.

"Invite them in."

"Don't be so stupid!" She yelled at me. "Why did they do this to me!" She breathed deeply. I watched her breasts rise and fall, and I had this sinking feeling that was as closed as I was going to get to those hills of snow.

"Listen, let me give them these drinks. Then I'll work it out."

"Work what out?"

"Damn it! Let me do it my way. OK?"

I stepped out of her way and she walked back out to the hall with the drinks. I removed my apartment key from my key chain and handed it to Chris. The passing of the key was not quite the enthusiastic, anticipatory scene I had envisioned.

"She's giving them drinks," I said to Chris.

"I can see that."

"I guess they're staying."

"I can see that, too. We need to leave. Now."

"No. I need to hang around here a little longer. Maybe I'll still get lucky."

"Fat chance. This is way past luck."

"Yeah, I know. But I have to stay."

"Hank, my friend, listen to me. You have to leave now."

"No, I can't. Go on ahead. I'll be all right."

"I really doubt that." He put on his coat and left.

A few minutes later Martha returned to the apartment. Her two Froggy friends were still out in the hall. "What are you going to do?" I asked.

"I don't want to be rude to you, but I can't send them away."

"Perhaps I should leave for a while and then return. How much time do you want to spend with them?"

She shook her head. Her stiff permanent hardly moved. "That's no good. I might as well level with you. I can't send them away. I can't tell you to come back in a few minutes. This is a real mess. Real embarrassing. I'm having an affair."

I knew the night was going too good. "There doesn't seem to be much to do. The decision seems to be already made."

"But I can't tell you to go either. I don't want to lose your friendship. I like you a lot."

Friendship and *like* were not quite what I had in mind for the evening. "Call me tomorrow. We'll talk then." Slowly, deliberately, conscious of each movement, I put one arm and then another into my jacket. I left confident of having won the situation in every way except the way I had originally planned.

When I closed the door to Martha's apartment and went out into the hall, the two Frenchies were sitting on the floor. Their drinks were next to them. One of the dark creeps mumbled "merd" at me as I passed him. I felt like kicking his teeth in, but didn't even look in his direction. Fortunately for all of us the elevator arrived quickly.

December 30, 1965. Afternoon

Martha called me early this morning and apologized claiming momentary insanity. Chris and I were still abed. When he realized who was on the phone, he departed for the bathroom and started a noisy shower.

"I don't know what came over me. It was the wrong thing to do." She made a sharp laugh. "I made the wrong choice, that's all. They came in, but I was so angry I wouldn't let them touch me. I was going to throw them out. They pleaded with me that their plane was leaving at seven this morning for Paris and they had no place else to go. So I let them sleep on the floor. I wish there were some way I could get you to forget that whole part of the night. Can you do that?"

"Forget? How do you forget things? Suddenly, poof! Memories are gone? I don't see how I can forget being thrown out. How about we leave it that you owe me one 'forget'? And that it had better not happen again."

"That sounds OK to me."

"What are your plans for the rest of the week?" I asked to change the subject. Also I was curious what she had planned for New Year's Eve, though I don't see how I can get out of my date with JoAnn. Unless JoAnn's date last night changed all that. *Too bad, Hank, I found a real man who spreads my legs without any usualness. And he can shoot a mile high.*

"I have commitments every night. Then I'm going home to Long Island for a week. I'll probably leave on Monday. Spend the college week off with my parents doing family things. When will I see you again? I really do like you."

"I'll call you Sunday evening before you leave. I'll be in New Jersey at my sister's house on Saturday and Sunday. I think I need some time to chew on this caper." She laughed at my pun and hung up.

Chris entered from the bathroom with wet hair and an under-the-eyebrows leer. "I won't remind you that I told you to be careful. She's nothing like Rusty. Rusty would never have done that." Up went his hand to fend off my immanent rebuttal. "All right. All right. I won't say another word. Call me when this Martha really does you in. I think you're much better off with JoAnn. She's your type of girl. Not this cold bitch."

We prepared breakfast in my tiny kitchen. I had some English muffins in the fridge that he insisted on fixing. "You have to cut English muffins with a fork, Hank. Never use a knife."

"Yes, Chris, I remember. I've been out with you plenty of times to a breakfast restaurant or slop joint where you returned your muffins because they were cut with a knife contrary to your explicit instructions. So this morning here's a fork. Do the honors."

He told me he had to leave by noon, had to visit a friend. Gender was not mentioned. Joanie and bambino were not mentioned. Something is rotten in Cazenovia. He also didn't ask to see JoAnn. Maybe he knows she would grill him with questions about Joanie and baby.

I was reluctant to call JoAnn anyway. Maybe she wouldn't be home to answer. That would force me to face the question of whether she had slept over some guy's place. Murphy who can shoot a mile? Well, this is part of the price of independence.

The other side of the price tag is that I can't tell JoAnn that Chris was here last night without being subject to a thousand questions myself. But then again, maybe it would do some good to let her see that her going out on a "date" made her miss talking to Chris. Either way I win. Decide later.

JANUARY 1966

January 3, 1966. Monday Midnight

New Year's Eve wasn't cold, just windy. Bill worked until eight and then left for his new flame in Brooklyn. The girl in Queens never forgave him for not visiting her on the night of the blackout. It was my turn to stay and punch us both out at nine. The hospital was as quiet as King Tut's tomb until Howard Carter popped his head in the door. I used the hour to work on a new book by Jessamyn West: *Leafy Rivers*. How can she describe characters so beautifully that they walk the pages of your mind?

After work I walked down to 14th Street and across to the IRT subway station for my trip uptown. The street was unexpectedly empty. Only three more hours before the transit strike was scheduled to begin (thank you Mayor Lindsey) and the subway would shut down (thank you subway workers union). Great union: screw the rest of you, we want our money.

At JoAnn's building I had to ring for the doorman who took forever. When he finally made an appearance, he looked a little funny, unfocused. I must have looked funny too on Park Avenue ringing a doorbell at a massive apartment building and waiting for someone to answer. The whole crew of doormen here are Irish. I wouldn't say that the Irish are drunks on New Year's, but then maybe this one wasn't representative of the whole race.

The elegant, old-fashioned elevator has a brass semi-circular control lever that looks like it came from a World War II naval vessel. Operating this delayed response relic requires a delicate dexterity to match the elevator floor with the hallway floor. You push the control forward or pull it back before the elevator lurches upward a few inches. Or feet. Then you pull the brass lever back and quickly return it to the original upright position in order for the elevator to drop a few inches. Or feet. This last maneuver creates a sudden stop with a distinctive sway that leaves little doubt that there is nothing between you and the basement but a length of twisted, old steel cable. How far the elevator lurches up or down is a function of the operator's deftness and judgment. My man was in deep shit if someone had come around to test his reflexes. He failed to align the elevator with the second floor hallway at least a dozen times. I finally asked him to stop wherever he could and I would step up or down the difference. That remark must have wounded his pride because on the next attempt he came within six inches of the mark. An accomplishment that pleased us both.

JoAnn's parents weren't home. After a fusillade of warm and welcome kisses we used her bed for some energetic sex. Then we descended her back stairs into the cool night and found a corner bar on Lexington for a few drinks. Nothing grand. Then back to her place (using the stairs again) to watch the ball drop in Times Square. Not a very exciting evening, but in many ways more rewarding than my date with Martha. Of course I said nothing. Neither did she about her night of freedom.

The next morning we drove the two hours to South Jersey to visit sister Rose (She Who Must Be Obeyed). She and Carl were in good spirits. We had a nice dinner, a bottle of Hungarian wine suggested by Andre helped the mood. Carl's florist business had done well over the holidays and he had a few light weeks to catch up and plan for the new year. After dinner Rose went through her standard groans about her county extension job and the "dense, stupid local ladies" who don't want to change anything about their lives. JoAnn and I talked about school and City.

As usual Rose gave us the attic room in their small house. It's normally cozy and romantic. Except I had one of my frustrating nights: everything worked fine until the last and then nothing happened. Probably not Murphy's problem.

OK, Murphy, it's time to shoot.
Right-o, JoAnn. Right on cue for you.
Oh, my. Hit the ceiling this time. Another record.
Hey, girl, nothing to it.

Full balls and angry thoughts left me tossing and turning through the long, quiet night. JoAnn slept the sleep of the innocents, snuggled up warm against me.

Early the next morning while the women slept, Carl and I took off in his old four wheel drive Ford truck for the Delaware River. We didn't talk much. Carl is a quiet man and I never feel the need to fill a void when I'm with him. We bounced and jostled along a potholed dirt track to the river's edge through a frozen, sandy marsh of swaying horsetails that were double the height of the truck. In many places they formed a canopy over the rutted, pebbled track. The inside of the truck was a junk pile of scraps, pencils, unidentified and unidentifiable pieces and parts. Years of collected debris. Each item had its own unique sound mostly in counterpoint to the tire and spring squealings. We were a moving Rube Goldberg symphony.

The sea of dry, brown horsetails opened up at the river strand and there before us was the broad expanse of the lower Delaware River. Carl cut off the engine. For a moment we were engulfed in a vast, limitless silence after ten minutes of total cacophony. The horsetails swished and snapped behind us in the cold wind off the water. The strand was a huge refuse heap of logs, lumber, pilings and trash: everything washed down from Philadelphia and Camden shipping.

Usually I visit the river with Carl during the summer. We arrive early in the morning to escape the scorching South Jersey sun and to beat other scavengers. In July the river marsh is full of life: rabbits, songbirds, lush green reeds and salt grass. From the river an occasional deep note from a ship's horn. The early morning sun twinkles, sparkles through the waving horsetails. Past this early summer morning freshness come the mosquitoes and sand flies. Mosquitoes: the New Jersey official state summer bird.

On this crisp January morning with its pale sun Carl was at the river seeking building lumber for his new horticultural sheds. I was searching for anything of interest. As we walked along the sandy shore, Carl selected a long timber here, a stout board there. These we moved out of the general tangle so that we could gather them later on the way back.

It was cold on the river. Damn cold. The small waves lapped and slapped against the soft yellow sand. My fingers and toes were in pain from the damp chill. I was more than ready to call it quits when I spied a treasure: a 55 gallon drum. I tapped it with my gloved knuckles; it returned a dull thud, not a hollow ring. It was full. Of what? We beat on the bunghole screw in the top cover until it finally loosened enough for Carl to unscrew it with his huge fingers.

He looked in and started laughing. "This is more for you than me." He stepped back for me to check it out for myself.

I looked in and saw a jellied substance. "What is it?"

Carl shook his head. His eyes sparkled in pleasure. The ground was littered with sticks. I found a small flat one and rubbed it against the side of my treasure to scrape off the river grime. It slipped smoothly into the hole and out came a mass of petroleum jelly. I had 55 gallons of Vaseline. We left the drum and collected the lumber.

After a hot and welcome breakfast of pancakes and syrup, JoAnn and I took off for my parent's house in North Jersey. I wanted to pick up my bicycle. Between the transit strike and a week of no classes, this type of two-wheeled locomotion may be useful. We arrived in time for lunch. My mother was pleased to see us. She reached up to kiss us both. She's even smaller than we are.

Dad was actually smiling today. Waved hello to JoAnn when she came in the house. I never see them together without thinking of that night two years ago when JoAnn and I were sitting on the living room couch holding hands and talking. He stormed in the room, his deep voice raised in thunder: "Don't think I don't know what you two are up to! I won't have that kind of behavior in my house!"

I was so embarrassed I couldn't even look at JoAnn. My mother was expecting us to stay over; she had moved Anthony out of his room and changed the sheets on his bed so that JoAnn would feel welcome. Any kind of "behavior" in my mother's house was unthinkable.

As soon as dad left the room, I went upstairs and brought down our bags. JoAnn was only going to stay the night before returning to the City, I had been planning to stay for the rest of the week before heading back to Dickinson College. We kissed my tear-streaked mother goodbye and left. I drove JoAnn back to Manhattan. The air in the car crackled with my anger. Her parents were out of town for the night, so we spent the evening at her place. Then next day JoAnn drove me downtown to Penn Station. From there I took the Pennsylvania Rail Road *Chief* to Harrisburg and then the bus to Carlisle. The whole week before classes I stayed in my empty dorm room. Better there than in New Jersey and that empty mess. Neither mom nor dad ever spoke of the incident again.

That was two years ago. Today we had a nice lunch with my parents. I asked mom to visit me in the City for a day soon. She liked the idea, but we didn't set a date.

After lunch dad helped me tie the bicycle on the top of the car. "The bicycle's for the transit strike?" he asked. I nodded. "Is it safe to use a bicycle in City traffic?"

"Usually not," I answered. I didn't want to talk to him, but I couldn't stop my words. "During this week I expect that the streets will be so clogged that traffic will hardly move. A bicycle may be the safest and easiest way to move around town."

He nodded. "JoAnn's a good girl." His cough started and he walked back to the house. Another conversation unfinished. A lifetime of half conversations.

JoAnn and I drove into Manhattan through the Hudson Tunnel. She dropped me at my apartment before she had to head uptown for her obligatory Sunday dinner with her parents. We didn't have time to clear away the pressure from last night's failure. With the bicycle in the room, there's hardly any space left. I can't leave it in the hall—it would certainly go the way of my little pumpkin. I still can't figure that out. Who would want a small pumpkin? Probably Mr Crapbeau upstairs performing some perversion.

I called Martha and we got together about 6:30. I rode my bicycle uptown to her place. She was open-mouthed when I walked into her high-rise apartment with a bicycle in tow. So much for a conventional life style.

She said she wanted to talk about the other night, and could we do it over dinner. Her treat. No objections from me to a free dinner. On Second Avenue we found a restaurant with open booths where you can stretch out your legs.

She lit a cigarette and started the conversation with her half-smile. "Well, what can I say about the other night? What an embarrassing mess."

I put my hamburger aside. "There was something you said that I didn't understand."

"Ha! You're not the only one!"

"You said you wouldn't let them touch you. What did you mean by 'them'?"

"Damn it! Why did I say that to you! What a mess I made of this."

"That doesn't answer my question and I think you owe me an answer. I'm willing to forget the whole thing, but I want reality."

"No, Hank, you don't. You say you do, but you don't. You're a romantic at heart. Misplaced in New York. And this situation is something you would not understand. I don't know if I understand it."

I just sat and stared at her. She snuffed out her cigarette in the ash tray and talked to the crooked butt. "OK, I'll tell you. But you won't like it." A big, tight smile without mirth covered her mouth. "I met both of them two months ago at a party. They're always together like brothers. They're not, but they could be they're so much alike. The right things were said, the right cues were passed, and we came back to my place and spent the night. The three of us. Look, it's not something I do all the time; it just happened." She looked directly into me, there was no smile and no laugh. "I knew you wouldn't understand this. You're going to judge me harshly, and I like you a lot."

I said nothing for a minute, my mind racing though my thoughts, rehearsing what I was about to say so that it would come out logically. "So when Chris left and then I left, they thought that we two had been there to make it with you. Isn't that a laugh?"

She wasn't listening to me. Where did she go behind those eyes? "We met a few more times. There wasn't anything in it. They're just fun to be with. I didn't know they were coming over the other night. Why would I ever want you to meet? And when you left, I felt so bad that I didn't want anything to do with them. If you want to know the truth, they became real angry that I didn't want to go to bed with them. Real angry. But I didn't want to anymore. So that's the story." Back to the smile and a new cigarette.

I sensed she was telling me a lie or parts of a lie. Something happened between them that night. Maybe she did say no to them. She said she didn't want to do anything, but she hadn't said that she didn't do anything with them. I know the rules of hair splitting with words, and her words weren't ringing true. In any case, I didn't push the issue. And she was paying the check.

I'm still not sure if she wanted me to go back upstairs with her to do more than fetch my bicycle. She claimed she was very tired. My bladder was bursting. In her bathroom I noticed a bloodstained sheet. Period time? She asked me to stay for a little longer and we talked of Christmas (sans mention of JoAnn) and school. She brought out her picture album of her trip to Europe last summer. A few minutes later she was lying in my lap babbling incoherently while I caressed her neck and breasts. But she was really out. I couldn't decide if I should take her to bed anyway. Confusing thoughts of Andre telling me to be more carnal, of her period time, of Martha becoming angry with me, of Rusty opening her blouse to me. Finally I left her on the couch covered her with a blanket (again!), took my bike and departed quietly closing the door with only the slightest click. Hank the Romantic.

What a case of the aches I had! All night and then some. Certainly not my weekend in that department. Fortunately JoAnn came over tonight. I managed doubles. And I didn't say anything about Martha. We learn. Slowly sometimes, but we learn.

Every time I've been out with Martha, the gods have thwarted me. What's wrong? 1/2/66. 1+2+6+6=15. 1+5=6. A six day. No wonder it was lousy.

January 5, 1966. Thursday afternoon
Transit strike this week. What a mess. This bike has been a real boon. With the weather sunny and warm for January I've been able to cycle uptown to JoAnn's several times. Everyone's amused when you arrive on a bicycle. Even JoAnn's parents laughed at my locomotion. At their apartment house I've been

able to leave my bike in the hall. With a private doorman and only two apartments per floor, the risk of having my wheels stolen is rather low.

Time to head off to work in a few minutes. Tootie has calmed down. Her squint-eyed, side-long glances have disappeared, her soto voce "tut-tut" complete with emphatic head shaking has waned, and the atmosphere at medical records has returned to normal.

An oddment the other afternoon. I was looking out the back window while donning my official hospital jacket when I noticed a shiny plaque on one of the brownstone buildings facing us on 17th Street. From that distance I couldn't read the print. I asked Doris if she knew what was inscribed on the historical marker.

"What plaque?" she responded. Her shift was nearly finished. She had her coat on and her purse was clutched to her chest as if the sum of her worldly possessions were stored in its deep confines. Her eyes remained fixed on the clock over the door. That circle contained the last five minutes before her 5:30 release time. Perhaps if she looked away, the time would escape the clock and leave without her.

JoAnn and I have had a pleasant week with movies, a trip to the Cloisters, the Central Park Zoo and the Frick Gallery. Now that's an eclectic collection!

The Cloisters up on the hill on the top of Manhattan Island stood lonesome and forbidding in the January light. How bleak and cold life must have been in the Middle Ages even for the wealthy. Stone fortresses may be secure against animals and arrows, but they provide no security against cold and damp.

Imagine life for the poor peasants who lacked even the stone walls to protect them from wind and snow. Zoe Oldenbourg makes a comment in one of her novels that the differences between rich and poor were less a thousand years ago than they are now. The rich and poor alike suffered from cold, malnutrition, diseases and hunger in times past. Today only the poor suffer these hardships. Can that be true?

At the zoo the polar bears, seals and penguins displayed perfect pleasure with the January cold in their cages. Outside, bundled in our own heavy coats plus gloves and knitted caps, we provided a harmonious counterpoint to the furry show and were out of place with the rest of our species.

We walked further into Central Park to the castle where we had lunch a few months before with Janice and Johnny. The lake lay stretched flat, frozen with dull green pitted ice. "Do you think there's any trace of our ever having been here last fall?" I asked JoAnn. She looked at me quizzically through one of her knitted scarves that was wrapped around her head and face. "What I mean is: We had such a nice time that afternoon. Does anything ever linger in a place after you leave? That sounds pretty stupid, I know. There's not much scientific chance of lingering presences. But our lives seem such a waste otherwise. We would be no more than polar bears playing in ice water."

She put her arm through mine; we walked on back to Fifth Avenue and the bus downtown. "Hank, the present holds the only reality. The past exists only as shadows playing in our minds. We have to live in the present and hope in the future. The past is for memories."

I know her answer is correct. Yet those cold, logical words leave me unsatisfied. There has to be more to life.

JoAnn told me she's been looking at apartments with Sara from school. I listened politely and nodded at the right places. That bought me some nice rewards but I don't really think anything will come from her pointless looking. Same old story.

We also managed to do some studying for exams this week. Tomorrow night I'm going out with Martha who returned from Long Island today. I told JoAnn that I needed some study time alone. "Whenever we study together we half study on and half study off. I need some steady study this week." She laughed.

Saturday evening JoAnn's parents want us to go to the theater with them after dinner at their place. Saturday dinner with JoAnn's parents always means a giant steak from the local butcher plus two vegetables. Annie the maid has Saturday night off. JoAnn's mother assumes stewardship over the kitchen, a position hotly disputed by JoAnn's father. They fight over how to cook the steak. He wants the meat medium, she wants medium-well. I can never tell the difference. The lines between her parents are delivered as set as a Shakespearian script.

A strange thing happened last night. Joanie called me from Upstate New York. "I wondered if Chris left his scarf at your place when he was there overnight last week."

"No, he didn't. But I do remember he had a bright blue and gold scarf on when he was here. I'll look around and call you back."

"No, that's not necessary. That's the scarf all right. He probably left it at my parent's house. In fact, I'm sure that's what happened. Thanks so much," she said about to hang up.

"Wait. Don't go yet. How is everyone? The baby?"

"Fine. She's big and brawly. Blue eyes like Chris." Silence. Finally I said good-bye and hung up. I had the feeling that she wasn't calling about the scarf, that she was calling me to check up on Chris. Something sounds very wrong.

January 9, 1966. Sunday afternoon

Thursday night I was real pleased to see Martha again. God, she's a sexy girl. Tight, small, muscular body with a nice shape ("cute" would be Andre's word), that wonderful red hair, and such a sharp wit. But whenever I'm near her everything inside me knots up. I say the wrong things and make the wrong moves.

We were sitting in her apartment on her couch, drinking a glass of wine and chatting about families when she dropped this bomb on me: "There's no way I could introduce you to my parents. You wouldn't fit in with them."

"I don't understand."

"Sure you do," she said with her tight smile. She was dressed in a tight blouse and skirt that left me totally turned on. Why didn't I just grab her and end the talk? I knew that was what she was secretly asking me to do. "You're intelligent and gifted, Hank, but that's not what my parents consider a good family background."

First JoAnn's father and now Martha's father consider me not good enough for his daughter. I was pissed and I blew up at her. "What are you talking about? My family's as good as any. We may be rich, but we aren't poor. My father's put us all through college. It's true my parents don't have college degrees and my father doesn't work in an office. Who would expect him to? He came up from poverty and an immigrant household that didn't even speak English. Hell, Martha, what do you expect?"

I paced the floor like JoAnn on one of her evening migrations around my apartment, and I rambled on and on. Probably making a fool of myself.

Martha sat back on her satiny couch and shook her head. "Sometimes I'm really dumb. I shouldn't have said anything. Let's forget it." She stood up, got her coat from the closet and we left for dinner.

Now I feel awful. First, I shouldn't have jumped off the handle because she told a truth about what others believe, albeit she did a pretty bad job of it. And second, I don't want to lose her. I keep messing up with this girl. I can't get close to her and I can't let her go. Needless to say, after dinner, back at her place, my feet became lead weights and wouldn't move in her direction to make the moves she wanted. I left with a mumble and an awful case of the aches.

1/6/1966. 1+6+1+9+6+6=29. 2+9=11. 1+1=2. A two day should have been better.

When I got home from work on Friday night, JoAnn had dinner ready for me at my place. There was even a candle on the card table and a bottle of wine with two glasses. Real glass, not plastic.

"Wow! This must be some occasion!" I said throwing my coat on the couch (not yet a bed) and kissing her hello and grabbing her bottom.

"Yes, it is. You're not going to believe this. I'm not sure I believe it. I've been pinching myself black and blue all day. You see, I signed the lease on my apartment today! Well, my mother signed the papers since I'm not twenty-one until July. But the rental lease is signed. That's my news."

"That's great. Can we drink a toast? An apartment with Sara?"

"Yes, and a third girl. We needed an extra roommate to swing the rent financially. Sara knows the other girl, her name is Sandy. Actually she not a girl. She's in her thirties." JoAnn had fixed pork chops and broccoli. She spoke as she served dinner. I was starved and shoveled in the food as she talked excitedly. "Sara and I will move in right after exams. Sandy started moving in today. The apartment has only two bedrooms. I expect since she moved in first, Sandy will take the one bedroom and leave the other to Sara and me."

"Is this the place on Ninth Street?" I asked between mouthfuls.

"Yes. I think that's why my parents finally agreed. It's only a few blocks from school. That and they learned Sandy is Jewish. Or maybe they gave up and accepted, al fine, the inevitable. As soon as Sara and I have time, we're going to pick out some paint and redo the place. We can start that before we move in. I'm only going to take a bed and a dresser and a desk. Travel light, so to speak. I've set January 22, that's a Saturday, as move-in date. Well, that's my big news."

"Do you want me to help you move in? Maybe I should stay away if your parents are steamed up."

"Of course not. I'm counting on your help. One of the reasons I chose the 22nd is that my parents will be away that weekend. You will help, won't you?" she asked with a sudden uncertainty.

We didn't even bother to put the card table away before we turned Dr Jeckle couch into Mr Hyde bed.

Saturday dinner at JoAnn's parents was served promptly at 6:15 in the formal dining room with candelabra. One of their monster steaks from the butcher around the corner. Totally delicious. Annie, their black cook and maid who has been with them as long as JoAnn outdid herself. I like Annie and she's a great chef. This was one Saturday when she stayed to cook. Averting fight time in the kitchen over how to cook the steak. Annie resolves these disputes in a manner that amazes me. When she cooks, no one bothers her. How does she do it?

Whenever I eat a formal meal at JoAnn's, I feel out of my element. Silver napkin holders, monogrammed cloth napkins, a myriad of slightly differing silver forks ands spoons, one glass for water, a second for ice tea, a third for wine, and a baffling plethora of other unfamiliar table amenities. My Jersey upbringing sorely lacked these points of etiquette. At home we used a spoon, fork, knife, plate and glass in whichever way seemed most effective at the moment.

JoAnn's father was in fine fettle about John Lindsey. "Damned liberal incompetent. He'll ruin this city before he learns how to govern it."

"I thought he was your congressman before his election to mayor?"

"A congressman is one thing. His bungling idiocy is diluted by several hundred others. Collectively they do less damage than any one of them let loose. But a mayor has full executive authority. If he can't deal with one of his local unions, then all the citizens suffer. Look at the money this pampered, spoiled WASP has cost us. Too perfect, too much the pretty boy to play the game right."

"Do you mean payoffs?" I asked.

"Payoffs, smayoffs," he answered between bites. "What's a few dollars compared to the millions lost to business? To the inconvenience for people who have to travel the public transit system to work? And this talk about building more 'Projects' on the East Side. Just what we need: Bring the slums down from Harlem. Why does this cotton-head think we have the slums where they are? When the ghetto comes down to Midtown, then drugs, crime and prostitution will come along with it. All this mess so that Pretty Boy Mayor can reap a few more votes for his ambition."

At the end of the meal JoAnn's mother snuffed out the candles with a small shot glass holding it tightly around the candle to contain any smoke. "Otherwise the wax goes up and coats the ceiling." She says the same thing to me every time I watch her carefully extinguish the candles. I wonder how she does birthday candles on a cake? Does she have tiny little shot glasses for each candle?

Theater was a Broadway comedy: *The All American Girl.* JoAnn's parents enjoyed themselves. Her father really liked the play because he fell asleep in the second act and started snoring. Apparently this is a normal state of affairs because

JoAnn's mother poked him in the ribs a few times as calmly as if she were changing sheets. I thought the play was silly and a waste of money. Fortunately theirs.

Andre just called. Wants me to come over and have Sunday dinner with him. His usual chicken paprikosh that he makes in a single pot. It will probably be a lot better than macaroni with my mother's frozen Ragu sauce warmed up.

January 10, 1966. *Monday evening*

Tried to reach Martha several times last night. No answer on her phone. She didn't show up after German class today for our regular coffee hour. Instead I had coffee (and tea) with John from German. At my usual coffee shop my waitress said hello and raised her eyebrow. I shrugged my shoulders. "No luck with girls today," I said. She smiled and blew me a kiss.

John's older than the rest of the students in class. He attending class on a GI program. A VietNam veteran studying pre-med. I asked him why he planned to go on to medical school. "Hey, that's where the money is."

Earlier this year I purchased his textbook, class notes and lab reports for Physiology since I have the same professor and lab instructor that John had the semester before. He charged me $40 for the lot which I thought was damned high. But he scored straight As in the class, so I paid him in hard earned Tootie hours.

I started by using his lab reports as a guide to my own. On the first report the snotty grad student who oversees the lab gave me a C+. On the second report I inserted John's figures and results over my testing. The simpering shit gave me a B-. On my third report, I submitted John's report with my name on it. His exact report. The same report the instructor gave John an A on the semester before, this semester brought me a B! Needless to say, I can't complain to anyone in authority.

John listened to my tale of woe over a cup of coffee this morning. "Hey, man, life's a bitch. And a bitch is never fair. Like a woman." I knew the conversation was about to switch to John's favorite topic: finding pussy. "You take what you can get and enjoy it. The rest you put off until the next opportunity. It doesn't mean a shit because deep down women are after their own things. You're only a means to their goals. Or a bit of fun for them along the way."

"That's a cynical viewpoint."

"Man, I'm just giving it to you straight. And speaking of nice, I've seen you around with a dynamite redhead. Sexy body. Bet she sits on your dick and rips it off, right? Who is she? I've got to meet her."

"I wish she were taking me apart. I can't seem to get it together with her. Every time we get close to doing something—bang!—the evening crumbles into chaos. Maybe I want too much."

"There's no more to girls than what I'm telling you. Listen to me: You tell them a few jokes, fuck their brains out and thank them when you're done. Stop this looking for something deep shit. There's nothing deep there. I'm telling you. And speaking of shit, how's your standing with the draft board? You're supposed to graduate this year, right? And you need that fifth year because you changed majors, right? I've met guys in your shoes. In 'Nam. They didn't get that fifth year. Instead they got two with a rifle. You better be sure your board doesn't demand their pound of flesh in June. Believe me: you don't want to fuck around with 'Nam. And if the army grabs you, you want to go as an officer for three and not a grunt for two."

I'll write my county draft board. Telling a joke and screwing Martha's brains out may be a lot harder.

January 16, 1966. Sunday night
Greek Thinkers exam tomorrow and I'm home hitting the books.

Never could locate Martha this week. Finally spoke to one of her roommates who told me she has been sick with the flu and stayed in Long Island. I had visions of her cavorting and contorting with her Froggie friends.

Last week in the NYU student paper there was an ad for singers for the Desoff Choir production of Karl Orff's Carmina Burana. Especially noted was the need for tenors. But so far I've had no luck contacting them for an audition. Now there's a piece I would love to sing! Leopold Stokowski will be directing the American Symphony Orchestra. Stokowski of *Fantasia* fame.

This situation with Martha is beginning to extend beyond my control. I'm afraid to try anything with her—I'm afraid of failing. These fears are nothing new to me; but I wasn't aware that I had them in such depth. I am also afraid that she will come to see my weakness and fear and use them against me. JoAnn never would, but JoAnn doesn't have Martha's streak of coldness. Martha is more rational than JoAnn, more self-directed, and more masculine in her thought patterns.

I should be able to say that I will overcome these fears and uncertainties as soon as I put my mind to it. I know I can. And yet…And yet…Any yet deep underneath lurks this morbid uncertainty.

Every time I attempt something with Martha the situation stretches out beyond my grasp. I see her Rusty red hair, her smart sexy body and I'm pulled toward her. At the same time my feet are moving backwards. It reminds me of a dream I had during the summer after Rusty's abortion. In the dream I was standing naked in my bedroom in my parents' house. On the bed was a huge snake. The viper's red eyes stared at me without deviation; its forked tongue flicked in and out with a steady rhythm. The snake wanted me. I knew I had to escape, to walk backwards slowly out of the room so that my movements would not rouse the monster snake to strike and destroy me.

When I tried to step backwards with my right foot, my leg moved forward instead and brought me closer to the bed. Total horror. Then my left foot refused to obey and it too took me a step closer. Parts of me conspiring to destroy me as my legs took me closer and closer to the snake. I woke in an awful fright with the image of that impassive, cold beast watching me.

The other night Andre listed patiently to my dream and discussion about Martha as we shared a glass of Bull's Blood wine in his kitchen. He shook his head. "Hankie, why do you always have to be so serious? Why do you need all this control? And why, my darling boy, are you going out with this cold bitch who drags you through the mud?"

I didn't have an answer for him. But who is he to talk with what he drags up the stairs half the night?

January 27, 1966. *Thursday night, late.*
Snowing tonight. A very pretty scene outside my window. White fluffy flakes falling in a slow motion cascade through the street lights in Union Square. I wish I didn't have this German exam tomorrow. I want to go outside and romp and kick up the snow and be a high school student again. But I'm so far behind in my studying and I'm doing so poorly in the class that I have to stay with the books. Groan.

Had a great date with JoAnn last week. We spent the night at the theater with *Marat Sade*. The most moving, thoughtful, mad play conceivable. We arrived at our seats just as the play started, although started isn't the right word. People wandered on to the stage with no darkening of the theater lights, no indication that the play had begun. These were obviously mentally retarded people recruited to do roles on stage commensurate with their limitations. At intermission I turned to JoAnn and asked: "How did they ever get these people to memorize their lines?"

"What people?" she answered confused.

"The mental patients in the play."

"Those aren't really people from an asylum," she whispered. "Look at your playbill. We're watching the Royal Shakespeare Company."

I was astonished. The acting was so real! Ian Richardson, Patrick McGee, Glenda Jackson. And what a play! So much meat to chew on. So many ideas. We went back to my place and spent half the night talking and singing (quietly) the songs from the play.

We moved JoAnn into her apartment with a minimum of fuss. As she predicted, she has to share one bedroom with Sara since Sandy appropriated the second bedroom for herself. They set up the apartment with single beds. That made the move very easy. A small dresser, books, stereo, clothes and female bathroom paraphernalia. Two trips in her car on a chilly afternoon.

The apartment is on the second floor and looks out over Ninth Street between Fifth and Sixth Avenues. Big, bright windows face naked branched trees. Promises to be lovely in the spring. JoAnn and Sara had painted the rooms cream and gray one day last week. I was not invited to the painting. "This is my project with Sara and Sandy. No men allowed." Story sounded fishy to me. Who did they get to climb on the ladders and paint around the cornices? Probably Murphy marking bulls-eyes on the ceiling.

Last night the phone rang about midnight and roused me out of a dead sleep. "Hank? Did I wake you?" asked JoAnn in a meek voice. "Can I come up to your place? Please?" I reminded her that the elevator closes down at one. Then I fell back to sleep until her key in the door woke me again.

She sat at the bottom of the couch/bed with her coat on. I stayed with covers pulled up to my nose. "I don't know what to do. I can't go to my parents and tell them that I made a mistake. They would never let me live it down. My father would gloat forever."

"Could we be a bit more specific?"

"Why is this apartment always so cold?" she asked with no expectation of a reply. "Can I get in bed with you and talk?" She was already in the process of taking off her coat and shoes. After that her skirt and blouse that she neatly folded and laid across the back of my chair. She hopped into bed with me, her bra and panties still on. She snuggled up to me. Bra and panties on meant sex off. She really did want to talk. "Hank, you're always as warm as a heater in bed. Oh, that feels good tonight. I'm so cold."

She had her arms around my neck with her head snuggled against my chest. I asked: "Are you here to rob my precious heat calories the way you drain off my bodily fluids? Or did you want to talk?"

"In a minute. I haven't slept in two days and you feel so good. Let me lie here for a minute first." Her minute turned to two. Then I felt her twitch as she slipped into a deep sleep. Great. I haven't been laid in days, she has her tits pressed against me, my dick is a broomstick, I'm wide awake and she's dead out. I disentangle myself and she doesn't stir from her slumber. Out came the extra mattress, sheets and blanket. I'm dispossessed from my own bed and left to my own poor devices.

This morning I was up with the garbage trucks. The extra mattress put away, sheets and blankets folded while she slept on. I was at my desk under the window studying when I heard a rustling from the bed. "Hank? Oh, I didn't mean to fall asleep on you. Come over here and make love to me." Well, that eased the situation a bit.

1-27-66. 1+9+12=22. 2+2+4. A four day. Good number for me. Four and eleven have always been my favorite numbers.

JoAnn insisted on taking me out for breakfast before I had to head out to the library and she to her apartment to change clothes. Her treat. We walked down South Broadway to a coffee shop on Eleventh Street. I took advantage of her free meal and gorged myself on bacon, eggs, hash browns, toast and hot tea. Best breakfast I've had in ages.

She talked to me holding her coffee mug in both hands. "We made a mistake in Sandy. Big mess. I had to leave last night it was so embarrassing. She brings her boy friends in and she keeps us up all night with her screaming."

"I don't understand. Her boyfriend is hurting her?"

"No, Hank." JoAnn lowered her voice. "She a screamer when she has sex. And she doesn't mind who hears her. We never talked about having boys— men—over. I don't think I mind in principle, but I don't know what to do about this."

"How can she stay up all night and go to work the next day."

JoAnn gave me the look that said: *You can't be that naïve.* The Andre scene again with a new protagonist. "She's a hooker. This is her job. Sara and I are going to get together this morning and decide what to do. I thought about bringing Sara with me last night to your place. What would you have done with the two of us? Of course we've never talked about whether you like having sex with dead people." She laughed as if that were the funniest thing she had heard in days. Maybe it was.

We parted with a kiss.

Speaking of Andre, he has a full time lover: a sophomore at Columbia, a business major. You would never guess by looking at him that Dorian is gay: He seems an ordinary, nice young fellow. A round, quiet face with sandy brown hair, average height and weight, a plain dresser with slacks, starched shirt and sweater. He's intelligent but not scintillating. He spoke intelligently on a range of issues when I met him although I can't recall any one thing that he said. Right now he lives in a college dorm apartment in the upper West Side near Columbia.

Andre had JoAnn and I over for dinner the other night to introduce us. Maybe he even wanted our approval. Tailless Corky ran back and forth down Andre's long hallway doing tricks at Andre's bidding. We laughed at him over a bottle of Hungarian wine. Poor Andre—he was so sensitive about everything. The wine had to be perfect, the crackers arranged just so on the plate, the cheese cut with a thin knife. It's amusing to see such a rational man the puppet of irrational forces within him.

I spoke to Andre briefly this afternoon before I had to leave for work. "I'm surprised to see you home early this afternoon, Andre. Up late last night, hmmm?"

"Very funny, Hankie. In fact I was at my desk before you woke this morning. Now and then even we Wall Street security analyst types are allowed a few hours early in the office. Actually today we had a luncheon presentation uptown that most of us walked out on. Hopeless company. Not worth a nickel of my client's money. Very technical stuff based on silicon. Ridiculous."

"Speaking of company, not the hopeless type, I hope, how are you doing with the young energetic Dorian?"

"Well, since you asked, Dorian, my young friend, my almost too young friend, is spending the day with his mother in Queens trying to convince her to let him move in with me." Andre's eyes twinkled.

These two twinkies have cooked up a scheme where Andre has a nephew who is in school with Dorian, and Dorian wants to leave his dorm and stay with the nephew. The uncle (Andre) thinks this is a good idea for his normally introverted (and totally invented) nephew. I tried to reason with Andre. "This scenario won't work. It doesn't even hold water with me. Invented nephew, phony uncle. Dorian's mother won't buy it."

"Hankie, you're being too critical and too negative. There's nothing wrong with this plan. Uncles have a duty to help nephews. This situation is perfectly believable."

Then I talked to him about the Martha mess. As always, he asked me why I had to get so involved. "And it seems to me that you have a great fear of being alone." I couldn't answer him.

Instead I switched subjects to JoAnn's roommate problems. "Well, Hankie, she can always come and live with me. I'm very discrete. I'll treat her like a brother. Or maybe a sister—depending on my mood. Who knows?" Great. Thanks for the help.

January 29, 1966. *Saturday afternoon.*

JoAnn called me at work last night and asked if she could meet me at my apartment. Since I had nothing planned, that sounded great to me. Work was slow, the walk home cold and damp. Her great big smile greeted me when I opened the door.

"Have you eaten dinner?" she asked.

"Yes, I had a pot of macaroni and peas before work."

"Can I get you a cup of tea?"

Hot tea sounded good. And she already had my old metal kettle on the small gas stove. Tea bags were waiting in the cups. Sitting side by side on the couch, we leaned back against the wall and sipped our warm mugs. She crossed her legs under herself and sat Indian-style. Talk time for sure.

"I don't know that I should be so happy. I certainly didn't live up to my expectations for myself, being self-sufficient and independent and solving my own problems. This morning after another long night of Sandy and her boyfriends, I went to visit my father at his factory in Brooklyn. He was surprised to see me. Actually he took one look, buzzed his secretary and told her to cancel his morning meetings and hold the phone calls. He sat me in a chair opposite his desk, told me I looked like hell, and asked me what was wrong.

"I was determined that I wasn't going to cry. I was only going to explain the problem and ask for his advice. No more—I'm not his little girl anymore. So I explained about Sandy and her boyfriends. His face turned beet red. God, he was angry. I said to him: 'Dad, this is my problem. Mine alone. What I need is advice on how to solve this myself. I want...'

"He cut me off. 'So, she's a whore, a hooker, who screws her tricks at night with my daughter in the next room and I shouldn't be concerned? You're in the middle of this—listening to her fucking and screaming every night—and I should only talk to you?'

"Hank, my father has talked rough to me, called me all kinds of names this past year, but I have never heard him talk like that, not to anyone. I turned as red as him. He was angry red and I was embarrassed red. I don't remember what he next said to me, but in a minute he was on the phone with Sandy.

"I was sitting in his brown leather office chair sinking lower and lower, mumbling to him not to do that. Their conversation started off pleasantly and then quickly became angry. Not hot angry, but cobra angry—icy business. I've never seen my father like that and I now know what people mean when they say the blood froze in their veins. Because that's what I felt.

"'Now you listen up good, little Miss Hooker. I've got a thousand dollars on the table in front of me...That's right, cash. And here's the show: Somebody is going to be a thousand dollars richer by noon. You clear out of that apartment and never return. In that case you get the thousand. Or at noon I'll call a detective friend of mine and pay him the thousand to give you a visit and get you out any way he sees fit. And sister, believe me, this is one man you don't want to mess with. Either way, the game is up and you're out by lunch...Yeah, you got the idea. You pick up the money at my lawyer's office. Make sure you bring your packed bags and leave the key.'

"He gave her directions, told her she had one hour, no more, and then he wished her a pleasant day as if they were the best of friends. When he hung up the phone, he gave me a big, broad smile that I haven't seen in years. 'What are fathers for?' he asked, spreading his hands apart.

"Five minutes on the phone and her took apart my maturity and solved a problem I was lost in. I know I should have been angry with him, but I wasn't. In fact, I think that was the most I've ever loved him. Then I told him there was no way that Sara and I could afford the apartment without Sandy. I knew, I just knew, he was going to throw that in my face, that he was going to demand that I move back home. Well, he didn't. He told me we would work the money problems out. My second shock of the day."

She uncrossed her legs and slid off the couch. "Is your tea cold? Let me get you some more hot water." She didn't return to Dr Jeckle couch but started her regular caribou migration around my room.

"He called his lawyer, made arrangements without laughing about my problem, and stressed the need for something called a 'Release'. Then he asked if I was busy for the rest of the morning. Of course I wasn't. My exams are over. So he had me file papers and help out his secretary until lunch."

"Was he trying to keep you away from the apartment?"

"Sure. What else? But I didn't mind the work. He insisted on taking me out to lunch. Then he gave me my third shock of the day. Zappo. He asked me the usual questions about school, but this time, maybe for the first time in years, he listened to my answers. Not giving me the usual vacant stare or demanding comments or condescending lectures. He asked me why I was doing this or that without being the heavy father."

"One minute he talks to you like a kid who can't solve her own problems and the next he talks to you like you're really someone," I commented hoping to deflect her migration movement and focus her back to my direction. It worked. She sat down next to me. No legs crossed. Ah, lady luck.

"What he said next I never expected." She looked right into my eyes. "He actually talked nice about you. Said maybe you weren't so bad. He commented on how hard you work to maintain your own apartment without help. That's a great improvement over anything he's ever said. He sat back and listened to me as I talked about you. He really tried to understand as an adult to an adult why I love you."

She kissed me sweetly and Dr Jeckle couch quickly transmogrified into Mr Hyde bed. Sorry about that, mother.

Oh, I forgot to mention. When JoAnn returned to her apartment that afternoon, Sandy was gone—lock, stock and barrel, as they say.

January 30, 1966. *Sunday morning*
Cold and clear today. The pigeons are flapping around Union Square. Probably dive bombing the various statues. Kamakazie diarrhetic flying rats.

Yesterday morning Andre, Dorian and I drove out to Long Island in a car Andre rented to visit Dorian's mother. Andre drove like a drop-out from driving school. He spent so much time trying to be flip and snappy that he didn't look at the road half the time. Maybe he was nervous. In case you didn't guess, I was along pretending to be Andre's nephew who lives with him. Suckered into the scheme to convince Dorian's mother that I want him to move in with Andre and I.

Once again I told them: "Dorian's mother will never fall for this scheme."

"Hankie, it will be a cinch. You really are a student, and you do live down the hall from me in your own room. So so you won't have to invent much."

Then they dropped the bomb. "Your name is Vincent."

"Why?"

"Because that's the name we invented for Andre's nephew," said Dorian. "Before we had to find a real person to fill the role."

"Why don't you just tell the truth?" I asked. They glared at me like I was the idiot of the week.

His mother is a surprisingly nice lady who fixed us a delightful lunch. The house was neither large nor fancy; but I found it quite stylish. Large south facing oriel windows let the wonderful sunshine pour in and brighten everything. A marvelous, clean January light. Over lunch she was as suspicious as I thought she would be. She peppered me with questions about school and classes. It was easy to supply complete, honest answers and she relaxed some. And obviously I knew her son. But every time she looked at Andre there was a querulous stare.

After lunch I wandered around her home to look at the books and records. Suddenly, behind me, someone called "Vincent!" It took me a moment to react, to remember that was my name for the day. A moment too long. She stood smiling at me.

"I know this is all a phony. Yet you seem like such a nice boy, sincere. You really are a student at NYU?" I nodded yes. "And you do know my son?" Again I nodded yes. "And is your name really Vincent?" I started to answer yes, but she raised her hand to stop me. "Please don't lie. It's so degrading. And you seem so sincere. I know about my son's personal life. I'm neither stupid nor blind. And you don't act like this Andre or some of my son's other friends." She said the word *friends* with a peculiar twist. I quickly became uncomfortable under her withering gaze. "Are you?"

"I'm not gay. Not even close. I have a lovely girlfriend that I've been with for over two years. And it's true I am a friend of Andre. I've always found him to be a decent..." She held up her hand again.

"Thank you for being honest with me. I treasure that in a man. And please don't feel the need to defend this Andre. There's nothing you can tell me about him that I don't already know." She relaxed into a smile, shook her head at some inner thought and left the room. She had a flowery scent that lingered in the air as if she were still there judging me. The rest of the afternoon passed smoothly. I gathered that Uncle Andre had received her blessing to take in her son Dorian with his nephew Vincent. What are these two going to do if mother wants to pay her son a visit? What a tapestry of lies. A tapestry made of tissue paper.

We returned to the City by late afternoon. On the way back I told Andre that Dorian's mother wasn't fooled about anything.

"Nonsense, Hankie. You preformed your part perfectly. Now Dorian can come live with you and your uncle Andre."

Then Andre asked if JoAnn and I were free to join them for dinner. They had something to discuss with us. I rolled my eyes. Now what? Hadn't I been part of enough silliness for one day? I told them that as far as I knew we were free.

As usual Andre cooked a great dinner. He had on a new kitchen apron and looked, in his words, *tres chic*. He and Dorian spent half the night hugging and kissing. I don't feel quite comfortable about that. Men kissing each other doesn't look right. Prudish New Jersey Catholic upbringing haunting me. JoAnn didn't mind one way or the other. Every time they kissed she grabbed me.

After a wonderful dish of ice cream topped with brandy and a last glass of the third bottle of wine, Andre finally came out with the reason for dinner. Actually it was more like a speech. "You know, my dear friends and guests, that if it weren't for living in this tiny, oh too tiny, apartment, I would never have met Hankie here. And of course I wouldn't have met the lovely and cultured JoAnn either."

"That's logical enough," I said with a slur in my voice. I was plastered on the wine, my mind a twirling, swimming fog.

"But this apartment isn't big enough for Dorian and I. We're going to have to find something else."

He looked at Dorian and winked. Then he turned to JoAnn. "And I hear that you've had your share of apartment problems, too."

"Problems is right," said JoAnn loudly, almost laughing.

"Anywho, what we want to ask you two friends is this: we would like to know how you feel about sharing an apartment with us. With four people, two couples, we can secure a big, fine apartment at a reasonable rent. Much better than this apartment, and yours Hank, and yours JoAnn taken separately. What do you say to that?"

JoAnn jumped right in: "That sounds great to me!"

"Well, we've been doing some shopping. We saw a lovely place in the upper 40s off Second Avenue. Two large bedrooms separated by a living room, dining room and kitchen. Lots of privacy. Plenty of room."

JoAnn was in hog heaven. I agreed but with less enthusiasm. Now, this morning, I'm not so sure. What concerns me is not Andre and Dorian. It's losing my freedom. If I live with JoAnn, I won't be able to date anyone else. Am I ready to be tied down to a relationship with JoAnn only? Am I ready to give up Martha?

FEBRUARY 1966

February 1, 1966. *Tuesday night*

My grades for last semester were not up to par. Aced my English class (not bad for someone who failed the Proficiency Exam) and Greek Thinkers; Physiology a B (mostly from poor lab grades using John's straight A reports); Organic Chemistry a C; and German a D. At least I ran through the alphabet.

Wrote as letter to the Draft Board of Essex County, New Jersey. Not a great letter, but I hope it had the proper mix of humility and patriotism. Our Draft Board is strict.

> *Gentlemen,*
>
> *I would like to request permission to extend my college deferment for an additional year. I switched majors from Psychology to Biology and lost a year in the process. I believe that I will be a better, more productive member of society with a college degree than without.*
>
> *I will present myself to Selective Service Center promptly on graduation and intend in no way to shirk my duty.*

This semester I did not sign up for the English class I had originally planned to take. If they don't want me as part of their department, then let them fill my spot with some dunderhead. I have to take German II and Organic Chemistry II and I need to raise my grades in both those courses! Comparative Anatomy, Greek Plays and Sociology round out the picture. A full academic load.

Classes start tomorrow. I am going to ask Martha out this weekend. Need to break the JoAnn monotony. Speaking of JoAnn, I told her yesterday that I wasn't so sure about this latest idea of Andre that all of us live together in one large apartment.

"Not sure? You were pretty sure the other night. What's wrong with living better than we do now? Andre's right. Why should I pay rent and you pay rent and he pay rent for places none of us is really happy with? We get a large apartment with lots of privacy and everyone pays less. You and I almost live together now."

"What will your parents say?"

"They'll object of course. I can cope with that. I moved out on my own with their opposition. I can manage this move too. And after the Sandy mess, they may even think a big apartment will be better for me. They won't like you in the place with me. But they can tell their friends that I'm living with a number of other students. We'll work this out. Why are we talking about me? You're the one who changed his mind. Why?"

"I'm not changing my mind. I never really agreed. And thinking more about the situation, Andre isn't that stable. We could be left with a big mess if he breaks up with Dorian. And I never liked noisy places with parties every night."

"Hank, this isn't about Andre or Dorian or me or my parents. You are the one who doesn't want to do it. OK. Fine. That's your choice. I see I'm pushing you into an involvement you don't want. OK. I thought we were getting closer together lately. I thought this would be good for us. Big mistake. My mistake."

Of course I told her we were closer together. No reason to head into the snake pit that discussion would lead to if I showed even the slightest agreement with her analysis. I been there before and felt those bites. She never really came out of her rotten mood after that nowhere discussion. The evening ended on a sour note, namely her leaving me to Dr Jeckle couch. Thanks.

2/4/66. 2+4=6. 666. I should have known it was going to be an awful day.

February 5, 1966. *Saturday morning*

Thursday evening I called Martha from Medical Records. I couldn't call her from my place later in the evening because JoAnn was going to meet me after work for a late dinner. Martha and I made a date for Friday evening to see a movie. "You told me once that you're a Friday Night girl."

"Yeah?" she answered with a laugh. "Guess we'll find out tomorrow."

When I came back to my apartment after a cold walk across Fifteenth Street, JoAnn greeted me with a big supper laid out on a linen tablecloth covering my card table. One thin candle flickered in the center. Dishes and silverware perfectly set. Her idea of a romantic interlude, I suppose. She even had a Schumann symphony on the record player.

Then she nailed me with her usual fifty question routine: How was my day? Was work busy? Did I finish studying for German? Did I like the soup?…On and on. Usual burdensome, weighty crap that leaves me mentally quagmired. And I'm accused of creating *usualness* in our *relationship*. Well, if this is her usualness, then maybe Murphy should have her.

Of course I didn't say that. She would have beaten me over the head with her verbal baseball bat forever if I had spoken those lines. So I kept my mouth shut, except for eating her delicious dinner, and let her rattle on with her dumb questions. I responded with an occasional grunt or hand movement. What I really wanted was Thursday night with JoAnn to be Friday night with Martha. Anything else was orchestrated filler.

Finally she threw down her napkin and threw me a royal blast. "Why are you being like this? And don't give me that dumb look that says: 'What are you talking about?' I cook you a nice dinner. I have your apartment completely cleaned for you. And you don't even have the basic manners to talk to me. OK. You have something on your mind that you don't want to talk about? Something too important to share with me? Fine. Then I'll leave. I know when I'm not wanted."

The Righteous Indignation Play Act I. Followed by exit, stage left with coat in arm. And obligatory door slam.

That left me alone with Schumann whom I've never been overly fond of. I changed him for Beethoven #7 and continued with dinner. Chicken in orange sauce with wild rice. Actually very good. My mind wandered and lingered on Martha, what would I say, how would I get her up here to the apartment, how would I undress her. My interest rose to an empty occasion. Maybe I shouldn't have been so stinky with JoAnn. A full bed is better than an empty one. And thoughts of Martha are not as satisfying as slipping The Chief between JoAnn's thighs.

Five minutes later Act II begins with re-entry by the departed, wronged lady with coat still draped over the arm. She probably never left the building. Just stood down the hall stewing in her own juices. I was seated at table, the candle lit.

"Can we talk?" she asked. I pointed to her empty chair, her untouched dinner. I told her I had a difficult day, a great deal of pressure from school especially damned German. I spiced it up with a story about Organic Chemistry Lab and a student who mistakenly put his whole hand in a jar of Martius dye. He removed it but couldn't wash the yellow dye off. He had to take the subway home, his hand on an overhead strap and looking like a creature from a science fiction thriller: *The Yellow Hand of Dr Martius* or maybe *The Creature From the Yellow Lagoon*. She was not interested in what was being said, only that communication was taking place and we were laughing. As John said to me: Make them laugh and you can screw them all night. Which I proceeded to do.

Friday afternoon JoAnn called me from her apartment and caught me just before I had to leave for work. "I've been thinking of you all day. Let's get together tonight."

"Well, actually I've been real tired today. Someone we know has had me up for the last several nights. I was planning on taking the train to New Jersey after work. So tonight may not be a good idea."

"So you're going out with someone else tonight. I felt you were distant last night. Now I know what it was." She was not asking me a question. And she was level-toned and very angry.

"No, that's not the situation at all. I never said I was going out with someone else. Where did you get this idea from?" Wriggling worm trying to avoid the hook.

"That same girl that slept over right after Christmas. That's who you're seeing. That's who you're seeing when I call and the phone doesn't answer." She never forgets a thing. Or forgives either. "The one you claim you never did anything with. You only slept side by side, brother and sister. Don't you think you could at least tell me the truth? Aren't I even worth that much to you?"

Somehow I managed to smooth her feathers. We made a date for Saturday (tonight). I stuck by my story of going to New Jersey. So now I have to produce a quart of sauce and meatballs or I'm dead. That's what I'm cooking now. Bought the chop meat and Ragu at the deli on Third Avenue. Rolled out the meatballs and fried them in my one sauce pan. Now they're cooking in the sauce for an hour. Later I'll have to wash these dirty pots and put them away, air the room out, and freeze the sauce in one of my mother's jars. A lot of work to cover an evening of total disaster.

I finished my part of pulling charts early last night. Bill promised to punch me out at 9pm. I owe him one next week. Martha met me outside the 34th Street Murray Hill Movie Theater. We arrived almost at the same time which was good because the wind from the East River whipping up the street numbed me to the bone.

We saw *Othello* with Lawrence Olivier. Fabulous. We were glued to our seats for five minutes after the end. Emotions beyond crying; the death scene overpowering. Even Martha who has the sensitivity of a Hedda Gabler was deeply affected. We walked hand in hand down Third Avenue to my place. A mile. A cold mile. We needed the fresh air.

Back at my apartment, I took out a bottle of Chablis that I bought for this purpose along with two glasses and we sat back on Dr Jeckle couch. The light from my small lamp caught the red in her hair perfectly. She took a sip and talked to the glass. "Last week I thought I might be pregnant. I was late. And I'm never late. I was worried because I use a diaphram and hell, that's not a hundred percent safe. I can't use the pill, the hormones drive me up the wall. Why can't they make something better? Why don't you do something about it? You're into Biology." She punched my arm and gave me one of her half-tight smiles. "Well, all that worry was for nothing. It proved to be a false alarm. My monthly friend, if I can call her that, came to the rescue."

"I know the feeling," I said and regretted the words as soon as they came out because she gave me a deep, questioning look. No way could I tell her the Rusty story: the missed periods, the fear, facing my mother and father, the hunt for someone who...No, I couldn't sink into that. I struggled to shake the swamp out of my mind. I took a deep breath, reached for her hand and bit the bitter onion. "I would really like things to become more serious between us." Inside, my stomach was quivering like a newborn lamb.

"So would I," she said. She leaned over and gave me a sweet kiss. "Wait for me," she said, leaving the couch and taking her purse with her to the bathroom. The door closed firmly and there was the sound of running water.

I paced the floor from window to couch. My brain was racing: Does she mean that I'm supposed to make the couch into a bed? Is she saying she wants to go to bed with me? Of course, what else, you dummy! Do I take off my clothes? What if I do and she's only in there to take a piss? Wouldn't I look like a jerk when she comes out? Or maybe she still has her period and she went in the bathroom to change her plug. Why is it always so easy with JoAnn?

She came out of the bathroom with only her blue bikini panties on. She was gorgeous in the low light: small, tight, muscular body with pale skin and that incredible fiery hair; firm breasts that didn't sag or bounce; her nipples pointing at me, asking for attention. I was paralyzed.

"You're still dressed," she said walking to the couch. She pulled off the bolsters and threw back my mother's corduroy cover. "I always wanted to know what was under this thing. Blue sheets." She slipped between them ands smiled at me as she stretched her arms above her head. "I told you I was a Friday night girl."

I took my clothes off in a New York minute and joined her in bed. Where

JoAnn would have her arms around my neck and her legs wrapped about me as soon as I cuddled up to her, Martha continued to lay stretched out, waiting. I kissed her breasts and moved my hand down along her wonderful contoured body to her blue panties. Then inside to feel her furry valley. Slowly I pushed them down.

Still she didn't move. I threw back the sheet, completed removing her one piece of clothing and kissed her sweet body from her feet all the way back to her lips. She responded with only a slight shudder. "Do anything," she whispered. Then disaster struck. Or didn't strike because what was supposed to rise to the occasion stayed limp. Not a shred of life.

JoAnn would know what to do: slip her hand between my legs and grab on for a while. No Chris problem there. But last night I was in bed with this goddess and she was waiting for me. So I reached down and pulled on the pud for a while. Nothing. I couldn't ask her to play with me. I couldn't say anything.

The situation simply fell apart. After a while, without any talk, we both got up from bed and started dressing. I took her downstairs on the last elevator at 1 am. Outside she said she would take a cab uptown by herself, no sense in my going back and forth. She kissed me good-bye and we agreed to see each other next weekend.

I walked around the block a few times until I was thoroughly frozen in the damp February wind. A few taxis and an occasional pedestrian, bundled up and hunched over, were the only life forms I passed. The nine flights of stairs warmed me marginally. I pressed my ear to Andre's door, but there were no sounds from within. My bedroom never seemed emptier. Only an hour before she was here waiting. Her sweet scent lingered on the sheets. What a disaster.

This morning I went out early to buy the paper and walk around the block a few more times. As I stood in the hall unlocking my door, I heard a voice behind me: "Mr. Intili?" It had to be Mrs. Keller. Who else old enough to be my grandmother calls me by my last name?

Her door was only open a crack, her chair still latched. I could see half her wrinkled face as she looked around the door. Gray hair spilled down over her eyes. "I can't open the door because I'm only dressed in my housecoat." Her thickly veined hand pushed the dry hair away from her face. "Did you hear all that noise last night? Someone was banging on the walls and throwing things in the middle of the night. I've been up ever since in fear that someone was killed in our little apartment house."

"No, Mrs. Keller, I'm sure no one was hurt. I heard it too. Definitely from upstairs. No one on this floor."

"Are you sure?"

"I'm certain. Upstairs. Probably Mr. Cranbeau."

"Oh, him. That fruitcake. Don't look at me that way. Just because I'm elderly and nearly confined to this small room doesn't mean I'm blind and ignorant of the ways of the world. No, the noise sounded so close. Woke me out of a dead sleep. Dead sleep. Now there's a bad turn of phrase for an old lady to use. Will you ask the doorman downstairs anyway? To make sure. Are you coming right back? Yes? Well, then buy me the Times and knock on my door when you return."

When I returned with her paper that she insisted on paying me for, she had dressed and had a pot of tea ready for me. Her hair was up in a bun and she looked very classy. I told her that the doorman/elevator operator hadn't heard a thing about any problems last night.

"That's so odd, Mr. Initli. I know I'm not inventing this. By the way, how is JoAnn, that lovely girlfriend of yours? You two must come to visit me when it isn't an inconvenience for you." Everyone likes JoAnn.

I wonder who else I woke last night with my class act?

February 6, 1966. *Sunday Afternoon*

JoAnn left here a few minutes ago to return to her apartment. She wants me to join her for supper this evening at her parents' place. She'll call me when she's ready and we'll meet at the 14th Street subway station to ride uptown together. Usual Sunday supper: Hamburgers, each weighed to exactly 3/8 pound, and whatever vegetable is available. Then ice cream for desert.

I was *extra nice* to JoAnn yesterday. *Extra.* She came over as cold as the stone walls at the Cloisters. I suggested dinner at my place with some of my mother's sauce that I had brought back from New Jersey. She gave me *the eye* which I ignored. No, she preferred to eat out. We discussed Chinese or Italian and settled on pasta. Her conversation was not marked by warmth of expression. Gloria's Restaurant came to mind. I hadn't been there since my birthday.

We walked the ten blocks uptown without holding hands. Hers were firmly thrust into deep coat pockets. And not because the weather was cold. Down the sandstone steps into the basement restaurant, I opened the heavy metal door into the small, poorly lit foyer. Even in the dim glow from strings of tiny Christmas lights (that seem to be on the walls no matter what the season) we could see that the dozen tables were full. We looked at each other asking silently if we wanted to stay in the warm, crowded restaurant and wait for a table, or if we wanted to brave the cold wind again and try Dino's down the block.

The waiter whirled his way between tables like a dervish in the tiny dining room, talking to this one, laughing with that one, promising a quick return to a third. He spotted us and came right over.

"Do you have a reservation?" he asked. His forehead furrowed in thought as he looked at me carefully. Then he smiled brightly. "Oh, it's our student! The birthday boy! How nice to see you again!" His eyes turned to JoAnn. "And this is your girlfriend? She's lovely. Why haven't you brought her sooner?" JoAnn blushed.

"You're so lucky to have a lady this charming," he spoke quietly to me. "Your name's Hank, isn't it?" I nodded yes.

"You have a terrific memory," I countered, but his attention had already turned.

"And can I ask your name?" he said in a warm voice that I could barely hear over the clinking and chatting sounds of the restaurant.

"JoAnn," she replied with an equally warm smile.

"JoAnn. Yes—that's perfect. A lovely name. My name is Todd and I'm the waiter here. Or at least I try to be. Isn't tonight an awfully cold one?" he asked. JoAnn nodded yes. Here we go again: the yes, yes, yes routine. How do these twinkies do it?

"Now listen you two special guests, we don't take customers on Saturday night without a reservation. We're always so busy." A desk-top bell rang several times from the back of the restaurant. A tocsin for Todd, a summons to perform his waiterly duties and cease trying to flatter customers. He ignored the sound. "But tonight I'll make an exception. You two squeeze into the restaurant and keep warm. I'll find you a table in a few minutes. Someone's bound to leave soon. Can I take your coat and hang it in the back?" he asked JoAnn. Yes, yes, yes. Maybe he took lessons from Andre.

"Todd!" shouted a voice from the kitchen. The sharp bellow cut though the dining room like subway lights in a dark tunnel. I recognized the voice as the young chef. Her head popped though the small window that separates the kitchen from the dining area. "My food is getting cold! Can you tear yourself away long enough to feed our customers!" The people seated at the tables laughed and shook their heads.

Todd worked his way back through the crowded tables avoiding people calling out his name or waving menus to get his attention. From the kitchen I heard whispered comments. A head popped back in the window looking at me. "Yes, it is," said the young chef. A second head, older, pushed aside the first. Gloria herself. "Ha!" she snorted and disappeared. More whispers.

"Mama!" shouted the first to a blast of cackling laughter.

"What did the waiter mean when he called you the birthday boy?" asked JoAnn putting her arm through mine for the first time that evening.

"I had dinner here on my birthday. Somehow he pried out of me what day it was. I guess he saw I was lonely that night and the place was empty. So he stopped to talk. They took me back and fed me a special dinner. I'm surprised he even remembered me."

"You had dinner here on your birthday? Alone? I thought you were out with…Well, I see I was wrong about that. I'm sorry. I'm truly sorry. Boy, did I call that wrong. I'll have to make that up to you. Somehow." She pressed up against me, whispering in my ear. No way was I going to tell her that I was here alone because Rusty didn't keep her promise. I could feel JoAnn's thigh against me. And I could feel something else pressing against the front of my pants. Nothing wrong with me in that department tonight. A little late, fella.

Needless to say, after that the evening was fast uphill. Todd was as good as his word about the table. And dinner was splendid. The chef came out to say hello. She wore and apron spotted with grease and food. She looked tired and not nearly as appealing as the last time. However, I wasn't nearly as lonely tonight as I was on my birthday sans Rusty and JoAnn. As they say, abstinence makes the heart grow fonder. And my birthday was a complete victory for my mother's couch and the forces of moral turpentine.

Over the veal and pasta dishes JoAnn was light and effusive about her apartment and how everything was so pleasant with her and Sara without Sandy. We returned to my place walking down Lexington Avenue hand in hand. Later she didn't lie back waiting for me to *do anything*. And yet I have to say that not a few times I wished Martha's thin, tight legs were wrapped around me instead of JoAnn's meatier variety. Well, one can't have everything.

February 7, 1966. *Monday night*

Very pleasant dinner last night with JoAnn's parents. They were in a fine mood, chatty and relaxed. Her father jumped on one of his favorite subjects: crazy young people. Last night it was Peace Corps. "What do these college kids think they can do, huh?" he asked over his dish of diabetic ice cream.

"Help people. We have so much and they have so little," I answered, trying not to sound argumentative. I poured an extra ladle of melted chocolate over my Hagen Daz vanilla ice cream. Definitely not diabetic.

"Humpf," he grunted. "We're already paying for programs to build roads and dams, programs that help less fortunate people learn how to plant crops and raise livestock. These countries need businesses and an agricultural base for the creation of capital and wealth. What can a young person fresh out of college with minimal skills teach them about business?"

"Maybe there's some good when we can show them that we're not all ugly Americans trying to exploit their country for our own gains."

"Exploit? Some exploitation! Do you really think they see it as exploitation? Maybe that's how it's described in the books you read, but it certainly doesn't square with my experience. They beg us to take their minerals and employ their unskilled and unmotivated labor. Wave a dollar bill and you can get anything you want in those countries.," he said waving his fork like an errant dollar bill. "They're starved for hard currency. Hell, I remember the time I was in Honduras to buy some sugar..."

He went on to tell an interesting story. But I'm certain he missed the thrust of the point I was trying to make.

JoAnn decided to spend the night with her parents in her old room. Outside the front door in the small hallway while waiting for the elevator, she kissed me sweetly on the lips, and told me she loved me deeply.

So I rode the IRT subway back downtown alone. The token seller at the 96th Street Subway Station entrance was sitting straight up on his stool, alert and awake, behind his glass window. No free rides this week.

Work tonight at the hospital was long and tedious. Pulling charts took forever. There seemed to be hundreds of them. Apparently, not all the world's menial labor lives in Honduras. Everyone and his foul smelling uncle must be headed for the various clinics tomorrow.

Walking back to my apartment after work, the damp, cold mind numbed my face. Being a winter fisherman in Maine has never been my vocational aspiration.

A strange thing happened to me as I crossed Second Avenue. First let me say that every day near Washington Square I encounter a street beggar dressed in ragged clothes, his gloves full of holes, a cloth hat in his hand, his face covered in bruises and unshaved. He displays a horrible palsy, a shaking and trembling that convulses his body so completely that to hold a metal clanking cup with its few pencils requires his total effort. Whenever I pass this pathetic mendicant, I drop a dime or a nickel in his cup and never take one of his pencils. As my mother would say: "There but for the grace of God…"

Tonight, walking home from work, I'm certain I passed him crossing Second Avenue. Except he wasn't a beggar any more. He was dressed in the same rags and his face had the same bruises. But he strolled gracefully across the street in long, confident strides. No palsy, no doleful expression. I watched him hoof up the avenue for several blocks without a care in the world. Chin out, face up, a look of determination and contentment.

I raced through calculations. Let's say during the day in front of NYU he draws in one person every minute to drop a dime into his cup. (Not an unreasonable number since I've watched him do at least that much business). That's $6.00 per hour. Three times what I make before taxes. If we assume eight hours a day, that's $48. No wonder he's sauntering on the avenue looking contented. How much of my hard earned money have I contributed to this phony? Or should I praise his business acumen to JoAnn's father?

On Fifteenth Street near the apartment house I met Andre walking Corky. We strolled around the block, skirting the side of Union Square. The streets were nearly empty. The cold wind made it a less than pleasant night for ambling. "Where's Dorian that he's let you out to pick up stray men?"

"By *stray men* are you referring to yourself, darling? I certainly hope so because my roving days are over. Well, at least for the present." Andre dropped the leash and Corky ran down the block, although ran is a quixotic expression to describe Corky's stubby boundings. A sharp whistle from Andre threw his dog into reverse like a train thrown off the track and jack-knifed around. The tan coated rover returned to us instantly. "Well, Hankie, since you asked, I'll tell you. Dorian, also known as the young roommate of my nephew Vincent…"

"Supposed nephew. And she wasn't fooled for a moment."

"Nonsense. You played your part perfectly. Everything came out co-pasetic. Mama is pleased and placated. You have missed your calling: You belong on the stage. Anywho, fair Dorian resides upstairs doing his schoolwork like the good little student he is. Can the same be said of you, Hankie?"

"You have a minute to talk?"

"Oh, a tete-a-tete. How charming. But not down in this freezing wind, my dear. Corky, are your evening ablutions complete? Yes? Can we retire to warmer climes?" Corky ran ahead of us to the building entrance; his short legs propelled his sausage, tailless body in tiny burps of movement. Andre clapped his hands and shouted to him in a high falsetto: "How nice of you to grant us your permission!"

Up stairs I said hello to Dorian who really was doing homework seated at the kitchen table. We chatted for a minute about school and classes before Andre broke in. "Hankie here has asked for a little talk with his Uncle Andre. Shall we retire to the living room?" Dorian sensed the talk was not for him and excused himself to return to his books.

Andre poured us both a glass of sherry. I told him about my failure with Martha. He listed politely and shook his head at various salient points. He poured another sherry before commenting. "Hankie," he said in a tone softer than usual, "why do you persist in seeing yourself as a machine? You and JoAnn have a fine sex life. There is nothing wrong with your plumbing. Did you stop and relax for a minute? Pour another glass of wine and talk of sexy things? Laugh at your anatomy? Tell her how much you enjoyed her titties and wanted inside her? Don't give me that look. I know what boys and girls do together. And please stop avoiding the main issue. Now tell me: Did you stop and relax?"

"No," I answered looking away from his steady gaze.

"Why not?"

"I don't know."

"'I don't know.' That's not a very mature answer."

"It's the only answer I have," I said in a whiney voice I couldn't control.

"Tell me this, my young friend: If your dickie decided not to rise to the occasion with JoAnn, would you pound the wall and wake the neighbors? Or would you wait a few minutes and have her try something more relaxing? Hankie, sex is not a job. Sex is for fun and pleasure. Doesn't sound to me like you were having much fun. Not that you would know what bedroom fun is.

"You're bright and humorous, but that's not the same as being sensuous and—damn, what is the English word—sybaritic. So what did you expect your dickie to do? You know that swinging weenie between your cute legs is a part of you. Well, maybe you don't know that. Your lady JoAnn knows how to relax and enjoy herself. You treat your pleasures as if you aren't allowed to enjoy them, as if they're not a part of your core reality as a man, as a person.

"Hankie, you're so cute. But very difficult. You should have moved in with us. JoAnn could have loosened up some of your violin strings to sing a sweeter tune. Then maybe you and your dickie would be on the same track. OK, let's not be catty.

"One more thing. I've warned you before, and I'm going to warn you again: This Martha is not for you. She plays in a far rougher league. Stay with JoAnn who loves you and wants what's best for you."

Another Andre lecture. His talk must have sparked something within me because I woke up this morning from a dream and I knew why I failed with Martha. The reason is so obvious; it was standing in front of me, staring me in the face the whole time. Sometimes I'm as stupid as the pigeons sitting on Horace Mann's shoulder in Union Square.

In my dream I was lying on the bed that Anthony and I shared until I was eleven (there's that eleven number again). Someone under the blanket sleeping next to me. I thought the shape had to be Anthony. But when I pulled back the cover, Rusty was stretched out smiling at me. She wore the same dress she had on in my earlier dream about the car in the garage, and she was once again huge pregnant.

Rusty smiled at me, her great grin that showed the gaps in here teeth. She spoke quietly in a voice I couldn't understand. I leaned forward to hear her better and then a force took over my body and started pulling me towards her. My snake dream again. I woke from the dream shaking in fear with the sheets wrapped around me.

In a flash I knew the reason for my failure on Friday night: Somehow I had mixed up Rusty with Martha in that one brief mention about the abortion before I asked her to go to bed with me. That thought of Rusty stuck in the back of my brain and tangled up my dick like being tangled in the sheets.

Knowing the cause, I know the cure. Next time I'll put more energy into erasing any thoughts except those for Martha.

February 8, 1966. *Tuesday night, late*
Late. I belong in bed. One of those nights where I can't close my eyes and sleep. As soon as I hit the pillow, a dozen problems pop up and dance around my head. I thought JoAnn might call or drop by tonight. No such luck. I'll have to arrange something for tomorrow night. Can't let the week slip by without some sex. Only homework for a companion brings on the Hawaiian disease: Lakanookie. Pretty soon I'll be inducted into the Hawaiian Royal Family as Price Plenty-Pully-Dickie.

This morning I passed my beggar on the northwest corner of Washington Square. He hopped and twitched, his face blotched and red, his dented cup held out. His gloves were black cotton, dirty and full of holes. In the freezing wind he was a piteous sight. Definitely my strider from the night before. I stood on the opposite side of the street and counted his take for fifteen minutes. Two people a minute dropped something into his cup. No one took a pencil.

I'm not a Business major, but clearly my calculations from last night were way off base. Even at a dime a person, he's making 20 cents per minute or $12.00 an hour. That's the low estimate! No wonder he's a beggar by day and a contented man at night.

Martha met me at the coffee shop this morning. I ordered my usual cup of tea and a Linder tart. She had coffee and her usual Winstons. More usualness. Nothing was said about my failure Friday night. Nothing. We talked classes and cold weather.

Unexpectedly, John came into the shop and sat down on the stool next to me. He had on his burly sheepskin coat that he snapped open in the warm inside air. "Hey, Hank, howareya? Damn, miserable weather, right? You going to introduce me?" Before I could react, he reached across me and held his hand out. "My name's John. I've seen you a few times with Hank and asked him to introduce us, but he won't. Probably a male territorial thing. Afraid I'll steal you away from him."

Martha took his hand and offered him her tightest smile. "I wasn't aware he owned me. You can call me Martha. Why not since it's my name." They nearly pushed me off my seat shaking hands. My waitress came over and poured John a cup of coffee. He didn't acknowledge her and she gave me a glare as if I was responsible for his rudeness.

"Get that letter out to your Draft Board?" he asked. I nodded yes. "Good. Can't trust those bastards. They're like a woman. You think she'll do one thing, then *bang*, off she goes on her own. The only thing you can do is follow your interests. Sure as shit she's going to follow hers. Your redhead here. Think you know what she's going to do? Hell, no. Mind of her own, direction of her own. Like being on a fiery rocket. Only thing to do is top ride the beast and enjoy yourself. Because there's no way you can steer it."

"Yes, John," I answered. "Letter is out to my County Draft Board. Very meek and mild. Nothing left to do but cross the fingers." I ignored the rest of his speech. Martha hadn't ignored his spiel. She seemed suspended in mid-motion, unsure how to respond.

"Hey, you two," said John leaning across me again, touching Martha on the arm, "How about dinner at my place Friday? Double date with my Kathy. I'll cook dinner for all of us. You folks bring the refreshments. Sound OK? My place isn't a work of art, but, hell, that doesn't mean we can't have some fun. OK?"

"I'll go for that," said Martha without even looking at me for confirmation. I agreed because there didn't seem much choice. Maybe after this double-date dinner we can get back to my place and finish up where we left off last Friday.

February 11, 1966. *Friday night late.*

I know I should be angry. Pissed off, furious angry. Spitting mad like Kathy heading downtown alone in the cab. Instead, I'm only tired. Bone dead tired. I want to write this diary entry and sleep. Sleep all day and all night. Sleep until I'm so much older that I no longer care or remember. Once again the gods have shown their disdain for my aspirations.

Last night I left work an hour early with the usual arrangement with Bill. I owe him next Friday night. Took a cab uptown to John's building, an old brownstone on 38th off Second Avenue. The building smelled musty, the hallways were dirty, what I could see of them in the dim light. I had to negotiate several flights of narrow, creaking stairs to reach his apartment on the third floor. Inside his place the windows off the main room and bedroom faced a trash-strewn back yard and the rear of the brownstone opposite. Not exactly the high rent district. I expected better from 38th Street.

John's apartment was one shade removed from a dump. Three rooms: a full kitchen off a large main room and a small bedroom in back. The apartment was furnished in Salvation Army Renaissance. An old couch that may have been fluffy at one time and was now sagged and faded. A radio but no record player. No books except school books. His dining room table bare wood and scarred with numerous cigarette burns and coffee rings. The room was certainly lived in.

To my eye it lacked definition and personality. And a good vacuuming. The only character in the room was provided by a pair of black and white kittens playing tag on the couch arm. Their gamboling was completely out of phase with the man and his sense of décor. Maybe John planned to use them in a physiology experiment.

He, Martha, and Kathy (a girl I had never met before) were already halfway into the first bottle of a rather harsh red wine. Kathy introduced herself as I took off my coat and gloves. Considerably taller than me (which doesn't say much), mousy hair, poor complexion, subdued clothes that couldn't hide an unremarkable figure. Hardly what I expected from big-talking John. Fortunately she was a good cook and the food at least made the trip worth the inconvenience.

Over dinner John started telling stories. Very funny stories. He had a hundred of them and spat them out like machine gun tracers. We laughed hysterically and blew our noses on paper napkins while he told stories about hunting for the perfect native girl in VietNam. I'll never tell the story correctly, nor do I really want to. Maybe the second bottle of red wine had something to do with the laughter. The point is that John was perfectly on script about how to treat a girl on a date. Unfortunately, I didn't understand my role in his play.

I offered to help Kathy clean up expecting Martha to chip in. She didn't. Instead, John asked her if she wanted to see some special awards he kept in his bedroom. She agreed with a bright "Sure!" and off they went leaving the dishes to Kathy and me.

Kathy washed and I dried. She talked about being a Sociology major at NYU. We agreed that our paths never cross which is why we hadn't met before. And, no, she hadn't been with John long, only a few months. This was their first time out with another couple. She struck me as a rather nice girl who didn't make much of an impression until you spoke to her directly and then discovered she has considerable depth. I wondered: How did she ever pair up with John?

Before we completed the dishes, John popped his head into the kitchen and asked to speak with Kathy for a minute. I stayed drying the dishes while they moved into the main room. I heard whispers back and forth that rapidly transformed into John speaking very softly and Kathy shouting in crackling anger. By this time I had moved out of the kitchen and was drying my hands on the towel. Kathy and John stood at the far end of the room near the couch. The two kittens had ceased playing during the main course and were now curled up together, sleeping against a pillow. Martha stood by the bedroom door dragging on a Marlboro. I looked over at her but she wasn't watching anything except her cigarette. She was as disturbed by the argument as the kittens.

"What kind of bullshit is this!" Kathy yelled into John's face. He answered too quietly for me to hear. "Oh, is that so? You're not going to treat me like this! I won't put up with it from anybody!" She poked her finger right into his chest.

He ignored her jab and whispered another comment that again I couldn't hear. I was beginning to feel very uncomfortable. Martha and I should leave if they're going to fight. Kathy's hand flashed upward and slapped John so hard on the face that the noise was like a car backfiring. "Pay for a cab? You can go to hell!" she screamed. She grabbed her coat from the back of the couch and stormed over to the door. "As for you," she said pointing a finger at Martha, "You little bitch. Don't you ever cross my path again!" Kathy exited with a door slam that shook the remaining plates in the sink.

Martha hadn't moved a muscle other than her cigarette arm that pivoted back and forth from her side. Where had I seen that movement before? John walked over to Martha and whispered in her ear. I knew something was awfully wrong, but I couldn't piece together the puzzle. Or maybe I did want to see the pieces falling together. I crossed over to the couch and picked up one of the sleeping kittens. A limpid ball of purr.

John came over to me and Martha followed. "Uh, Hank, you see, the situation' is like this…"

"Yeah, like this," said Martha in her hardest voice and her tightest smile. "I don't need any pussy cats tonight. And that's all you are. A damned, whiney pussy cat. Good for nothing but stroking. And that's not what I need tonight." She walked away a few steps and snuffed out her butt in the metal ash tray on the table. She lit another. Her eyes were glazed. She hadn't drunk that much.

"It's like this," John continued in a quiet even tone, the same one he used with Kathy. "Martha and I want to spend the rest of the evening together. You know. Hey, nothing personal. These things happen."

I was still stoking the kitten that had never fully woken. "You want me to leave?" I asked Martha.

"Right," she spat out the words from the other side of the room. "Leave, exit, vamoose, good-bye. That's the idea. The sooner the better."

John nodded his head in agreement. I gently lowered the kitten back on to the couch next to his twin. I took my coat and gloves from the back of the couch and left without slamming the door. No Froggies sat in the hall this time. Might as well have.

Down at the street corner I met Kathy trying to hail a cab from a stream of traffic. "Going downtown?" I asked. She looked at me; her eyes flashed in the cold streetlight. She didn't answer and returned to her hand waving. I tried again: "Want to share?" A cab pulled up to the curb. She bustled herself inside and slammed the door shut behind her. Guess she didn't want to share a ride.

Thinking about the situation, neither did I. So I walked the mile back to Fifteenth Street through the frosty evening with vapor-mouthed pedestrians and the honking cars as companions.

Past Twenty-Sixth Street I debated going into in Gloria's and saying hello or chatting or anything that smacked of home comfort, family acceptance and that sort of stuff. It was almost midnight when I looked in their front window. No small, multicolored Christmas lights shone in the darkness. The restaurant lay closed and empty. Nothing there for me.

On Sixteenth Street in the block before my building I saw Andre and Dorian out with Corky. I didn't want to meet them and was about to turn away when Dorian and then Andre waved at me. Too late to avoid them. Andre set Corky loose and he bounced along to greet me. I stooped down to pet him and avoid their eyes. No use. They knew in an instant something was wrong.

"Why, Hankie, you're upset," said Andre with unaccustomed warmth. Usually he greets my moods with sarcasm. We strolled around the block several times with Corky as he performed his evening ablutions. They listened to me tell the whole story of the evening without a single interruption.

"Hankie, these things happen all the time to people. That's the way the world is. You accepted those game rules when you chose to go out with this Martha. I won't be so catty as to rub it in your face that I told you to watch out for this girl. But I did. You bought your ticket and you've seen your show."

"I'm not sure that's going to help him, Andre," said Dorian. We were standing in front of our building, stomping our feet in the cold. Corky looked up at us with his wide brown eyes wondering why these odd creatures were standing outside when warmth lived ten feet away on the other side of the big door.

"Well, my love," answered Andre, "Nothing is going to help my nephew more than a good dose of reality."

"You mean the reality that unless we go inside right now," I said with chattering teeth, "We'll miss the last elevator and have to walk up nine flights?"

"Very cute, Hankie. But you're avoiding the point. As usual."

Nonetheless, he did lead the exodus into the building to catch the last creaky elevator. The old man was not pleased at having to interrupt his dressing for the outside to take a last load of passengers almost to the top floor.

"Can Hank come inside with us for a cup of tea?" asked Dorian.

"Of course. A most excellent suggestion." Andre put his hand on my arm and guided me down the hall. Corky ran past us, his nails clicking on the tile floors.

Seated around Andre's kitchen table, Dorian prepared a pot of tea while Andre continued his lecture. "You're not going to like me for saying this. You probably won't listen with more than half an ear. But I'm going to tell you anyhow. You are a brilliant person, one of the most naturally smart people I have ever met. This hurt that happened to you tonight, this pain, this heartbreak, you did this to yourself. Deliberately."

"Like shooting myself in the foot?"

"No, not at all. Regular people do that. You've done something special. Far beyond stupid, far past your charming naiveté. You created a real monster to chase after, capture and torture yourself with for abandoning the mysterious Rusty. Then afterwards you wallow in self-created pity. Hankie, you spin webs where you are both the spider and the fly." He stopped and sipped his tea. He smiled at Dorian and thanked him. Dorian stood behind Andre and rested his hand on his shoulder.

"I see my lecture is landing on deaf ears. I knew it would. So I'll leave you tonight with this one thought: You belong playing in JoAnn's ballpark. She plays the style of baseball that is right for you. Whenever you leave that for someone like this Martha, then you will fall and injure yourself. Deliberately. Well, nephew Hankie, my young lover and I need to get to bed. And I suggest the same for you. Will you and the lovely JoAnn have brunch with us on Sunday? Meet us here at 12:30?"

I listened to him politely and finished my tea. He watched me closely as his words spun round and round in my head. And back in my room, I knew, as certain as I've ever known anything, that if he was right, then I've treated JoAnn very badly.

2-11-66. 2+1+1+6+6=16. 1+6=7. That's not a bad number. But this was sure an awful day.

February 13, 1966. *Sunday evening*
Saturday morning I was up early after a night of very poor sleep in spite of my protestations about wanting to stay abed with covers over my head forever. Tossed and turned with thoughts of John on and in Martha. Spreading legs and grasping arms. What a complete failure.

Called JoAnn about nine in the morning. Sara answered. "No, Hank, she's not here. I don't think she's been in all night. She wasn't here when I got back about two this morning. She was out with you, right? Uh, oh. I think I just said

199

something I wasn't supposed to. Maybe I'd better leave a message for her to call you when she gets back in. Sorry." Terrific. I lose Martha to John and JoAnn spent the night with Murphy who shoots a mile. Anyone but Hank and his Usualness.

Spent the rest of the morning cleaning house and cracking the books for a change. Both activities spiced with phantom conversation starters with Martha who I was sure was going to call me to apologize claiming another sinister force. I had my answers well rehearsed between washing dishes and scrubbing bathtub;

No, this time you've insulted me too much.

I demand an explanation.

I already gave you your one forget.

You have something to say that I haven't heard before?

Martha didn't call.

The phone rang right after the Con Edison bell tower on 14th Street chimed noon. JoAnn's voice was as dry as crusted pigeon droppings. "Sara said you called this morning. Glad to hear you finally got home. I called you several times last night up to midnight." She sounded anything but glad.

"I was at Andre's until 1:30." No lie there. "I've been home this morning doing schoolwork and cleaning for a change." I tried to keep my tone light even though my brain felt like settling cement. Between the vice jaws of Martha's rejection and JoAnn's disappearance, any sense of manliness and triumph had been squashed out of me.

"That still leaves a lot of holes in your story. Of course, I'm not supposed to ask what you do or where you go when we're not together. That would be stepping on your precious freedom. I'm supposed to sit home like the good little girlfriend and wait for you to summon me to your presence. Well, maybe good little girlfriends become tired of being made fools of. Three years together and I find myself playing back-up sex partner." Her voice had continuously risen in volume. One pissed girl.

"Have you had lunch yet?" I asked to change the subject. "We could meet at the deli on 12th Street."

"I don't give a damn about lunch! Why do you always treat my feelings in a trivial fashion? And I can't meet you at the deli; I'm not at my apartment."

Great. Calling me from Murphy's motel room. He lying in bed propped up on an elbow, running his finger down her naked back, listening to the phone call and laughing at me. *Why bother with him, JoAnn? I can shoot a mile, he only dribbles out. Anyway what do you want with Chief Limp Dick who can't perform with a beautiful girl in his bed? Let me show you what a real winner can do, not some little pussy cat.*

"I wasn't trying to avoid you. I just thought the phone is not the best place to talk. That's why I asked to meet over lunch. But if you're busy with someone else, then maybe we can find another time."

"Busy with someone else? What are you talking about?" she asked in a milder tone. "Who else would I be busy with at my parents' place especially when they're here? Oh, now I understand. Sara didn't know where I was, and you thought I was out with…Isn't that ironic. Last night I think you're out with that other girl and this morning you think I was out the whole night with another guy. At least the score is even for once. Assuming you really were at Andre's all evening and not out with that girl you've been chasing for months. An assumption I very much doubt."

Silence on the phone. I didn't know what else to say. The lack of talk sagged the phone line heavier than any weight could have. Finally I asked: "How about later this afternoon? My place?"

"My mother wants me to go shopping with her. Maybe after four, provided I'm not busy later." Ice in her voice. She was making me grovel for her time.

"I was hoping we could go out this evening."

"Are you asking me for a date? Your calendar is empty for the evening but your balls are full and you need some sexual relief?"

"Yes, I'm asking you for a date."

"I'll think about it. Maybe I'll be there at four and maybe I won't. I'll check my own calendar and see if it happens to be empty!" Slam the phone down.

I filled the afternoon with a visit to the record store on 11th Street. Flipped though the bargain bin and settled on a Vivaldi for $1.98. Concerto for two violins. Soaring with cascades of perfect notes. Then an hour with Mrs Keller across the hall discussing her latest issue of *Soviet Life* over a pot of tea and some excellent Danish butter cookies. "Look at these young folks on their farm. So full of life, so much dedication to their country. Why can't we be like that?" And as always she asked about JoAnn. She likes JoAnn. Is there anyone in the world who doesn't like JoAnn!

Four o'clock became five. I toiled with my German translation. Five became six. I struggled with glycol chlorination. I had been too upset for lunch and I was starved. Mother Nature always wins. Scrounging through the freezer, I found some pork chops. I fried these with sliced apples, onions and wine. Set up the table for two and waited reading a new book by Jessamyn West.

This morning I waited for Martha to call and was disappointed; this evening I sat there waiting for JoAnn again disappointed. A double negative day. No worse—negative squared. I kept telling myself: Deep down I know JoAnn will show. She's giving me the righteous indignation and anger routine.

Around seven she arrived in a big, new fluffy coat that she shrugged out of and threw on Dr Jeckle couch. "My mother decided I needed a new coat, and you know how she is about shopping. We had to go to a dozen stores. Oh, I see you have dinner ready. Good. I'm famished."

We ate and drank silently. Me because I was damned hungry. She to drive the wooden stake in deeper. "How was your mother?" I enquired to break the silence.

"My mother was in an unusually fine mood." JoAnn was working on her second glass of wine and the magician El Vino had begun to thaw the mountain of ice. "We had lunch out at a particularly elegant place, went shopping through most of the afternoon, spent an hour at my place, and then had late afternoon coffee with Sara. Yes, mom was in a very fine, unusual mood. My mother is actually pleased that I'm living on my own. Apparently things have been much better at home for her without me there. A double benefit.

"I told her about Andre's offer to move in with him. That really surprised her. I mean, that I would discuss it with her. She said she and dad wouldn't be pleased to have me living with three men. I answered that two of them had only limited male qualifications. She turned red with embarrassment and laughed. Of course she added that she was glad I hadn't moved in with you which had been their great fear."

"Naturally," I commented.

"No, not what you think. Both my parents have spoken much more positively about you lately. She said she didn't want me living with a man—she wanted me married before I moved in. Then the bomb of the afternoon: She asked me if you and I had ever talked about marriage." JoAnn looked me square in the eye. "I told her no, that's never been discussed." Then JoAnn dropped her eyes and returned to her dinner waiting for me to reply to the subject of marriage.

Time for me to bite the bullet—a different bullet. I took a last sip of wine and told her the whole story about Friday night at John's. Everything. Needless to say, I didn't tell her about Chief Limp Dick the week before. Honesty is one thing; craziness another. Talking about that mess would have led to the lies about going to New Jersey.

"So that's what's been going on. It certainly is nice to hear a story from you that has the ring of truth. There's been a scarcity of that lately. But why are you telling me this? Why is it any of my concern?"

"Because I'm not going to see her again…"

"Big deal. Not much chance of that happening."

"…and I want to talk to you about a one-on-one relationship, maybe another discussion of joining Andre and Dorian in…"

"I always thought we had a one-on-one relationship." She returned to the full face stare. "You encouraged me to leave Dickinson College and transfer here to New York University. I fought my parents and did that. I did that to be closer to you, and you start seeing other girls. You don't want to be pressured, you don't want to be pushed. You're like a child that gets a big piece of cake and then wants another. But when you taste the new portion and find it's full of pepper, you want to go back to the first one. I'm not going to be used that way by anyone."

"JoAnn, it's not that simple."

"You're not listening to me. That's another thing I don't like. I have to listen to you, but you don't listen to me. Oh, you hear the words, but you don't hear my needs. And you certainly don't seem to care about them even if you do hear them. I am not going to be a sweet piece of desert for you to play with. That's so easy to happen because you're so strong and so secure. You know what you want and you have the strength to try for it. I'm not that strong. I know that. But I've begun to see that a relationship between us isn't going to work unless we both have an input. I want relationships based on honesty."

Secure. The word rang in my ears. The last thing in the world I felt was secure. "All right. I promise. No more dates with anyone else. And I will try to listen better to your needs and wants. That's on my side. On your side: no more Murphy."

"My side? You just don't hear me, do you? You abuse me and our love. You toy with a relationship that means, that meant, a great deal to me. And all you can talk about is Murphy?" She stood up. I groaned inside that the great migration around the room was about to start. Instead, she pushed in her chair and spoke directly to me, spat the words in my face. "What I do with Murphy or what I don't do with Murphy, or with anyone else, is none of your damned business.

You had me exclusively and totally for three years. You were my first and only. Maybe you still are and maybe you aren't. But what you have made clear to me this weekend and this night is that you do not appreciate what you have. Or what you had. The real issue here is very simple: My worth.

"You know what I see in your eyes, Hank? You think I'm yours tonight. You think you only have to say a few nice words and then I'm going to pull back the covers on the couch and jump into bed. You want me to soothe your worries about other men and then soothe your cock that you had planned for your redheaded bitch. Well, I don't think I'm going to sell my relationship with you that cheap anymore."

JoAnn walked over to the couch and picked up her new coat. My chest took a blow as surely as if she had hit me with a baseball bat. She was about to leave.

"Now wait a minute, JoAnn, what I wanted to say was…"

She shook her head forcefully and her long hair flew in all directions. Her arms were already in the coat sleeves. "No! I don't want to hear it! You'll say the right words and I'll stay and do whatever you want. And nothing will be different. Not this time. I'm leaving. I'm not saying that I'm leaving forever. Maybe if you can show me that you really want me and you really care about us, then maybe, maybe, I'll come back. I'll decide when that happens. Because it sure isn't happening now." She started to cry and her voice broke. "Damn it! Don't you know how much I love you? Why do you treat me like dirt? I can't have that. It destroys everything." She turned away and opened the door.

"Please don't go," I said.

"I have to go," she said sobbing. "I can't stay." The door closed behind her with an awful finality.

I didn't move. I sat glued in the chair. I figured she would walk down the hall, cool off, and come back the way she always did. Five minutes later I crossed the room on tip-toe and opened the door as quietly as possible. The hallway was empty.

Back in the apartment I washed dishes alone and closed the closet-kitchen double doors remembering JoAnn's special way of asserting: Well, that's that, now let's move on to other things. Only JoAnn wasn't there to move on to other things.

Later that evening I went to call her. My fingers wouldn't dial the number, my hand froze on the receiver. I couldn't think what to say. My usual lines weren't appropriate. *Maybe she's right,* my brain kept repeating. *Right about you, right about her.*

What do I do? If I do nothing, she'll leave me. But I can't think of anything to say. There has to be a solution, but I can't piece it together.

February 17, 1966. *Thursday late.*

I stopped by the coffee shop after German and was about to go in when I saw Martha seated at the counter. I backed away from the door and took a long, slow walk around the block. At my jewelry man's kiosk I bought a pair of earrings for my mother's birthday. When I returned to the coffee shop, Martha was gone.

When I sat at the counter, my waitress sauntered over. "Your redhead girl friend was here. She stayed for almost an hour working hard at a cup of coffee and a dozen cigarettes. She looked like she was waiting for someone. You?"

I shrugged my shoulders. "Oh?" she answered with a raised eyebrow. I ordered hot, sweet tea and a Linder tart. We talked about the cold weather and I showed her the red coral earrings. She agreed my mother would love them.

Fortunately she didn't mention JoAnn. I couldn't have stood the pain.

If you liked this book, please go to my website and learn about other writing.
www.henryintili.com.

Also available from PublishAmerica

NOW THAT I KNOW
by P.J. Christian

Now That I Know is a love story that leads to tragedy to the point of suicide. It is about a girl who suffers great pain from making a life-altering, destructive decision to have an abortion and the downward spiral that follows. She aches and spends many days stuck in anxiety, wishing she could undo what she did, because she *now knows*. She tries many ways to compensate for the despair, but this only leads to more sorrow to the point she believes life is not worth living. In her darkest moment with the intention, method, and suicidal plan, all is lost, and dying would be the only way to ease the pain. In that instant someone loves her enough to reach out, pull her out of the depths of hell, and give peace, new meaning, and purpose to her life.

Paperback, 110 pages
5.5" x 8.5"
ISBN 1-60441-570-3

About the author:

P.J. Christian has written sports articles for newspapers and two articles about her experience as a traveling nurse. Inspired by God to write this book about this very dark, hidden secret of her past, she writes to share how God can take a broken, worthless life and transform it. Now that she knows about abortion and the life-changing reality of Jesus Christ, she offers that knowledge to you.

Available to all bookstores nationwide.
www.publishamerica.com

THE DAY SATAN REPENTED

by Cicero Ernest Curry II

Imagine growing up in the Bellows family where an eternal curse has been placed on them throughout the generations by a witch doctor. With each succeeding generation, only one male could be born within their family unit. The wives of these men could not give birth to any females because the witch doctor caught her husband in bed with his mistress.

These men have been watched throughout the ages by Satan who has in fact designed this curse for his eventual return to walk upon the earth. Known as Lokanetra, he is disguised at first as a great miracle healer. Then, as his fame grows, he brings together the leaders of the Middle East, ending the raging conflicts that have ravaged the region. Through Satan's final act of deceit, his main objective is to have a son born by way of his spirit-filled seed with a virgin wife.

Paperback, 128 pages
5.5" x 8.5"
ISBN 1-60474-692-0

About the author:
I am a sixty-two-year-old writer who can remember being a twenty-three-year-old who had a dream of writing a novel someday. I am socially active living in the beautiful city of Portland, Oregon. I have been married for thirty-three years and I have eight children and five grandchildren.

RECOGNIZING SATAN

by Audrey Kenner

Many troubles we face in life have some explanation; we can attribute them to bad behavior, past experiences, trauma, mental illness, even insanity. But what about when such explanations fail? What of a loved one changing inexplicably into a different person altogether? And what is it when someone who barely knows us deliberately targets us to unleash his ill will? One explanation is demonic force. One solution that's lost its popularity is exorcism. Throughout history and even today, demons have inhabited human bodies to do evil. Satan exists today, challenging our faith, hoping that we're ignorant of the awesome power of Christ. *Recognizing Satan* exposes how the devil operates in the lives of both sinner and saint.

Paperback, 253 pages
6" x 9"
ISBN 1-4241-9599-3

About the author:

Audrey Kenner was born in Chicago, Illinois. She met her husband Brian at sixteen. Brian felt the call to the ministry two years later and was ordained; they married one year thereafter. Audrey attended Columbia College (Chicago). They have been married for twenty-seven years and they have two children and three granddaughters.

Also available from PublishAmerica

SEPHARDIC FAREWELL
by Joseph Hobesh

Late fifteenth-century Spain, Queen Isabella and King Ferdinand issue the Expulsion Edict. Non-Catholics have two choices: convert to Catholicism, or leave Spain with nothing. The monarchs provide Columbus funds for his first exploratory sea voyage. Against the historic sweep of Columbus' voyage, the expulsion of the Jews, and the exploration of the New World, one family chooses to remain in Spain, living as Catholics, while another emigrates to Turkey to continue their Jewish faith.

Uprooted by the edict, the Halavi family is dispersed. Joshua Ben Halavi sets sail with Columbus, while Benjamin and his father, David, settle in Constantinople, establishing deep Jewish roots.

Paperback, 247 pages
6" x 9"
ISBN 1-4241-6247-5

The San Miguels, whose Jewish roots have been well-hidden for many years, choose to remain in Spain as Christians, their fate a mixture of Inquisition horror and New World success. From the historic voyage of Columbus and the colonization of the Americas, *Sephardic Farewell* follows these two families, portraying their lives through the sweeping events of the fifteenth and sixteenth centuries.

About the author:

Born and raised in New York City on the Lower East Side, Joseph Hobesh worked as an electrical engineer until 1996 and is now retired. Being of Sephardic ancestry, the subject of the Jews' expulsion from Spain has always held immense interest for Joseph, and he has been working on this project since 2002. Married with five children, including a set of twins, Joseph resides in Lafayette, California, with his wife, Anita, where in addition to writing, he is an avid senior softball player, and grandfather.

Available to all bookstores nationwide.
www.publishamerica.com